GOLDDIGGER

THE LEGENDARY NELLIE CASHMAN

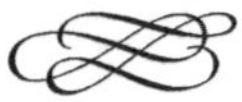

KATHLEEN MORRIS

Ebook Edition ISBN 978-1-7379866-9-0

Paperback Edition ISBN 978-1-7379866-8-3

Hardcover Edition ISBN 979-8-9874563-0-9

Dunraven Press February 2023

Cover Art & Design by Syric Lost

ALSO BY KATHLEEN MORRIS

The Lily of the West

The Wind at Her Back

The Transformation of Chastity James

Fallen Child

Risk

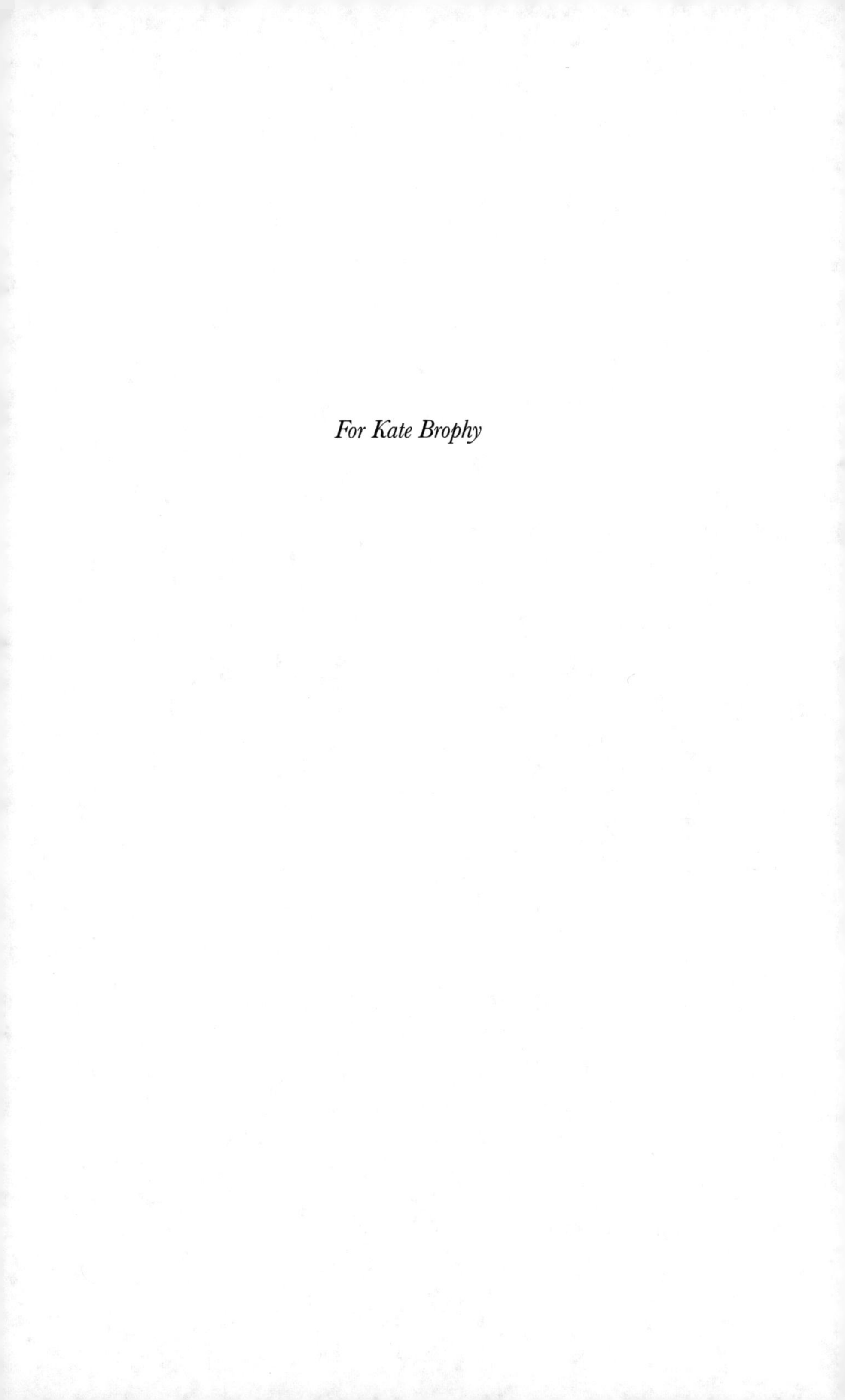

For Kate Brophy

PROLOGUE

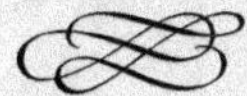

Alaska, 1924

I am a woman with a reputation. I'm an angel, maybe even a saint. That's what the newspapers say, and don't we always believe what those self-proclaimed savants tell us?

All the years on the road, the restaurants, the stores, the claims and the treks have taken their toll. I ache for a long while in the mornings, and my nights are often sleepless. I can't seem to shake this cough and I don't have the gumption I used to. I'm going to be eighty soon. Years have never mattered to me, but I guess there's something to what they say. You get old, you slow down. Or shut down.

Soon now, I'll have to head into Fairbanks and from there take the boat south. I'll stay with the sisters at St. Joseph's Hospital in Victoria for a bit, see if they can talk to God about this tiredness and cough, ply me with tea and toast and get me up and ready for a spring trek. God ought to listen, or at least St. Joseph, since it was the money I raised that built most of that place. I've helped out quite a few places here and there, schools, churches, and always gave a helping hand or two to people in need.

I'll have some time, between the tea and toast. To write it all down, if for no one but myself and God. Not a confession, never that. A chronicle.

Angels. Saints. Even they make mistakes, that's how journeys begin. Mine certainly did. Come along now and let me tell you of my life.

CHAPTER 1

Boston, 1866

I was born the year death came to Ireland. It wasn't my doing but for a long time I prayed on my knees because I thought it might have been, and there was no one who assured me it wasn't. When I was five, my mother took my little sister Fanny and me onto a ship and we outran death, *An Gorta Mor,* leaving it sure as the waves pulled us towards America and life. My father had not been so lucky.

Boston was full of us Irish, all looking for salvation and work and to say we weren't welcomed with open arms by those already here was an understatement. We Irish were a rough lot, brash, brawlers, drinkers, Papists, singers and poets too. Some more forgiving employers took chances with the family silver, the pouring and the scrubbing, and many of us found jobs in the big houses. My mother was a bit luckier. She was a seamstress and a good one, with some education, unlike most of the country girls, and before long we had established ourselves in two rooms on Federal Street, the same two rooms we still live in now, and my mother became a dressmaker to those who mattered in Boston society, unlike ourselves.

There was no one else in St. Joseph's when I slipped inside

after work, the soaring ceilings shadowed with flickering votive candles. A faint scent of incense blended with the smell of wax wafted through the silent space as I lit my two candles and knelt, closing my eyes. I'd never talked with Saint Anne before, but today seemed a good time to start, since she protected women, along with Saint Christopher, with whom I'd had many chats in the past.

"Holy mother, hear my prayer. I ask for your help to guide me, along with Saint Christopher, along the path I wish to tread. It is a big world and I wish to be part of it, to find my place in it, and I feel it's not here any more."

The words stopped flowing from my mouth, but more swirled around in my head, and I know the two saints heard me. I wanted to go West, into the unknown, the land of opportunity, and yes, possible riches. To see the other ocean, mountains, and vistas without soot-stained buildings and streets clogged with people. To breathe air that tasted of silver and purity, to find . . . I wasn't sure exactly what, but the need to search for it was choking me and I could no longer bide my time. I would find it, whatever it turned out to be.

I opened my eyes and my two candles had burned halfway down. A soft susurrus on the stone floor beside me and a gentle hand on my shoulder broke my trance.

"Nellie, my child, are you all right?" Father Ryan smiled down at me, blue eyes kind, his white hair a wispy halo around his head, reassuring in long cassock. I'd been coming here to this old chapel since I was twelve. I found it one afternoon on one of my long walks, and the serenity I found here, along with this kind man, had been my guide through many a crisis, from nightmares to my so far limited life choices.

I stood up, my knees creaking, pins and needles running down my calves, pushing my hair away from my face. "Yes, Father, thank you," I murmured, looking around at the empty chapel. Dusk was fast approaching and the candles were points of lights in the small dim chapel.

He took my arm and we walked down the main aisle. "You know I'm always delighted to see you, my dear. May I help you with anything this fine evening?"

I poured it out: my dreams, the desire to travel, the exciting possibilities, even the fears of the unknown, as well as those of convincing my mother to do this wild thing. To his credit, he listened and simply nodded. When I was empty, he smiled.

"I will miss you, Nellie Cashman," he said. Astonished, I looked at him. Was he approving of my madness?

"I've seen this coming for some time. Follow your heart. You are a determined, resourceful and intelligent young woman. You'll do well, and take care of your mother and sister. You have my blessing, and safe travels."

I threw my arms around him, to my surprise and his as well. Flustered, both of us, he ushered me out the door into the crisp spring evening. It was as though a granite boulder had lifted from my shoulders. It was over two miles to Federal Street, but I don't remember my feet touching the cobblestones.

* * *

We lived on the third floor, and the ever-present smell of boiled cabbage and potatoes, along with the reek of soiled nappies and the whining of children, followed me up the stairway. I had come to hate the place and its aura of hopelessness.

I stopped into the bathroom we shared with three other families on the floor, and splashed cold water on my flushed face, peering into the cracked silvered mirror. More of my long dark hair had come loose during my walk and I repinned it atop my head. I stood back to check and that was the best I could do without a hairbrush, my blue eyes staring back at me as I gave the mirror a lopsided grin. Not even this place could stopper my newfound feelings for long. Upon opening my own door, those feelings were superseded by the rich aroma of beef stew and my mother Fanny's welcoming smile.

"Well there she is, now," she waved her spoon at me from where she stood over the pot on the stove. "How was the day doing your ups and downs?"

I smiled at her reference to my elevator operator job at Tremont House and kissed her cheek, powdery dry with the usual scent of lavender water. "Ah, well, up and down, don't you know. That smells delicious."

"Wash your hands and fetch your sister," she said, ladling the stew onto plates and setting them on the small table, just big enough for the three of us, but laid with a pretty lace tablecloth nonetheless. Fanny had standards.

My pretty little sister, Young Fanny, was curled up with a book, as usual, in the bedroom the three of us shared, which had, amazingly enough, worked out well for many years. We went into the front room, which not only housed the kitchen and small eating area, but was quite large by Boston tenement standards, allowing for two large worktables where my mother created some elegant frocks for Boston society ladies, and she had a large following. My sister Fanny had become quite the lacemaker over the years, and her work adorned many of the dresses my mother made, as well as the delicate silk lingerie which was a big seller. Now that we'd both finished school at St. Mary's, young Fanny had been able to spend more time on her lace and delicate adornments and business had been very good. I was all thumbs with that sort of thing, and after a stint as a livery attendant, where I'd tucked my hair into a bun hidden by a cap and passed as a boy for a year, I'd talked my way into my job as an elevator operator at Tremont House Hotel, most of the available young men still not home from the war. It was a fairly elegant place, the Tremont, and I'd learned a lot about the world outside our rooms and school, observing and chatting with people from all over the world. But that was going to change soon, and I knew it like the dread of a fragile bell whose clapper is about to meet its side with a resounding clang. Men would take my job, and many others that women had held.

The stew was delicious and we did it justice. My mother and sister chatted but I found myself unable to join in. I had bigger things on my mind. My mother had been watching me and finally put her fork down, focusing her attention on me.

"Out with it, my girl."

"What?" I blinked, but I'd actually been waiting for it.

My sister cleared our plates, nudging me with her hip knowingly as she passed, stacking the plates in the sink and sitting back down.

"Nellie's got an itch," she smirked. "And it isn't the boy down the hall."

I wanted to smack her. I'd confided a few ideas but all Fanny knew were boys and she flirted incessantly with the whole neighborhood, slim as the pickings were, to my mind. Her biggest dreams only involved having a pack of children, and being a brood mare wasn't on my list of possible futures. I crossed my fingers and put my hand in my lap, taking a deep breath instead.

"Mama, I want to go west. Get out of Boston and go to San Francisco. They discovered gold there in California and lots of other places. The West is where people make their fortunes, and not just exist in a couple of rooms." I waved my hands around to encompass the area I lived in, and while I stopped for breath, I could see the storm clouds gathering on both my mother and sister's faces. I held up my hand before they could say a word and plunged on.

"Hear me out before you say no, please, both of you." I turned to my mother. "How long do you want to sit in this room, winter and summer, sewing beautiful clothes for rich women, and never having any for yourself? Freezing in the winter with ten feet of snow, and roasting in the summer with these windows that we never leave open because of the soot and noise? Being ashamed of our heritage, instead of proud? Staring at the brick walls outside and never running through a meadow full of green grass again, like we had in Ireland?" I saw her eyes fill with tears but I couldn't let myself care.

"We can do this, Mama. It's not a dream, we can make it reality. You've worked hard to take care of us. Let me take care of you, but I can't do it here, running an elevator. If it means taking a risk, it's a risk we'll have to take. I talked to Father Ryan today, and I prayed on it for weeks now. You always told me God helps those who help themselves. Well, I think he wants to help us, but one thing I know is that we have to do some lifting of our own."

She was silent, the tears running down her face, and I took her hand in mine. "You took the biggest risk and saved us all, leaving Ireland. But Boston isn't the end of that journey, it's just a stop in time. We've gained all we could here. Now we need to move on."

My sister shoved her chair back. "What about me, Nellie? What about me? I'm going to the dance at the parish hall with Sean O'Connor Saturday night and I think he's going to propose. What am I supposed to tell him? 'Oh no, we're going to be wild Indians and go gold mining or get on some wagon train' with my mad sister? I want out of here too, and that's how I'm going to get out, by marrying Sean. He's got a good job with the Astors as an under-butler." She glared at me. "You don't care about men, anyway, you'll just be an old maid because you scare off anybody that looks at you sideways and you think they're stupid."

Well, that was mostly true, I thought, but it wasn't the time to say so. Before I could even a draw a breath to start my argument, my mother stood up. She was still a pretty woman, even with the gray in her hair and the stoop she'd developed, bending over sewing all day. I hated what it had done to her.

"Girls, I have something to say." She looked at both of us. "For some time now, I've been thinking there has to be more than what we've found here. Somewhere people don't sneer when they hear my accent as I open my mouth, where they don't say "Irish" and look the other way like we're contaminated. In spite of that, Boston took us in, and we've done well enough here. You girls have had an education and we haven't gone hungry. But, your father, God rest his soul, wanted more for his children and for me. I think Nellie's right."

Fanny made a whimpering sound and my mother reached over and took her chin between her thumb and forefinger, turning her face towards us. "Sean O'Connor is an idiot. You can do much better than that, my darlin'."

And that is how three months later, we found ourselves on a ship bound for Panama, crossing the isthmus and boarding another, sailing into San Francisco Bay. It hadn't been an easy voyage, but much better than the dimly remembered horrors of the trip from Ireland. When those misty green hills of California came into view through the fog, they looked just like the hills of my home, at least to my childhood memories. I sank to my knees on the deck, thanking my mother, St. Christopher, St. Anne, dear Father Ryan, but most of all, myself.

CHAPTER 2

The moment I stepped onto the wharf to welcoming smiles, I knew what they said was true. San Francisco was much friendlier to the Irish than Boston had ever been. Maybe it was because people who came this far from their native land had earned respect, or that the old hidebound prejudices didn't reach this far. Maybe both. Whatever it was, it was grand to not see the usual signs "No Irish, No Dogs" everywhere. The truth of it is, I thought, most dogs are preferable to Englishmen or Bostonians in my experience with all three.

We took rooms at a nice boardinghouse on Fifth Street, where many of the other residents were Irish too. For a week or so, we were so relieved to not feel the floor moving under our feet, we didn't venture out much, but that soon changed and we strolled around the city. Every time we turned a corner, we became more convinced that we'd made the right move. Beautiful houses, shops, Union Square, the Opera House, all very close to us, and accessible in a way that Boston had never been. What a wonderful city this was, so full of life and energy, all sorts of people from all over the world, and very few of the prejudiced and snooty Bostonians that thought the Irish were lower than their hunting dogs, which was a welcome relief. Even pretty young Fanny, who hadn't been as happy as Mama and I, leaving her erstwhile beaus, soon came back to life and was her old smiling self, especially with the many handsome young Irishmen that seemed to be everywhere.

Particularly so once Fanny met one of our neighbors at dinner the second night of our stay, a Mr. Thomas Cunningham, a handsome young man with twinkling eyes and ample amounts of pure Irish charm. To be sure, I liked him myself, but I could tell Fanny was smitten and any lingering dreams of her Sean O'Connor vanished like wisps of fog in an onshore California breeze. My sister's happiness would ever mean more to me than any gentleman ever would. She had no need to worry about any romantic competition from me for Mr. Cunningham.

Our boardinghouse wasn't just a home, but a place that encouraged congeniality and friendships with our fellow housemates. When you share meals with others, you learn a great deal not just about them, but from them. In Boston we hadn't had that experience and we all enjoyed this new conviviality and the news and information it brought as well.

"Please pass the biscuits, would you, Mr. Cunningham?" Mama said. "And where was it you said you were employed?" She was a sly one, mama, especially after one look at Fanny's lovestruck face.

"At the United Workingmen's Co-op Shoe Factory, Mrs. Cashman," that young man replied with a grin. "'Tis a fair place with opportunities for those with ambition. Just last week I was named a supervisor, would you believe it?"

"Isn't that wonderful now," Mama said. "This is truly a land of opportunity, isn't it?"

Samuel O'Hara, a florid-faced man who laughed a lot, smiled across the table at her. "Ma'am, I will testify to that. I'm about to depart for the gold fields. Got me a claim stake.

It may be the streets in America ain't paved with gold, but I tell you true, my pockets soon will be."

My ears perked up at that. I'd heard stories about gold and silver mines even back in Boston. For some reason, they didn't simply interest me, they struck a chord in me I hadn't even known I was ready to listen to before now.

"Where would you be going, then, Mr. O'Hara?" I said, hiding my eagerness, but my mind was buzzing.

"Virginia City, missy. There's a bonanza up there. Whole place is like a cosmopolitan city on the hill built with silver ore. They call it the Comstock Lode. Nothing like it, I tell you. Just there for the taking for anybody with the balls," he paused, "oops, sorry ladies, I meant to say the stamina to take it."

Mama frowned but O'Hara was bombarded with questions from half a dozen other men at the table, and the rest of the dinner conversation was all about mining, Virginia City, Pioche and other places I'd never heard of before this night. I listened avidly. By the time dessert was served, to my regret, the conversation had died down while everyone devoted themselves to chocolate cake. Still, if I wanted to go anywhere, I needed the money to do it. I turned to Thomas Cunningham.

"Do they hire women at your shoe factory?"

He smiled at me. "Why, yes, Miss Cashman, they do. Are you interested?"

I smiled back. "I most certainly am, Mr. Cunningham. Be assured that you'll find me a most willing and able worker."

"I have only known you for a day, but I do believe that is true, Miss Cashman," he said.

And that is how, on Tuesday morning, after the usual spot of interviewing and dithering, I reported for work at the United Workingmen's Co-op Shoe Factory.

* * *

Tom Cunningham was right. The shoe factory paid good wages and I was a quick learner. While I had no intention of making shoes for the rest of my life, each payday I put more money into my bank account after helping Mama with expenses. She and Fanny had once again started a dress-making business and it was much more profitable than the meager wages they'd earned in Boston, and they were selling directly to the women they clothed. The shoe factory was a short walk from our boardinghouse, even though many mornings I had to make my way through the fog, occasionally so thick I'd walk right into a lamppost. Usually by noon, the onshore breeze had taken care of the fog, but even on warmer days, it was chilly in the evenings and I never dawdled coming home. I was always happy to leave the noisy and smelly shoe factory for the day and the walk cleared the tiresomeness of the work from my head.

Every night at dinner, and sometimes at lunch counters or wherever people congregated, I listened eagerly for news of mining and exploration far away from the city. The taverns and bars would've likely provided me with a great deal more information, but they weren't places I felt comfortable going into. Times were changing, and standards were different in California and the west, but still, respectable women rarely made appearances in these places. I didn't care so much about respectability, truthfully, but I wasn't quite ready to step into rowdy taverns or be considered a "loose" woman.

I bided my time, saving money and learning. Samuel O'Hara was long gone, but other men came and went, and talked constantly about gold and silver strikes, the different camps and towns that had sprung up to accommodate miners and fortune hunters and there was plenty to learn. One thing I learned for certain was that big city life wasn't for me. I had a yearning for wide open spaces and there were plenty of those out there, according to my fellow boarders.

Although I spent my weekdays at the shoe factory, on the

weekends off, I roamed the city, often alone, chatting to everyone I met that looked interesting, friendly or had a tale to tell. We Irish and most other immigrants were readily accepted but I came to find that the Chinese did not fare so well, and there was much unfounded ill will towards many of them, similar to the prejudices the Irish had borne back East. I found this dismaying and I have always found these resentments against anyone considered different, whether it's the color of their skin, or their language, customs and accents, to be reprehensible and unjust. Although I had seen not nearly as much as some, I already knew that learning from everyone and every culture different from your own was the pathway to wisdom, acceptance and opportunity.

At night, I read the newspapers and all the books I could find about the beautiful country just outside my view, especially the precious ores it hid beneath its surface. I was eager to learn all I could about the West and the opportunities that abounded here. I was so preoccupied that when Fanny and Tom Cunningham announced their engagement, I was taken aback for a moment.

"But, Fanny, you hardly know him," I said. "It's not like you know his family or anything about where he came from. Are you certain?"

Fanny laughed and held my hands, kissing my cheek. "Nellie, you've been in your little world, I declare. We've been here over two years now. Besides, I know everything I need to know about Tom, and he about me. We were destined to find each other on this western shore, and I love you for bringing us here."

I kissed her back and held her to me, this darling sister of mine. She was right. I'd been in a daze of making money and thinking of my own future, not hers.

"I'm sorry, love. I wish you both much happiness. Soon there will doubtless be little Cunninghams roaming about. Will you be getting a house then?"

"Oh yes, Tom's already bought one, Miss Practical," Fanny laughed. "With room for Mama, too. She adores him."

Well of course she does, I thought. I likely would too if I'd taken more time with him. Well, now that he was going to be family, I'd make sure to rectify that.

The wedding was lovely and so was the bride. They moved into their new house, blissfully happy. For the time being, Mama and I stayed on the boardinghouse, as she wanted to give the newlyweds plenty of space to begin their lives together. She was always a sensible woman, my mother.

"Would ye be so kind now, Miss Cashman, to pass the tatties?" A newly arrived gentleman asked one evening. "It's been a long time I've been travelin' and haven't had the opportunity to sit down at a well-stocked table."

I obliged, handing him the large bowl. "Surely. Where is it you've been, Mr. Sullivan?"

He launched into his trials of mining in Virginia City, which I'd been hearing a lot about ever since Mr. O'Hara had left to seek his fortune there, and I was all ears.

"'Tis quite a place, Virginia City. Every manner of sophistication, don't you know. Mansions on the hills, these silver barons have, the like of which rival anything you'd see here or anywhere. Restaurants, opera houses, the place is booming. Under it all is where the money comes from, Missy, but it's not easy to get to as you'd think. Takes a toll on a man."

"Can you file a claim?" I asked, ignoring my mother's frown.

"Course you can," he answered, between mouthfuls of potatoes. "Getting it out's the harder part, but it's there, that I can tell you."

"Are you going back?" I asked.

He laughed. "'Course I am. I know a good thing when I see it. Just have to get some supplies and I'll be gone again."

Of all the places I'd heard about since we'd arrived here, Virginia City was the closest and the richest of all the mining towns. When I went to bed that night, I couldn't stop thinking about that mountain city Sullivan had described, rising from the riches of the silver beneath it, built on grit and dreams. The Comstock. The new silver towns in Nevada were producing more than the famed Gold Rush ever had, and new millionaires were made every day, while thousands still flocked in to try their luck.

Three weeks later, I went to the bank, packed my things, and bought a ticket on the Central Pacific to Reno. Everyone was against the idea, especially Tom Cunningham and my family.

"You'll rue this decision, Nellie," my mother said, shaking her head as though I was going to the very gates of hell.

I kissed her cheek, the salt of her worried tears on my lips. I picked up my bag. "I have to see this for myself, mama. There's a world of opportunity out there and I need to explore it. Don't worry about me. I'll be back before you know it."

CHAPTER 3

1868

"There you go, sir." I deposited the plate full of steak and potatoes on the table. "Will you be needing anything else, then?"

"No, ma'am, this looks grand," the bearded miner replied. He looked as though this was his first foray into town in some time and I hoped he enjoyed his food. "Thank you kindly."

I retreated to the kitchen for the next orders. The Silver Mine Café was a busy place, which I knew only too well. I'd been working here for six months, both cooking and waitressing and my feet could certainly attest to that. It was worth it, though. I learned more about the mining trade by listening to my customers' conversations than I would've in a year of shoveling dirt out there with them, though occasionally, on my day off, I did that too. Silver was elusive, and I quickly learned that the best and to some, the only way to get it out of the ground was to use heavy equipment and refining processes that the lowly lone miner could never hope to afford. Most of them went to work for the big mining consortiums and spent their days underground. The entire city was honeycombed underneath by the mines and tunnels that produced the riches that generated the lifestyle of the thriving society above it.

While it hadn't dampened my ardor to try mining for myself, I became fairly certain that the way to finance any of those who did, from big to small, was to feed and supply them. I made more money working at the restaurant than most of these miners ever would. The owner had opened three more restaurants in the short time I'd been here, and was in the process of building himself and his family a lovely Victorian house just up the hill.

That night, on my knees beside my bed in my small room at the boardinghouse, I prayed like I hadn't since we'd left Boston.

"Thank you for bringing me to this place in your wisdom, Lord. I'm learning more each day, and discovering ways to use the gifts you've given me. There is never an end to that discovery on this earth or in our heaven, nor to the souls that need saving, mine and everyone else's. I'm trying to do my best. Mother Mary, watch over your humble servant. Amen."

The next morning I gave my notice at the café and packed my belongings and cash in my bag. I'd learned as much as I could in Virginia City. Besides, I missed my Mama and Fanny. This was the first time I'd ever been away from them.

The road down to Reno was just as frightening as I remembered on the way up, the coach clinging precariously to the side of mountain. It wasn't a long way as the crow flew, but for mere mortals in peril of their lives and those of their horses and passengers, it took a great deal longer. The railroad from Reno into San Francisco across the Sierras and Donner Summit, beautiful as the views were, wasn't a lot better and given the steep grades on both sides, the engines straining and moving just about as slow as the poor horses and mules. I felt like an old hand, having done this before, in comparison to some of my fellow travelers, but even so, occasionally my heart beat faster too, and I caught myself fingering my rosary beads before we hit the valley floor.

I couldn't help but chuckle to myself. If I wanted to pursue precious minerals, I'd better get over those trepidations quickly. They hid in the deep mountains, those elusive metals, and it was almost as though they were being guarded by the little folk from the old Gaelic tales, laughing at us humans and leading us a merry chase as we tried to hunt them out, making the journey and even the destination, as harrowing as possible. Fortune favors the brave, so they say, and there's a good reason for that, I was beginning to discover. I had a feeling my time in Virginia City was just the beginning of many revelations to come.

* * *

"TJ, you are most handsome young man in the world," I said, bouncing my chubby laughing nephew on my knee while Fanny concentrated on her chicken and dumplings in the kitchen. I'd told her I'd make dinner but she was having none of it. She was five months pregnant again but she was as stalwart as ever, my sister, even though I knew her back was bothering her, and keeping up with TJ was a new adventure every day.

They were adventures I was happy to share with him, and ever since I'd returned from the Comstock, I'd been delighted to do my part, along with Mama, who doted on the child, too. I think Mama was hoping for a dozen children from Tom and Fanny, but I was not. Perhaps Mother Mary or the Pope would be angry with me for that, but my sister had never had my strong constitution, and she was always prone to influenza and colds. I knew little about medicine, but I knew having too many children too quickly certainly would do nothing to make her stronger. I remembered some of the thin overworked Irish women in our Boston neighborhood, always chasing thin, dirty unruly children for a dinner that didn't provide much more than boiled potatoes and greens, if they were available.

I kept my perhaps sinful thoughts on childbearing to

myself, of course. I knew they would not be welcomed, certainly not by my family and very definitely not by Father Shanahan at St. Patrick's.

After I returned, I stayed at Tom and Fanny's house, along with Mama. There was plenty of room. Tom was a prosperous man who planned ahead, and had built extra bedrooms. They'd be filled with children in the years to come, I was sure, but for now, it was a haven for a wayward aunt and a doting grandmother. Tom was a most kind and thoughtful man, and I could see the love between him and my sister every day, from the touch of a hand to a quick peck on the cheek. My sister had found her heart's desire here on the other side of the continent.

I was still searching for mine. I wasn't quite sure what it was, only a longing to explore and see the world, along with a feeling that there was something wonderful to be discovered just over the next mountain or the next river.

I had saved my money, from Virginia City as well as the shoe factory, and rather than get another job, I roamed the city, visiting coffeehouses, shops, restaurants, and parks where everyone gathered. Conversations abounded, and I participated in many, while quite frankly, listening in on others. I thought of it as an academy, only the subjects were vastly different than those taught in any formal school. My interests lay in other areas.

My favorite place was Shepherd's Coffeehouse on Mission Street, across from the San Francisco Chronicle's office. It was a cheerful place, warm wood paneling on the walls, and the crackle of the apple logs in the fireplace on a foggy day, with the enticing aroma of freshly ground and brewed coffee. Here I would show up at least every other day and read the Chronicle, along with the California Evening Republican, sometimes from the night before, or very late afternoon. Those papers were as close to a library as I could've gotten at Harvard, at least for me. My chances of ever getting into Harvard Library would've been limited to being part of the Irish cleaning crew at night. But here, the newspapers provided me with the information I craved. There weren't many other women who frequented Shepherd's, but I rarely encountered any resentment or raised eyebrows.

When summer came on, along with Fanny's beautiful baby boy, I was ready for another expedition to that enticing world beyond the Sierra Nevada. Tom hired a nursemaid and suddenly Mama and I found our services weren't as needed as they had been, although of course they were always desired. Still, I thought it was time Tom and Fanny had the house to themselves and their children. The poor things hadn't ever been truly alone, although it clearly hadn't led to any inhibitions, considering the two full nurseries.

"Mama, I've been thinking."

My mother was no fool. "Nellie, that statement coming from you always precedes something I'm not certain I want to hear. You've always been the most impetuous girl."

"This one you'll want to hear, Mama. There's this place, Pioche, Nevada. Biggest silver strike in Nevada. The place is booming and I've figured out a way for us to get in on that boom."

My mother set her teacup firmly in its saucer. "And how would that be now, Nellie?"

"I'll tell you, Mama. Trust me. We can make a great deal of money because Pioche needs what we have to offer."

She agreed to be my partner, my dear intrepid mother. For weeks, we prepared, buying supplies of food, utensils, linens, clothing, tools and of course, boots from Tom Cunningham – everything we could plan for but of course, missing many things we'd need, as we'd come to find out. At last the day came when, all our cargo loaded, Mama and I took our seats on the Central Pacific and we were off to Pioche. To be honest, I was having some second thoughts after hearing news stories of the area, but I'd invested much of my savings and it was too late to back out now, so I kept those misgivings to myself.

At Paradise, we left the train and boarded the freight wagon I'd contracted for, pulled by six horses and piled high with our boxes and goods. After two days on that wagon, the somewhat uncomfortable train seemed like a palatial carriage from a fairy tale in comparison. My mother slept on my shoulder and I marveled at the two drivers who somehow managed to stay awake, despite our brief stops, one of them overnight for the sake of the poor horses, a respite nearly as uncomfortable as the jolting wagon. When we finally entered Pioche itself on a grey afternoon, we saw a man gunned down in the street by two others who nonchalantly walked away. Our wagon passed by his body and I said a quick blessing for the poor man's soul as I watched his blood spread onto the dusty road. Mama clung to my arm, her fingers digging in.

"Nellie, what in God's name possessed you to think this was a good place to set up business? These people are animals and we could be killed by a stray gunshot. We should turn this wagon around and go home tomorrow."

She wasn't wrong. This place was no Virginia City. Pioche was a lawless town, no sheriff, no deputies. While I was ambitious and wanted to get in the thick of the mining boom, what I was witnessing made me worry we were in over our heads. Almost every building we passed was either a saloon or a brothel, easy to tell because of the underdressed women on the porches of a third of the buildings, to say nothing of the drunken men free with their guns outside the others.

"What sort of godforsaken place is this?"

The first driver laughed. "About the worst one I've ever been to, madam, and that's saying something, since I been to Bodie. Still, there's some good people here. You'll find them.

Leastwise, I hope you will. In the short time I've known y'all, you seem to have good heads on your shoulders."

That was true, I thought, *as long as we kept them intact instead of drilled with a bullet.* It wasn't a comforting thought but one I'd come back to many times after that afternoon, a maxim that kept my head firmly attached, and my Mama's too.

CHAPTER 4

1872

Panaca Flats was no paradise, not even close. I stood on the upstairs veranda of our Miner's Boardinghouse and sipped my coffee, and watched the hills as the sun began to rise.

Downstairs in the kitchen, I could hear the rattle of pots and pans as the girls began to prepare breakfast for our guests. I knew I should go down and provide a hand, but they were doing a great job, and I had more pressing concerns this morning. I had to meet the freight wagon from Paradise with our next shipment of saleable goods from San Francisco, as well as the wagons from Utah bringing food and supplies for the kitchen.

Running a boardinghouse for thirty-odd miners wasn't a job for the lazy, and the store I'd set up to sell clothing and supplies took even more time, even though Mama was actually enjoying her role as the chatelaine of that venture, set up on the ground floor of the boardinghouse. We were making a handsome profit on both the boardinghouse and the store but not a day went by when we weren't somewhat concerned about our safety, in spite of the loyal boarders who had taken to being our defenders.

Panaca Flats wasn't as dangerous as central Pioche itself, but trouble could erupt in a heartbeat anywhere in this area, especially between the two big rivals – Raymond & Ely Mining and Meadow Valley Mining. They both hired gunmen to enforce their policies and "protect" their workers but nobody was really fooled by that. When a miner got hurt or sick, he ended up at my kitchen door, where I ran a medical clinic and impromptu diner for those who needed it, and often supplied them with new boots and other necessary items. Mama would grumble my openhandedness was eating into profits, but after the first time I smiled and said "what does it profit a man to gain the world and lose his soul", she threw up her hands.

"Nellie, you and Father Scanlan will never get that church finished if you give away the money to do it with every day. The two of you, I swear, thinking you can save the world."

"I'm not concerned with the world, just the little piece of it I can see that needs to be kinder, Mama. I can't ignore what I can help fix." I'd been raising money in donations from the miners and the businesses in town to help Father Scanlan build a church.

Somehow, that became my motto from then on. Running a business was all well and good, and I had to admit I had a bad case of gold fever, but walking over somebody that needed a helping hand just wasn't something I could do. There was lots of money but little compassion in Pioche, Nevada. I was just beginning to find out that was true for much of the world, but it was never going to be true for me.

We ventured into the downtown Pioche area occasionally, to Brown's Opera House and the ice cream parlor, among other venues. Pioche was booming, there was no question about that, but there was also no doubt that it wasn't a safe place, even for a town that grew up from a mining camp.

After breakfast, while the miners were leaving for their long day, Sean Whitstone stopped me in the hallway.

"Miss Nellie? Can I ask you something?"

"Of course," I said. Sean was one of the Cornish miners, the "Cousin Jacks", but he was a gregarious fellow, unlike most of them, more on a par with some of the talkative Irishmen.

"We'd like to have a meeting here at the boardinghouse tonight, after supper. Mining business. Maybe in the dining room?"

"I don't see why not, Sean."

He smiled. "Thank you. Tonight then. We won't make a mess or anything, I promise."

I laughed. "You do, you clean it up, Sean."

I spent the rest of the day down in Pioche at the freight office, overseeing my supplies and didn't give Sean's request another thought, until the house had quieted down after supper and men began showing up in twos and threes, quietly entering the dining room. After a half hour or so, there were over fifty of them in there, most standing or sitting on the floor, the chairs occupied by early arrivals. I stood outside in the hallway and listened. I wasn't sure what it was about, but I knew this was no ordinary gathering.

There was a lot of talk, in English, Gaelic which I knew, and Cornish which I didn't, but the gist of it all was a union was being formed right here in the Miners' Boardinghouse under my nose and on my premises. I couldn't disagree with these men and their plight. Far from it. They worked brutal jobs, long hours with poor pay, and no compensation for any injuries or any thought to their families if they died down there. Even the Comstock was being unionized, I knew that, as were the Colorado silver mines. The times were changing for the ore barons and it was past time they did.

After sitting on the stairs for over an hour, I opened the doors and entered the dining room. Faces turned to me in alarm, most of them dirt-stained and all of them apprehensive. The room reeked of hard-earned sweat, pit dirt and desperation.

I held up my hand. "You all know me, well at least most of you do. Have no fear that I will divulge anything I've heard here this night. You have a just cause, one I agree with."

Sean Whitstone came to stand beside me. "You need to leave, Miss Nellie. You can't be a part of this."

I shook my head. Men could be so silly. "I am a part of this, Sean, since you all decided to use my house for your meeting. Lucky for you, I must say, rather than some other venues around town. Since you've all been talking for an hour, I am now taking a turn."

He blinked, stared at me for a second or two, and nodded his head, whether with regret or agreement, I didn't know. It didn't matter anyway.

"Listen, you lot. You're embarking on a dangerous path, one more perilous than you know, and for anyone who supports your cause, which now includes me. Raymond & Ely and Meadow Valley will oppose you with everything they have and you have to be smart and communicate your needs to them in a manner they won't see as threatening, at least not at first. Let's hope you don't get to that point, but you likely will. Before your needs become demands, and their opposition becomes lethal, you must find middle ground. I don't voice these cautions lightly. I'm Irish, like many of you, and I know what oppressors can do. The English proved that a long time ago and we don't want to see anything like that occur here."

It was pretty quiet after I finished my piece, but a lot of heads were nodding in assent, and many looked at me with newfound respect.

Sean touched my arm lightly and nodded towards the door. "I apologize for this, Miss Nellie, but I'm also grateful that we met here and for every word you've said. We needed to hear that. Do you think Father Scanlan would support us too?"

Lord God save us. Did they want everything, these boys? Apparently, they did.

Father Scanlan likely would. "I will ask him, Sean. For now, carry on but heed my words. And, next time? Have your meeting somewhere else. There will be trouble and I don't want it on my doorstep."

He nodded. "I understand. I never meant to endanger you or your mother."

"I know that," I said. "Still, you must learn to think ahead, Sean, especially if you want to lead these men to a better life. Now you are responsible."

Negotiations began with the mining companies but nothing concrete seemed forthcoming. The next few weeks passed with no trouble, at least no more than the usual gunfights and the bodies being buried in the cemetery which was rapidly expanding, trouble enough.

The night when Sean Whitstone was gunned down on the front porch of the Miners' Boardinghouse, along with three other men I'd seen at the meeting in my dining room that night, made me rethink everything I'd done in the past year. Changes that attempt to provide people with better lives are often met with lethal violence from those that have no interest in anything but profit. The daily display of death from that and the casual attitude toward the ending of human life was not something that I wanted to have in my life, no matter how well my business was doing.

Sean's blood still stained the pine boards on the porch of my front door when I sold the Miner's Rest to an ambitious young man from Leadville at a very handsome profit.

Sometimes you had to look clearly at the future you wanted. Mine was surely not in Panaca Flats, Nevada and I needed no celestial help to realize it. Besides, I was eager to see my sister and her expanding family and I could never do that in this place. Mama needed to go back to San Francisco where she wouldn't worry or work so hard and could get back to the important business of dangling her grandchildren on her knee.

It was time.

CHAPTER 5

1874

San Francisco certainly had its cosmopolitan comforts. There was no disputing that. I enjoyed the crab dinners and the fine wines as much as anyone at the candlelit restaurants that overlooked the Bay. I loved strolling the streets with their myriad shops and bookstores, blissfully free from worry about stray gunshots or having my skirts covered in mud. It was comforting that our morning fog was the biggest concern, a concern that dissipated by noon just as the mist did.

Fanny was happy and content with two fine young sons now, and they were a delight to Mama, who spent most of her time shepherding them and advising Fanny on the best methods of child-rearing, at which Fanny often rolled her eyes at me. I ventured no opinions and found various methods of exiting the household especially when conflict was likely. None of it was ever allowed to reach the ears of Tom, now an important man at the shoe factory, and the household was increasingly prosperous with his endeavors.

The Pioche venture had been enough of a financial success that I had no worries about finding a job, and I had no desire to return to the shoe factory, even under Tom's benevolent supervision. I wasn't sure what my next opportunity would be, but the world so far had been kind in presenting them to me. Mama didn't quite seem to think along the same lines, particularly when it came to what she saw as my loveless existence and fecund responsibilities.

"Nellie, you're an attractive woman and young men have been presenting themselves to you constantly," she said one morning. "I do not understand your disinterest in them, not even accepting invitations to dinner or evening gatherings at respectable homes. It is time you looked to your future, my girl."

I tried to explain to her that I wanted to make my own future, independent of a husband or anyone else that tried to make it for me, but she dismissed my thoughts with a wave of her hand.

"Nonsense. When you meet the right gentleman, it'll be the same for you as it was for Fanny. Just look at how happy they are. You will be as well if you relinquish those unwomanly fantasies you've created. Just leave it to me, and don't be so truculent."

I stopped trying to explain myself to her after that. It wasn't just that she and I came from different generations, with lives fashioned on different continents. For me, it was something that wasn't fully formed in my mind yet, much less trying to explain or justify my position to anyone else. In fact, I grew defiant when pressed to do so, and rather than argue, I kept my opinions close to my chest. For a certainty, I knew only this: I wanted to go where others had not, to venture into the unknown, to make a life independent of society's rules and whims, especially those that pertained to women. I knew we could do anything a man could do, given the opportunity. I fully intended to make sure I had those opportunities. Perhaps that meant I would have to forgo the pleasures of a husband and children, because those were pleasures that for me, would slowly become the chains that would fetter me, and my desires and dreams would die.

One spring afternoon, my mother insisted we all get portraits done at the most stylish photography studio in San Francisco. I reluctantly complied. It was a torturous afternoon and once I saw that photograph of me in a sumptuous gown, with a feathered headdress, I felt as though I was about to be smothered by the convention of it all. Rather than making me happy and eager to find a husband, my mother's idea reignited the clandestine rebellion inside me.

To keep her from constantly badgering me, I accepted some evening invitations to this party and that, being bored silly with the inane conversations and the men who could lift nothing heavier than a champagne glass preening themselves before us females, single or not.

A mustached young man actually wearing a monocle which kept falling out unpredictably cornered me near some palms and I had no way out. "So, Miss Cashman, did you have an opportunity to see 'The Magic Flute' at the Opera House? I swear it was deadly boring to me, but I hear the ladies love it."

"No, Mr. Floyd, I did not have the pleasure of Mozart last week, I was too busy horse racing and training my fighting cocks."

He blinked and his monocle fell into his glass. "You're quite the kidder, aren't you?"

I smiled. "No, actually I have a terrible sense of humor. If you'll excuse me?"

To clear my palate, so to speak, rather than sherbet, I began spending my days at my old haunts, particularly Shepherd's Coffeehouse on Mission Street, among others, and reading the newspapers, eager for tidings of another ore strike or the latest area that might be one. My mother was not thrilled.

I loved this place, with its mullioned windows, dark wainscoting and the mouth-watering aromas of fresh baked goods, to say nothing of the enticing smell of fresh ground coffee beans from exotic places. My companions were mostly men, since many women, or perhaps their families, felt those places weren't quite genteel, and quite certain that reading the news of the day could be distressing to the fairer sex.

Soon we had assembled a coterie of sorts, me and a few gentlemen, some of whom were a bit rougher around the edges than others, but all good and amiable sorts. Three of them I'd met in Pioche – Ted Brandywine, and the McGill brothers, Matthew and Big Mac. Ted was a savvy Welshman, and the McGills were Cornish. Matthew looked out for his brother Big Mac, a giant of a man who looked threatening but was a little slow and had the gentle demeanor of a kitten. They'd all left Pioche not long after I had, and I remembered them well from the abortive union meetings at the boarding-house. Tommy Sweeney was a red-haired firebrand from Dublin, who'd been hunting for a strike since he landed in America, so far disappointed but always eager and the first one with the news of the day. Tim Rickman was from England, an eager lad, clearly the youngest amongst us all, and possessed of a wicked sense of humor which kept us all laughing. I thought of them as my boys, and thoroughly enjoyed their company, although I never referred to them that way as these were stalwart proud men looking to make better lives for themselves.

One afternoon my old acquaintance from the boarding-house, the adventurous Patrick Sullivan, came in and sat down in an empty chair at our big round table. At first he didn't recognize me, but as his eyes traveled around his fellow coffee drinkers, they landed on me. He'd changed a bit, more weathered, and had a beard but the blue eyes were still merry and his smile just as infectious.

"Nellie Cashman, is that you?"

I smiled. "I do believe 'tis, Patrick Sullivan."

"Well, well," he said, and got up from his chair and advanced toward me. I made sure to put my hand out just in case he was thinking of embracing me, and thankfully he grasped it with great enthusiasm. "I am happy to see that pretty face again, but rather surprised to see it here." He looked around the room, while the rest of my companions laughed.

Ted Brandywine, sitting beside me, snorted. "You better get used to it, friend. We think of this as Nellie's table. You may be welcome, if she approves."

Ted cocked an eyebrow at me and I nodded at Sullivan. "Take your seat, Patrick, and tell us where you've been these years since I've seen you."

He gave me a quick bow and resumed his chair, clearing his throat. We waited.

"Leadville, Cripple Creek, Bodie, Pioche, even an ill-fated venture into the Utah canyons which led to nothing but amazing vistas blurred by the sweat of my brow," he said. "Chasing the yellow is as fruitless as the unicorn, until you've found one, a course. But I've heard tell of a couple new possibilities, if anyone's interested?"

"Boyo, speak your words," Tommy Sweeney said. "And ain't that the reason now we rest our behinds in these chairs day after day? Possibilities? I do believe you've come to the right place."

Patrick ordered a coffee and a bun and turned to his transfixed audience. "Well, what they're sayin' is the biggest gold strike ever in this world in the Transvaal, South Africa. To say nothing of the diamonds."

Everyone started talking at once because we'd heard a rumor about that this very day and now here it had surfaced again. There was no doubt the lot of us had gold fever, me included, and news like this set our blood on fire with it. Patrick Sullivan looked around the table and saw the effect his words had on all of us, listening to the frenzied conversation. It went so far as to getting on a ship, discussing which route was fastest, across the Isthmus and the Atlantic or the Pacific. There was no consensus on that because really no one knew, nor did I.

After a few minutes, Patrick held up his hand. "Wait."

Everyone stopped talking and turned their eyes back to him. What other revelations could this new arrival have for us?

I hadn't said a word, but my mind was working furiously. Africa? I had visions of elephants, jungles, black-skinned magnificently fierce warriors and lions, rather than gold, but to me that was nearly as exciting and a world that frightened and thrilled me at the same time.

"There's another new strike, my friends, one much more accessible, one without a long sea voyage, but who can tell what awaits us in the far north, a land frozen half a year, and arguably much more impassable than an African savannah?" Patrick seemed to be enjoying this, dragging out the suspense, and his audience was rapt, even me.

"The Cassiar."

And with those two words, the die was cast and the thoughts of jungles, warriors and lions dissipated like San Francisco morning fog. Our thoughts instead reverted to white water rivers, mountains, and forests, the very territory we knew well, and places we knew shielded and yielded the precious ores we were looking for. We knew it, or some of us did, anyway. I had a fleeting thought of those dwarves hiding in the mountains laughing at us humans but the lure of the fortune that awaited pushed it from my mind.

It wasn't that far, the storied Cassiar, so the maps said. British Columbia, just north of us, more or less. Still on our continent. No need to take a steamer to an unknown foreign continent where no one knew the language or the terrain. The Cassiar was here, accessible and we could get there fairly easily. Or so we thought. Maps were one thing, terrain was another.

Gold was on our minds, and not necessarily the sacrifices we'd have to make to find it. I was no exception. In fact, that I was willing to go and said I'd do the cooking may have convinced the rest of them. That was something that would come back to haunt me, many pots of imaginative stew later.

In the few weeks that followed, with Mama adamantly opposed to my venture, of course, we filled every day with buying supplies and planning for our trip. Every obstacle that cropped up, from the weather to gossip and warnings in the papers, we dismissed. I was going to the Cassiar, because it called to me like nothing ever had before, That, and the enthusiasm from my fellow travelers led my footsteps up the ramp to the boat one foggy morning. We needed to get to the Stikine River before the ice melted in April and there was no time to lose.

I'm coming for you, I thought as we sailed away from the wharf. *Hope you're ready for me.*

CHAPTER 6

PATRICK SULLIVAN

Nellie Cashman. There was a woman like I'd never encountered before. I knew it from the first moment I met her during my short stay at that boardinghouse on Fifth Street. Something about the gleam in those big blue eyes, the sharp inquisitive glances she gave anyone who had information she found interesting, that quick turn of the chin when confronted with an opinion she didn't care for. Strangely enough, pretty as she was, she held no physical attraction for me, but only that of a fascinated fellow human, a friend or a brother, if you will. She would provide no soft breast for a man to lay his head upon after a hard day, or a wife who gives you pats and kisses of encouragement at breakfast or dinner. I knew I needed that pliant support from any woman unlucky enough to ever accept my proposal but so far I'd resisted those lures.

No, Nellie was Diana the Huntress, and I could even imagine her carrying a bow, a carcass slung across her slim shoulders, facing down any threat whatsoever. Perhaps it was fanciful, I freely admit that. Still, there was something about her that just wasn't like anyone else. Maybe it was her belief in herself and of course, she made no secret of her Catholic faith in her god, a philosophy that I'd learned the hard way wasn't for me with no basis in reality, hope or anything else. Despite that, I liked her a great deal. That she would be a part of our journey to the Cassiar went a long way when it came to convincing me to be a part of the expedition. Especially when she volunteered to do the cooking because all of us had heard how very good her cooking was. Turned out we'd need every ounce of that food, our own fortitude and maybe even Nellie's divine intervention.

CHAPTER 7

1874, BRITISH COLUMBIA

Victoria came into view on the fourth morning out of San Francisco. The tall green forests and hills were a welcome sight. I stood on the deck beside Ted Brandywine and Patrick Sullivan, who handed me a tin cup of coffee.

"It's beautiful," I said. "Reminds me of Ireland, but with big dark trees."

He laughed. "Yes, the whole damn place has a lot of those, you'll be finding. The English bastards didn't cut them all down here."

He wasn't wrong. Not just trees, but the whole island seemed to be in bloom, although it was early March. Once we disembarked from the steamer and walked into town, we were enchanted with the explosion of flowers and blooms, many on trees and more in baskets hanging from lamp posts, in window boxes and garden plots. Spring came early on this temperate island and it was a welcome sight. Also, for me, it was somewhat worrisome.

As we walked into town to find a hotel for a night or two, I couldn't help but fret about the spring thaw of the Stikine River and the sense of urgency wouldn't leave me, dampening my delight in the abundant flora. As we stood in the lobby getting our room keys, I turned to the boys.

"Matthew, please take Mac and visit the supply warehouses this afternoon. Tommy, if you would head to the wharf and see about ships to Fort Wrangell. Tim, if you would, see what we can find in tinned goods and produce that may last for months in this cold, if such a thing exists. Patrick, if you could –"

"Nellie." Patrick Sullivan put his hand gently on my arm. "We all know what we need to do, darlin'. For right now, let's get our land legs, have some breakfast, and take a breath. Nothing at all will change in a day, not even the ice on the Stikine."

I looked at the rest of them, their faces, clearly relieved at Patrick's words. My cheeks flushed. He was right.

"Forgive me," I said. "I don't mean to sound like a shrew giving orders. I have no right. I'm just anxious to get there, as I know we all are."

We settled in our rooms and met downstairs, downing a hearty breakfast and ready to get on with our business. I kept my mouth shut, at considerable expense, and everyone dispersed to get on with what we needed for our trek. By noon, Tommy Sweeney and I had ordered food, mainly tinned goods, flour, lard and potatoes, to be delivered to the wharf the next morning, while the others arranged passage on the thrice daily ships to Fort Wrangell, along with mining supplies and other essentials. The waterfront, warehouses, and the city itself were bustling with the influx of prospectors and people headed to the Cassiar, and the vendors and businesses had geared up for not just our arrival, but the hundreds more that were arriving weekly.

The McGills discovered a store that provided fur-lined leather gloves, hooded jackets called parkas, and thick wool underwear and socks, all of which we purchased, grateful for the advice of the sales clerks, who knew their business. I bought four pairs of thick wool trousers, and I knew my days of wearing silly and cumbersome skirts were gone, certainly for now and perhaps forever, unless I found myself back in what my Mama would call "proper society", not that I cared much what anyone in that category would think of me and my scandalous legs. I had already packed my two pairs of Tom Cunningham's sturdy leather boots, and those trousers fit into them very well indeed.

We all met for dinner at a chop house near the waterfront, crowded with fellow travelers on the same path as we were. As we sat enjoying our coffee, I saw two black-clad sisters walk past, and I threw down my napkin and hurried out to intercept them. I had no idea there were established orders up here, although I should've. Still, I wanted to get acquainted. The sisters were nuns from St. Anne's convent, and they invited me to have tea with them. I was grateful I hadn't yet donned my new trousers but was in a respectable skirt, and I eagerly accepted their invitation.

It was a delightful evening, and I met many of their sisters as they showed me around their home. It was a welcoming place, redolent with the aroma of candle wax and lemon polish, not as austere as some convents were. Sister Mary Margaret and I spoke at length about their plans to build a hospital, and their efforts at fundraising. I volunteered a few ideas of my own, from the Pioche days and Father Scanlan, along with some of my less lurid stories of that place, which the sisters found amusing. They found my plans for the Cassiar relatively alarming for a woman alone, but I quickly assured them that I was not alone, and that I could depend on the boys. Still, they seemed apprehensive but blessed my journey.

"Remember to always put your trust in God," Sister Mary Margaret said as I was leaving. "We will all be praying for you."

"Thank you," I said. "When I return, I will bring you

contributions for the hospital, because there's likely to be many a miner who will have need of such a place in the coming years. Investing in your future isn't something that's on their minds right now, afire with gold fever, but they will come to see I'm right."

"Unfortunately, you are, Nellie. We will appreciate any help you can provide us. Safe journey to you."

We left the next morning on the steamer to Fort Wrangell, up the inside passage, and soon civilization as we'd known it was left far behind. Soon there would be no sturdy deck, but only snow beneath my feet and moving forward would depend on my own strength, not that of a steam engine. Butterflies of excitement and yes, fears, flitted in my stomach but I turned my face into the brisk wind and sent a wish and prayer into the salt spray.

CHAPTER 8

Tall totem poles lined the seacoast, towering over the land below as we came into the harbor of Fort Wrangell. Painted in bright colors, and carved with intricate designs, these were beautiful things I'd never imagined existed. A friendly deckhand explained some of the markings to me.

"This is their land here, the natives, Miss, and those poles represent their gods or so they say. There is the wolf clan, see the figurehead? See there, the eagle, oh look at the wings, ma'am, then the salmon, the deer, the bear, and even the orca."

"What is an orca?"

"Oh ma'am, that is the black and white whale, the one with teeth," he laughed. "We see them all the time. They swam by the ship yesterday and if I'd known you'd never seen them, I would've alerted you."

"Oh, I so wish you would've," I said. I wanted to see this creature, the whale with teeth. I was enchanted by this beautifully harsh land already and eager to see more of it.

Tim Rickman materialized by my side. "Christ Jesus, I want to see one of those sea creatures meself." He turned to the deckhand. "Any chance they come into the harbor?"

"Sometimes, sir," the young deckhand said. "But I don't see any now. It ain't every day they come around."

"Next time," Tim said, and nudged me with his elbow. "Now we know to keep a sharp eye out, Nellie. We won't be caught napping the next voyage. It's been a good passage. No one fell overboard and froze to death in one minute, as the captain warned us could happen."

I couldn't agree more. The captain's speech as we left Victoria would never leave my mind. The icy winter sea gave no quarter to anyone unlucky enough to land in its waves. One look at that grey turbid sea convinced me and I had no intention of being a sacrifice to its depths.

At the wharf, we disembarked, and some of the men stayed to watch over our cargo being unloaded and make plans to get to the mainland while the rest of us went to reconnoiter Fort Wrangell. A curious place, the original fort had been built by the Russians, who had fought the local natives many times to remain in possession. Then, the British had taken over and now, it was American land, but many traces of the previous occupiers remained. The entire water-front, and indeed, most of the town itself, was teeming with people, bustling about, either purveyors of goods and services or those who were buying them, provisioning for their treks to the interior.

If Victoria had been a genteel tea room filled with flowers and ladies in hats, by contrast, Fort Wrangell was a rowdy saloon filled with the odors of beer, tobacco and unwashed men. Some were on their way south, but most were like us, on their way up the Stikine River to the Cassiar.

We claimed a table at the largest saloon, knowing that was the best way to get the lay of the land, as Patrick called it. Beer and liquor flowed as freely as water, and the conversation was running at a fast current as well. We all knew you could learn more about the true events and circumstances of a place from listening to those who'd been in it for a time, so we kept our ears sharp and our mouths mostly closed.

It didn't take us long to find out that we would need a small boat to take us and our supplies to the mainland and the mouth of the Stikine River. From there, we would be on our own. It was a hard trek to the Cassiar, and within an hour, we knew we'd need help. We also learned how to find it.

* * *

"Stop, Chris, stop," I laughed as the huge furry dog washed my face with his tongue. He settled down but stayed at my side as though we'd been destined to be together from the first moment we saw each other, his blue eyes flicking to me at the slightest word. I'd finally fallen in love, but it was a sweet gentleman of 150 pounds who traveled on four feet and had a lot of hair that wouldn't need a barber. Mama would be unimpressed but I was quite delighted.

Chinay, our Stikine Tlingit guide, gave me a faint smile. "He cares for you, Nellie. That is unusual for these dogs. They are workers, not pets."

I smiled. For me, this dog was already far from being just a worker and Chinay knew it.

"I understand."

He sighed, very discreetly. The Tlingit were not big on showing emotions. "You will need at least three more dogs, perhaps four, as this one is clearly a leader. We will harness him up front."

We found Chris's littermates, two males and two females, and that rounded out my dog sled team. I liked them too, they were good dogs but they didn't strike me as Chris had. They slept outside in our brief stay, but Chris had appointed himself my guardian, and slept beside my bed. I'd christened him St. Christopher, but Chinay had been quick to point out that a one-syllable word was necessary for sled dogs, and I'd shortened it, never forgetting the dog's namesake.

At the river, we'd found the Stikine Tlingit Indians to be of great help, as many had before us. We'd purchased dogs and sleds and, in our case, the services of Chinay, who had agreed to guide us up the Stikine to the Cassiar. I came to find out this was fairly unusual, as many of the Stikine Tlingits took a dim view of the white men who were coming in droves to rob their country of its minerals and leave damages behind, both environmental and human.

Many of Chinay's clan had done the same, taking full advantage of the white men who flooded into their territory in search of gold, even while others had not. I could not know the others, but this man I trusted. He was as alien to me and my Catholic faith as a man from another dimension, but I was a good judge of character and knew we were lucky he'd been there when we landed. This was a man of integrity and in the coming weeks, I found my instincts were correct. Had it not been for him, we likely would have perished as so many others had.

The rest of the men had done as I had, banding together and buying dogs to carry the supplies on three more dogsleds loaded with our supplies. From here on, we were on our own for anything we needed.

Up the frozen river we went, the sleds running easy on the solid ice. It was 160 miles to Buck's Bar, named after Buck Choquette who had first discovered the opportunities in the Cassiar, and we traveled as fast as we could, worrying constantly about the melt and the weather. I resented even stopping at night for rest, so eager was I to arrive in the Cassiar, accompanied by my constant concern about the temperature and the melting ice. Chinay was wiser than me, and insisted we stop even when I would've gone on, and I knew in my heart he was right.

"People who have gone past their physical limits also lose

the ability to think in the right way," Chinay said to me as we sat beside our little fire one night. "This is not a place that forgives foolishness. If you have the right thinking, it will work with you. If you ignore its wisdom, you will die."

I stroked Chris's head, smoothing the soft fur. "I understand, Chinay. And once again, I thank you for teaching me the ways of this land I've come to uninvited."

He made a sound in his throat that could've been a chuckle. "Nellie, you are a person of worth. I am proud to help you on the right path. For many of your countrymen I could not say the same."

I could not have been more honored. When I was falling asleep with Chris beside me, his warmth like a benediction, my last thought was how fortunate a woman I was to be able to experience all this.

* * *

"NELLIE, for god's sake, wake up!" Ted Brandywine's voice was more a shriek than a gentle wake-up call. "The ice is melting early."

I rolled over, laced up my boots and hastily folded up my blankets. It was dark outside, only the faint light of the stars but enough to see the entire camp was awake and packing, Chinay and Tommy Sweeney quickly harnessing the dogs, and the others throwing packs and blankets into the sleds. The white men looked panicked but Chinay was calm as usual. Over all of our activity was the ominous sound of ice smashing into ice, very like boulders smashing into each other, crushing everything in their path, just as Rip Van Winkle's storied bowling balls had done. Even if we couldn't see it, it was very close, as was our certain death if we were on this river when those giant pieces of ice overtook our helpless crew.

Within minutes, we were underway towards firmer footing.

Chinay had said the evening before we were only a few hours from Buck's Bar and should reach it by noon today, but I hadn't realized how important it was that we might. Now I did.

Chris led my sled and like always, he was the leader of us all. When he broke into the deep snow on the bank of the Stikine, he slowed down. The snow was soft this time of year and the dogs and the sleds sank into the depths. We plowed onward as there was little choice, but much more slowly. At least, on Chinay's advice, we'd distributed our supplies and the food we were carrying between the three dogsleds, as a precaution just in case anything went wrong. I was reminded of my Mama saying, 'don't put all your eggs in one basket, missy' and every time I thought of it, I smiled to myself. Mama was always right.

Dawn was beginning to break, and what we saw behind us was terrifying. Huge slabs of ice slammed into each other on the river itself, the dark green water beneath sloshing high onto the frozen chunks, the current pushing them outwards towards the banks and further downriver as well. The McGill brothers were on the last sled, pulled by six dogs, and just before they reached the banks where the rest of us struggled in the snow, they were hit by a giant slab of ice and plummeted backward, dogs, sled and all, into the churning river.

Patrick Sullivan, laboring beside me, turned and put his hand on my arm. "Keep going, Nellie. We'll get them." He handed me the reins of his sled.

He and Chinay stepped off into the snow, met up with Ted, Tommy and Tim whose sled was on safe ground, and they all headed to the rescue. I felt helpless, but kept the dogs moving forward inch by inch, while keeping a loose hand on the reins of the second sled. Most of all, I prayed, more frightened than I'd ever been for the fate of another. The odds of the McGills surviving the icy water, to say nothing of the dogs or supplies, were very slim. I could go no further. I halted both the dog teams and stared down the banks in the breaking dawn light. What I saw chilled my soul.

Men and dogs were captives of the icy waters, pulled down by the heavy sled, while the others strained to reach them. Patrick Sullivan jumped in and caught hold of Matthew's parka hood, pulling him to safety, while Tim and Tommy went for Big Mac, but they couldn't grasp him as fast as the current pulled him down beyond their reach, without being swept into the current themselves. I saw Tim's anguished face as he was held back by Tommy.

Ted and Chinay jumped into the river and pulled out their knives, the blades glinting in the sun, and cut the harnesses of the sled dogs, but only three of the poor creatures were able to instinctively struggle towards the snowy banks, shivering as they came to join me. The sled itself sank into the crush of water and ice and was never seen again, nor was Big Mac McGill.

The men staggered out of the water towards me, and Chinay, teeth chattering, told me to put Matthew McGill on my sled and cover him with blankets. The others, near frozen, pulled blankets over themselves and trudged beside Tommy Sweeney's sled as we made our way up the banks of the Stikine.

Once we were on safe ground, we stopped and I myself built the biggest fire we'd ever managed so far on this voyage, the men who'd been in the river stripping off the wet clothing once the flames were high. I made pots of hot tea, and rubbed limbs for hours, bringing back warmth from outside as much as the tea did for the inside, while they huddled together for body warmth. As dusk fell, we said a prayer for the soul of Big Mac as we huddled in our blankets, intent on surviving the night and keeping our toes and fingers free from frostbite. There was little time for tears or reflection. We had just learned in the hardest way possible what life could be like in the Cassiar, a tragic lesson none of us would ever forget.

CHAPTER 9

The Cassiar mountains loomed over us as we trudged into Telegraph Creek two weeks later. Dirty, disheartened and in mourning for Big Mac, but we'd made it. There wasn't much here to welcome us or anyone. The place was still in the grip of winter and somehow we all resented that. The climate was easy to blame for the death of our friend, and we took full advantage of that and anything else that displeased us, unfairly or no.

Miners came out of their disheveled tents and welcomed us, because most of them were looking for food, not much of which we could afford to share. It had been a hard winter in the Cassiar and clearly a lot of the people who'd come here had come unprepared. I'd found that to be true, sadly enough, in every mining town I'd been to or even heard of. What riches I couldn't find in the ground, I learned once again, I could certainly provide by giving people what they needed. That could be an even better source of income than digging in the dirt, although I loved that and would never give it up. From our hard-earned supplies of potatoes and tins, we sold some to them for the gold they'd hoarded, making us no different than they were. Gold was a wonderful thing, but starving to death before you could spend it on your dreams was quite another.

We camped at Telegraph Creek for two nights, gleaning information from the miners there, and decided to push on to Dease Lake, the site of many of the new strikes. It seemed the Telegraph Creek area had been thoroughly mined. Another 100 miles, dogs and all of us exhausted, we arrived and set up a new camp at Dease Lake. We didn't know what to expect, but it didn't take us long to find out. There were rich veins in this area, and we staked claims like we were stabbing frogs in a creek, according to Tim Rickman. Some of his other analogies were less repeatable, although amusing.

As summer came on, we found we weren't wrong in our assessment. The gold was here, so were we, and we planned to stay. By August, I decided to build a boardinghouse, and convinced some of my crew as well as others, to help in that effort. I couldn't help but think of the snows to come and our travails on the Stikine. Tents were not enough to make it through the winter. We needed more than that. The walls went up, as did the tin roof, and by the time the first snow flurries fell, the doors were on and my boardinghouse was a reality. It was a safe haven for us all, something we'd all longed for.

"Nellie, that was the best stew you've ever made." Tommy Sweeney licked his spoon and set it down in his empty bowl. "I know my sainted mother would agree."

"As she should," Patrick Sullivan said, smiling at me.

I was grateful they liked my cooking, but it was becoming fairly limited.

"Boys, I'm thinking I'll head to Victoria for the winter, as I'm a delicate member of my sex."

I waited while the hoots and hollers quieted down, since everyone knew that was nonsense. I'd worked as hard as any of them had since we'd gotten here and they all knew it well. Still, there was no denying the fact that we were running out of staples and rather than wait on the possibility of a supply team in the spring, it was best to plan on getting our own. Besides, the welcoming fireside of the Sisters of St. Anne was prominent in my memory, and I had something for them. We'd prompted all the miners to donate to the cause of a hospital, and the money would be a welcome addition to the planned construction.

The trek back down to Fort Wrangell was much less perilous than the journey we'd taken up to the Cassiar, but it was only moments after waving goodbye to the boys that I missed them and our settlement. It would be months before I'd see them again and they and Dease Lake were now a part of me. I hoped the hunting was good and they would have no problems in the long harsh winter. By November's end I was back in Victoria.

* * *

EVEN THOUGH IT was nice being back in civilization, with its warmth, comforts and food prepared by someone other than myself, a part of me missed the mountains, the snowy expanses, and the utter peaceful quiet of Dease Lake every day, and worried about how the boys were getting on. The Sisters of St. Anne offered me a room for the winter, overjoyed at the contribution to the hospital fund, and rather than spend money on a hotel, I took them up on their offer, insisting on helping them in any way I could.

I wrote to Fanny and Mama and enjoyed their letters in return. Everyone was doing well in San Francisco. Christmas season wasn't quite as merry at the convent, even though a few of the sisters and I had a rather raucous Christmas Eve with a bottle of brandy I secured, but it was definitely a time of reverence and reflection, the like of which I'd never been privy to before. Many of the sisters were Irish like me, and our shared memories of Ireland and the famine, most of them sadly poignant, gave us all pause on how different our lives were now.

In February one snowy night, a pounding on the outer courtyard door roused us from the dinner table. To my surprise, in stumbled Tim Rickman, his parka covered with snowflakes, chilblained cheeks red from the cold.

"Nellie," he said, as Sister Agnes led him into the dining room. "There's trouble at Dease Lake."

Before the poor man collapsed, we sat him down in a chair and gave him hot tea and soup. A few minutes later, the tale emerged.

"It's not that we don't have any food, Nellie. It's the kind of food. We're out of tinned goods and vegetables, and the last of the potatoes are gone. We live on elk, deer, and hardtack. We have flour for biscuits. But that's not enough. Scurvy will kill them sure as a knife or a bullet. Teeth are falling out, and some are so weak they can't manage to get up more than a few hours a day. The blizzards are so bad no supplies have gotten through from Fort Wrangell. We have to find a way to help them. I knew you'd want to know and maybe could find a way to help."

The next morning, Tim left in the tender care of the sisters, I went to the warehouses and purchased sauerkraut, vinegar, potatoes, canned vegetables, pickles and as many rather wrinkled limes, lemons and oranges as I could with the money I'd saved up from the summer. I arranged for transport to Fort Wrangell the next day.

Tim insisted on accompanying me on the steamship to Fort Wrangell and I didn't disagree. Snowstorms buffeted the ship and my old fears of falling overboard into the unforgiving sea haunted me, so I stayed in my cabin for most of the trip. I thought of myself as brave, but I had learned I was no match for Mother Nature when it came to northern weather. Once at the Fort, we wasted no time in transferring our precious cargo to the pinnaces for the trip to the mountains.

Captain Rogers at the Fort insisted that I not go on this pointless journey, but his pleas fell on deaf ears when it came to me and Tim. We stood in his office, the woodstove providing more than ample warmth, the snowstorm raging outside. He seemed a reasonable man, if not an overly compassionate one. Perhaps in contrast, I was neither of those things and he clearly thought me a mad and overly emotional woman.

"Miss Cashman, I've already sent two supply rescue missions towards the Cassiar, both of whom, one just last week, had to turn back. The blizzards this year are especially fierce. It isn't possible to reach Dease Lake under these conditions. Those men will have to take their chances because I can't risk any more men to try to help them."

"I understand, Captain," I said. "However, I'm going. Those men are my friends and colleagues. I appreciate everything you and your men have tried to do, but I know in my heart that I have to make the journey, and I intend to do so. We leave in the morning."

"Madam, if I could, I would detain you, but I have no authority when it comes to sheer foolishness."

I smiled at him, and put my hand on Tim's arm, who was about to say something that actually could detain us both. "I appreciate your sentiments, Captain, but I can assure you I am very far from a foolish woman. I am going to the Cassiar and there is nothing more to be said. Good day to you."

By the time the pinnaces had dumped our supplies in the snow and sailed away, my bravado the day before had begun to wane. We had sent word ahead to the mainland, but for the moment, Tim and I looked at each other in some despair, because there was no one here to greet us. Perhaps Captain Rogers was right. How could the two of us manage this without some help? Perhaps this was an insane journey. I sat down on one of the crates, the snowflakes thickening once again and began to pray for some divine guidance because we surely needed it right now more than ever before. Tim sat down beside me.

"They'll be here, Nellie. We sent word."

I looked out at the white landscape. "Ah, Tim, I pray you're right."

An hour, maybe two, passed with no sign of anyone when I heard a jingle of bells from the collar I'd fashioned for Chris, and the dog materialized out of the falling snow, knocking me clean off the crate, his tongue bathing my face in greeting. Quickly behind him came Chinay, Ted Brandywine, who looked on his last legs, two other miners I didn't know, and two Tlingit Indians, carrying snowshoes on their backs. I sank to my knees in the cold snow, Chris's warmth on my lap, and cried tears of thanksgiving.

CHAPTER 10

Four weeks later, every muscle in my body afire with pain, I sat beside my friends at our cookfire, Chris at my feet, as we shared our meal of elk and beans. We'd snowshoed up the Stikine, hauling our crates of provisions with human harnesses and headbands, sometimes making only what felt like only mere feet in a day, the blizzards seeming to blow from every direction, impeding our progress. Had it not been for the Tlingits and their amazing sense of place and direction, we'd have been lost and roaming in circles from the first day.

"How far, do you think, Chinay?" I said. "Another four weeks, or more?"

He looked at me over the fire, his dark eyes somber. "More."

I was afraid of what he would say, but there was nothing to be done but push on, for us as well as the miners up at Dease. It was as it would be.

There was a rustle in the trees to the west, Chris's hackles rising along with his growl, and Ted Brandywine took up his rifle, standing sentinel. Couldn't be a bear, they were tucked into their dens, and the wolves were smarter than to come into a campsite. The noise increased and a troop of soldiers, their uniforms hardly discernable beneath the snow that covered them, came into the light. They looked like half frozen lost snowmen.

"Nellie Cashman?" their leader called. I stood up and acknowledged it was indeed me, holding up my arm. "Ma'am, we're from Fort Wrangell and we've come to rescue you."

It was an absurd moment, following yet another trying day. Why did men always underestimate women's ability? I couldn't help myself and started to laugh, and after a few seconds, so did every man in my troupe. The officer looked quite taken aback.

I composed myself. "Forgive me, sir. But, as you can plainly see, I am in no need of rescue, nor is any man with me."

There was a long silence, followed by a few muffled chuckles. In the dim light I couldn't tell for sure, but I was quite certain the officer's face had taken on a much pinker hue.

"Please gentlemen, join us. We have roasted elk and beans, and we are happy to provide you sustenance after what I am sure has been a long and strenuous day."

They left the following morning, taking with them my apologies for Captain Rogers. I hoped they had a safe journey. Ours still had many more miles to go.

Weeks later, we approached Dease Lake with some apprehension. I saw some smoke coming from the chimneys of the boardinghouse and a few more here and there from some of the shacks and tents, but the whole place was silent, and only the cry of a hawk disturbed the air. We hurried into the boardinghouse and were met with the stench of sickness and death, redolent in the chilly air. The fires weren't tended well enough to bring up the temperature to a livable level even with parkas on. On the floor were pallets, occupied by bodies, some breathing, and some not.

Patrick Sullivan rose and staggered towards us as we stood in the doorway.

"Ah, Jaysus, Mary and Joseph, it's a fooking angel, is what it is," he said, before he fell face down on the wooden floor.

We spent the next hours canvassing the tents, shacks and cabins and assessing the levels of sickness, and in a few cases, hauling out the bodies of those who had passed. We administered lime juice first, forcing it down painfully swollen throats, then sauerkraut and potatoes which I hastily heated in the iron cauldrons I'd left last October. Green vegetables followed and there wasn't a man who survived that winter in Dease Lake that ever forgot.

It was a grim business, but in the end, we saved most of them. Scurvy and starvation were a deadly combination. Once the human body becomes debilitated to the point where it cannot function, perhaps for reasons unknown, lethargy sets in and death can follow in a horrifyingly slow fashion. I vowed from that day forward, to provide proper sustenance to people no matter who they were or where I might be.

* * *

THE SUMMER of 1875 was profitable, especially from a mining standpoint. All of us at Dease Lake worked our claims, without any heavy equipment, just our sluice boxes and other means, and our stashes grew. That winter I stayed on, ordering in our needed supplies early in the season, and we were well stocked for the winter. The boardinghouse grew, adding on additional rooms and refining the ones we had. The kitchen was bigger, as well as the insulation, from roof to walls, and we weathered the winter without incident. It was much tamer than the year before, but that was how things went in the North. You had to be prepared for anything but some years you got lucky.

Chinay and his friends came and went, sometimes

bringing in supplies and at other times game and local produce, all eagerly received. Our relationships with the Indians here were very cordial, but I was well aware that was not always the case in other areas, and I was very careful to point out to the men that these people were no different from us and deserved our utmost respect. Many times it was the native knowledge of the terrain and the weather that made the difference between life and death. It certainly had proved true for me.

By mid-summer of 1876, the yields of our claims were slowing down. The boardinghouse and store were doing well, and people still arrived weekly, but it felt as though the rush was over. There was still plenty of ore in these mountains, but for me, the passion I'd had when I first ventured here was beginning to wane. I knew it was time to go home, at least for a time. I missed my family, and letters were no substitute for loving arms. I sold the boardinghouse for a tidy sum to a gentleman from Seattle who'd arrived in June with stars in his eyes and lofty plans in his head. We both felt it was a fair transaction and I felt no need to include my hefty profit in my long-delayed confession whenever I saw my next priest. Business was business, I'd come to learn. Mining was something much different. One provided income, managed properly, while the other was a game of poker, with its attendant gains and losses.

I loaded up my sled, harnessed my dogs, led by dear Chris as always, and headed out for Fort Wrangell after the first good snowfall, before winter could really set in for the long months ahead.

The boys I'd first come here with stood beside me, except for poor Big Mac, and as I hugged each one, the tears began to flow from every eye. It felt like I was leaving a part of my heart here in this harsh place that had become a home.

"God bless you, Nellie," Patrick Sullivan. "You've made life livable here for all of us. God knows what we would've done without you. We'll meet again, I have no doubt, you Irish sprite. It's because of you we're all here in one piece to see you off." He turned to the rest of them. "Course, without your cooking we're like to starve to death before Easter, but don't be giving it a thought."

They all laughed, as did I, but all our cheeks were wet. "I love you all, and I'll miss you more than I can say. I only know this, you rascals: I'll see you all again, and I know that like I know my own name."

I turned to Chinay, my trusted companion, who had come to take the dogs. "Take good care of Chris and the team. I don't need to tell you this, because I know you will like no one else. You never know where the road will take you, my friend, but I think we'll meet again, at least I fervently hope so."

"Safe travels, Nellie," he said. "Chris, or his grandsons will be here for you when you return."

"You're an optimistic lad," I said, kissing his cheek. "But I'd like to think you're right."

CHAPTER 11

1879

Bored. I never thought I would utter that word, but it fit me perfectly right now. Oh, I had plenty to do – taking care of Mama, watching the children for Fanny, volunteering at the food kitchen, raising money for the church, socializing here and there at restaurants and parish festivities. It just wasn't enough. I missed my dogs, and the serenity of snow and solitude and I kept thinking about the Cassiar, and even Pioche and Virginia City. There was more out there, and I'd been to some but there were many more places I hadn't been. Sometimes my feet itched to be on the way to something new, something exciting, something with the promise of a tomorrow that no one had yet dreamed of, except for me.

"Aunt Nellie!" TJ grabbed my skirt, hands sticky with strawberry jam. "Come play with me."

And so I did, putting my thoughts away, at least for a time. This was now, and this was where I needed to be.

Weeks later, I ventured to Shepherd's coffeehouse, a place I'd avoided since I returned from the Cassiar. I stepped inside, not recognizing anyone except Bridie Shanahan at the counter.

"Nellie, it's so good to see you again," she said, handing

me a cup of the dark Columbian coffee I was so fond of. "It's not often I see anyone from a few years ago. You sure made a name for yourself up there. Angel of the Cassiar, no less."

I picked up the coffee and made a face. "Ah, not so much as all that, Bridie. I just did what needed to be done, as anyone would have."

She started to disagree, but I stopped her. "See anyone from the old days in here lately?"

"Not usually," she admitted, "but strangely enough, Tommy Sweeney came in just this afternoon. He's over at the table by the window, the one you all used to sit at."

I took my cup over to the table and set it down. There he was, that sturdy lad. Bridie had it right.

"How are you?"

At the sound of my voice, he jumped up like he'd seen a ghost and wrapped his arms around me. We stood there for a moment, neither of us saying a word, because really, we didn't need to. He pulled out a chair for me and I sat down, my heart full. One look at him and I was back at Dease Lake, the life I'd loved and left.

"It's so good to see you," Tommy said. "Wasn't sure if you were back here or in Victoria, or who knows where?"

Over the next hour, we caught up. My news wasn't compelling, but I hung on every word he said. Matt McGill had broken his arm, but the Tlingits had set it and it was back to normal; Tim Rickman had fallen in love with a Tlingit girl; Patrick Sullivan and Ted Brandywine had struck a rich claim. Tommy himself had done all right but decided he'd had enough of the snowbound mining life.

"You have any plans?" I said.

He shrugged. "Sort of reconnoitering, like. Thinking about starting a freight service, but haven't quite decided where. Somewhere warm, that's for certain."

We both laughed. "Going south, then?"

"Been hearing about some strikes in Arizona, some place

called Tombstone, and a few others. The whole state is a mess of them, from the little I've heard so far. What about you?"

"I'm getting a bit restless, too," I said. "My mama's been quite ill but she's getting better every day. Truth is, I haven't kept up with the news, mining or otherwise. This is the first time in months I've been in here."

Tommy gave me a sideways glance. "Why not?"

I sighed and leaned back in my chair. "Temptation, likely. Didn't want to run out on my family when they needed me. But, as I said –"

He held up a hand. "'She's getting better every day.' Maybe the time is ripe for a change, Nellie."

For the next three weeks, we met up every day at Shepherd's, poring over the mining newspapers and anything we could find from Arizona. Tombstone had possibilities for Tommy, but I wanted a more settled town, like Tucson, as I'd learned my business model ran to restaurants, supplies, and boardinghouses as well as ore. The Southern Pacific railroad was on its way east to Tucson, and already went through to Yuma. The day we bought our tickets to Yuma, we celebrated with a whiskey at the bar next door to the coffeehouse. In three days, we'd be on our way to Arizona, and we were both buzzing with excitement.

I wasn't quite so excited when it came to saying goodbye to my family. There were five little Cunninghams now, and even with the help Tom could afford, my sister Fanny looked exhausted. Mama was back in good health and was there with them too, but five children was a lot to handle. I tamped down my guilt before it could turn into remorse, and kissed my sister goodbye, holding her small frame close.

"Remember. Anything happens, or if you need me to come, I'm there for you, Fanny. Always."

"I know, Nellie. But I've chosen my life, and you have a right to do the same. You're unique, and you deserve to follow your dreams, wherever they lead."

I hugged Tom, the children and my mother, her cheek still scented with lavender. Tommy arrived with a wagon for my trunk and off to the station we went. A sudden tremor went through me as we drove away, and I hoped it was just anticipation, not a premonition of things to come for any of us.

* * *

THE DESERT WAS like nothing I could have imagined. I found its stark beauty wonderful, the openness of the landscape, the brightest blue sky I'd ever seen, and the vastness of it all, as though it was a place where earth and sky melded together to celebrate God's perfect union. It sung to me, that open country of endless possibilities, and oddly enough, as opposite as it was, it reminded me of Alaska.

When our stagecoach arrived in Tucson, another revelation was unveiled. This small town was a treasure molded from its own uniquely perfect architecture, the molded adobe walls, buildings and facades blending into the land itself. If I'd wanted to be among Catholics, which I did, I couldn't have come to a better place. There were even a few Irish here in this far-flung outpost as well, and everyone seemed to live in harmony. I knew for certain that learning Spanish was going to be a necessity and set about it, quizzing everyone I met, often much to their amusement at this silly Irish woman.

I decided to open a restaurant here and settled upon a location in the church plaza, St. Augustin's across the street, and set about opening my restaurant, which I ambitiously named Delmonico's. Tommy, after a week, was off to Tombstone and the silver strikes in its area, promising to keep in touch with me on what he'd find.

I was set for my grand opening and went to the offices of the Arizona Citizen, meeting a cordial gentleman named John Clum. He was an adventurous sort himself, coming west and had quite a history, I'd come to learn. Because of his profession, when I introduced myself, he stood up and gave a small bow.

"I am honored to meet the Angel of the Cassiar," he said, beaming at me. That irritated me, as it often did, but I swallowed my retort quickly. I needed his good will and berating the man would do me little good in that regard. I wasn't sure why my own notoriety felt like grandstanding to me but I didn't want any of my activities to be public, even though they clearly were beginning to be just that.

I forced a smile. "Mr. Clum, thank you for that. I would prefer if we could keep this to ourselves from now on, if you would indulge me. I did nothing but that which anyone would have done, and frankly, find it embarrassing to trade on that expedition, which was done with altruism alone and no expectation of fame."

He held my gaze for a few seconds and then nodded. "I respect that, Miss Cashman, and I understand. No more will be said by me, certainly not here. But, if I may say so, my esteem for you has just risen proportionately in view of your request."

He coughed and adjusted his printer's cap. "Please, have a seat, and tell me how I may be service?"

In the end, the advertisement read: "Delmonico's. Best Meals in the City of Tucson." I quickly learned that in truth, many of the best meals in the City of Tucson were Mexican fare or of some influence, and I swiftly hired two new and talented cooks that specialized in that cuisine, which everyone was more accustomed to and loved, myself included. They taught me as we worked alongside each other. We now had a menu that catered to all tastes. Business was good.

I'd come to love the desert, because to me it wasn't empty, but a place where you could breathe. There weren't many trees, that was true, but I learned to appreciate the prickly arms of the saguaro cactus and the clean fresh smell of sage and mesquite. One chilly morning in March, I unlocked the door to find Tommy Sweeney standing there with a big smile on his face. I sat him down to a plate of Manuela's huevos rancheros and when he finished, heard his news. It seemed Tombstone was booming even more so than anyone could've imagined.

"Nellie," he said, the last forkful done, "Tombstone is where you need to be. Silver is everywhere, it's like the Cassiar was with gold. You should set up a restaurant or a store there and you'll make money without having to put a pick in the ground. Even better than here," he looked abashed, "not that Delmonico's isn't great, but in Tombstone, they'd be lining up for your food and any other business you want to start. People are pouring in every day and it's amazing. There's ice cream parlors, grand hotels, gambling palaces like you can't imagine, specialty stores with fancy clothes and even a bowling alley. Follow the money, that's always been our motto, hasn't it?"

I couldn't disagree, it certainly was true, and the path to financial success, miner or businesswoman. Both avenues had served me well in the Cassiar. Within days of that morning, I was making plans to go to this boomtown. My curiosity was piqued. If that town wasn't all Tommy said it was, I could always move on to another and more profitable one. There was no dearth of those in the West, that was one thing I knew for certain.

CHAPTER 12

1880

Tombstone was certainly booming, and it was a raucous place. Thank Mother Mary it was not on the level of Pioche because law enforcement was alive and well here and that helped a great deal. I would have hightailed it back to Tucson if it wasn't. Tommy wasn't wrong about the level of sophistication the small town had either. There was everything a person could imagine available in Tombstone and generally people were friendly and outgoing. I couldn't compete with dresses from Paris, suits from New York or wine from Italy, so I decided to go with what I knew.

I promptly went about renting a space on Allen Street and set up a store called Nevada Boots and Gentlemen's Furnishings, and contacted Tom Cunningham to send me all the boots he could manage, along with other suppliers of clothing. In a mining town, these things were necessities, and constantly needed resupplying. I'd move on to ladies' furnishings if the men's provided a profit. There were certainly a lot of ladies in Tombstone, some not as genteel as the rest, but all of them would be eager to buy a new hat, a satin corset or some soft kid boots.

Next door a space became available and I rented that too,

and began selling food and produce under the name Tombstone Cash Store, advertised as "fresh daily from Los Angeles" which wasn't quite true, but true enough I felt no need to hurry to the confessional booth. I sold quality merchandise, whether it was a pair of pants or peaches, tinned or fresh.

I hired two pretty girls, one blonde and blue-eyed little Penny Arledge for the clothing store. Her father was a hard-luck miner who'd dragged her to Arizona with him on his quest for silver, and to the best of my knowledge, had yet to find any on his own and spent his days in the pit. Penny had a sharp eye for just what a man needed, but that only went as far as selling them clothes and boots, because she also had a sharp tongue when it came to anything else.

Conchita Alonso became my second self at the shelves of Tombstone Cash. She was a fiery little beauty whose parents had a farm in the Sonoita valley. Conchita knew produce like she knew her name, and what to do with it besides. I alternated between the two establishments, along with my two stock boys, Joe and Ben, two teenagers who were enamored of both the girls, who laughingly treated them both like eager puppies. They unloaded and stocked for me when the wagons came in. Tommy Sweeney stopped in every week or so. He'd staked a few claims and was doing well. Tommy always did well. Life in Tombstone was being established. I found it quite interesting, and profitable. I split my time between the two enterprises, overseeing both to be sure our inventory and sales were correct. Business was very good.

"Miz Cashman, I presume?" A dapper gentleman in an elegant frock coat smiled at me, palming a peach and holding it to his nose. "The lovely Irish lady who brought my favorite fruit to this misbegotten outpost of civilization?" His honeyed southern accent was musical.

I couldn't help but smile at him. "Indeed, 'tis me, sir. And whom might you be, peach lover?"

He laughed. "Dr. John Holliday, ma'am. Peach lover

extraordinaire. I am from Georgia, after all. Yesterday my friend Wyatt gave me a peach he said he bought from you, so I knew I had to come and discover these treasures for myself."

"Delighted you did, sir. I have other treasures you might care for as well," I said, and waved my hand over the produce boxes and the rest of the store, which held a wide variety of tinned goods, as well as cheeses and fresh-baked bread and croissants from the French woman down the block.

He turned to the woman that followed him into the store. Her dark blonde hair was piled high on her head and fastened with a feathered lilac hat that matched her dress. She smiled at me and I smiled back.

"Darlin," Dr. Holliday said, "smell this peach."

She rolled her eyes but did as he asked. "Well, Doc, you were right. And you," she said to me with an accent that sounded almost Russian, "must be Miss Cashman, of peach fame. I am Kate Haroney and very pleased to meet the latest woman who has captured Doc's fickle heart, or perhaps I should say nose."

She held out her hand, not something you always see with women, and I grasped it firmly, as she did mine. This was a woman who knew her own mind, as did I. I liked her immediately.

They left with a bag of peaches, cheeses, and a box of warm croissants. From the way they looked at each other, they were anxious to get back to their domicile and consume not just my food. It was customers like this that made my efforts more than just a business.

Some mornings, I left the girls in charge and met up with Tommy and we picked away at the hard earth to get it to yield its treasures. Old Ed Schieffelin said the silver was there for the taking and when you sank a pick into it, it went all the way up the handle. That was nonsense, of course, but I always came away with something to add to my stash, after giving Tommy his share. It was a boon because I was supporting the building of a Catholic church, Sacred Heart, and we needed every penny we could raise.

To Tommy's dismay, I also helped out almost every sad case that came to my door, whether it was a miner who'd broken his leg, or anyone who needed a decent meal or a stake to get back home when his dreams didn't work out. I only did what anyone should, if they had the capacity to do so. It was ingrained in me and I knew I'd never stop, nor did I wish to.

Pretty soon I had an impromptu hospital set up in the back room of the clothing store, and word spread. Nearly every day someone would show up with a broken bone, pneumonia or other ailment. Some of the ladies of the evening began to show up, many with the same ailments, including plenty of bruises, and I had no qualms about treating them same as any other. People make unfortunate life choices, but for many, it wasn't really a choice, but necessary. For the venereal diseases, I had few remedies to offer that were actually effective. Whoring was a chancy business, and the road often led to a short life. Comfort I gave, along with hope and prayers, but I often wondered how effective the last two were for these women or their customers.

Tombstone bustled and rustled, and so did all of us at my establishments. Along with contributing my own funds to the building of a church, and a better hospital than the meager one I could offer, I began to think up entertainments whose profits could go to those efforts. Talent abounded where people least expected it to be, but I'd learned since the Cassiar you could never tell what someone had been before they arrived in a place, and Tombstone was not only the exception, but the prime example.

We put on musical evenings, only a contribution into the coffee tin asked, and soon ventured out into theater. Not only were there many who were talented performers residing unknown for their talens in the vicinity, but there was a hunger and a passion for entertainment, on a much more sophisticated level than I'd imagined.

The Earp brothers were early customers, and early contributors to my ventures, as was John Clum, my old acquaintance from Tucson, who had arrived nearly the same time as I did, establishing a newspaper called the Tombstone Epitaph. They were valuable supporters, outstanding citizens who desired a town that was safe and livable, and some of the Earps were deputy marshals and sheriffs in the surrounding area.

There was a lawless element in Tombstone and Cochise County, and most of it was sanctioned as well as perpetrated by a group that called themselves The Cowboys. They felt the law didn't apply to them, and John Behan, the sheriff of Cochise County, for some mad reason ignored their illegal activities. The Earps, Town Marshall Fred White and Mr. Clum, among many others, disagreed. There were occasional spats and gunfights, but unlike Pioche and other mining towns, the peace was usually soon restored and life in Tombstone went somewhat placidly on. I did my best to keep out of the fray and any politics behind it. That was a fight I had no interest in entering, especially after Pioche. I'd seen death, whether it was lawless murder, or the kind that could happen in a frozen river and wanted no more of it. There were more pressing humanitarian issues to see to.

One evening in June, we launched our first theatrical play, a much-shortened version of Romeo and Juliet that we set up in the schoolhouse. I had talked Penny into playing Juliet, and she made a lovely doomed ingenue. For Romeo, I bribed handsome young Morgan Earp into the role, promising him tins of his favorite smoked clams and for his wife, the Swiss chocolates she adored.

The play was a huge success, raising over $300 for the church and hospital, and before the final curtain fell, I was planning our next one. Miners and gamblers, especially when things were going well, were great benefactors.

"Nellie, you ever need another actor, I'm your man," Morgan said, throwing his arm around me. "That was the most fun I've had in a long time. Glad you didn't make me wear tights, though."

"You were wonderful, Morgan," I said. "I was thinking MacBeth next. Ever read it?"

Wyatt and Virgil came up behind him. "Our little brother was Mama's favorite, Nellie. She shoved books down his throat from the time we were out catching frogs. He can handle that one," Wyatt said. "If not, Doc can tutor him. What about that, Morgan?"

"That's not a bad idea, Wyatt," Morgan said. "Doc knows everything."

Wyatt laughed. "Indeed he does, brother. That man is a walking library, and if he doesn't know it, Kate does."

Virgil frowned. "Those two know a lot of things, but I guess I'd trust them when it comes to Shakespeare. Not much else."

"Virgil, I was thinking you might make a brilliant Julius Caesar," I said, and Wyatt and Morgan laughed, slapping him on the back. "A true leader that never backs down."

Virgil was a stoic man unlike his brothers in that regard, but I had to disagree with him when it came to Dr. Holliday and his companion. They were both unfailingly polite and kind to me and I was a good judge of character. Whatever they'd done, I liked them. Besides, they both contributed heavily to my endeavors and that, to me, told the tale.

CHAPTER 13

In October that year, our Town Marshall Fred White was killed by one of the Cowboys, Curly Bill Brocius. He was not convicted of this crime, but let free, which seemed to me to be a miscarriage of justice. Virgil Earp was appointed to fill his place and peace, of a kind, was restored while many of us mourned Mr. White, my friend John Clum included. Sad as it was, I had too many things to look after to get caught up any further than I already was in local politics because it tended to create issues when it came to my other efforts, running the businesses, fund-raising for the church and mining. I'd learned the hard way that sometimes that was a dangerous mix.

After the first of the year, I ventured into Bisbee, a mining town not far from Tombstone, to see about possible business ventures there. Bisbee was a charming little town, built on the hillsides of the area, with the huge pit mines right there to the south of the downtown. I thought a hotel and restaurant could be a viable opportunity. I decided to wait on that and concentrate on my efforts on Tombstone. Perhaps in the future, Bisbee would be a good option for me, but not now.

In the spring of 1881, I received bitter news. Tom Cunningham had died of tuberculosis, and my sister Fanny and their five children were devastated. I went to San Francisco, and their situation was dire. Tom, wonderful man that he was, had not made adequate provision for his family, nowhere near enough to let them stay in San Francisco. There was nothing to be done but to whisk them off to Tombstone to live with me. Although I loved them dearly, having five raucous children hadn't been on my agenda. The first thing I had to do was find an adequate house for us all, while enlisting my sister Fanny as our housekeeper and helper in the stores, along with the two oldest boys, TJ and Michael. Now I had a family to look after, the one thing I'd avoided in my quest for an independent life.

I soon found that although I hadn't birthed these children, they became a wonderful part of my life that I didn't have and I adored them. Being reunited with my dear sister was a blessing and I hadn't known how much I missed her until she was there with me every day.

"You know, Nellie," Fanny said one morning after I'd supplied Virgil Earp with an apple and fresh baked bread for breakfast over at the marshal's office, "you like food, and you enjoy cooking it so much, I think you should open a restaurant."

I laughed. "We've already got two businesses going here, Fanny, and between that and the children, we can't do anymore."

Fanny retied her apron. "I think a restaurant might be more profitable than the clothing store. We won't be getting boots from Tom anymore so," she stopped and swallowed. I put my arm around her and put her head on my shoulder.

"I know, dear, I know."

She pulled away after a minute, but her eyes were dry. "We have to think about the future. A restaurant makes sense. We've already got the produce contracts and suppliers here at

Tombstone Cash. Maybe even a boardinghouse. Lord knows we are bursting at the seams with the children in the three rooms above the store. Maybe we need more space and bigger ideas to match it."

Just so, the Arcade Restaurant and Hotel were born. True to my mantra, we advertised "Finest Meals in Tombstone" and also extended our offerings to the back kitchen (without the nice tablecloth and ambiance of the dining room), a plate for 50 cents or free if people didn't have it. Things went well, and business was good. I advertised in both the Nugget and the Epitaph, dividing my money between Cowboy-supported business and Clum's Epitaph, champions of the Earps and the Vigilance Committee to end lawlessness (much of it from Cowboys) in Tombstone and Cochise County.

Tombstone was in turmoil between the two factions and sometimes even in the restaurant, I had to intervene between one party and another to keep the peace. I cautioned Michael and TJ to stay off the streets when the Cowboys rode in, and only hoped they had sense enough to do so. Michael in particular was my little risk-taker, raptly listening to stories about Geronimo from John Clum, and trailing Wyatt and Virgil Earp around to hear stories about outlaws.

"If Michael or TJ follows you into the Oriental, you make sure to shoo them away," I said to Wyatt one evening when he and Mattie were in for dinner.

"You know I will, Nellie. They're curious lads, that Michael especially. Every time I turn around, there he is."

"Don't I know it," I said. The subject in question was stacking dirty dishes on a tray and pretended he hadn't heard a word, but his ears were red and he made a hasty exit to the kitchen. I'd have to make sure he had things to keep him busy besides stalking his heroes.

Vigilant fund-raising efforts finally paid off, and the Sacred Heart Church opened its doors in Tombstone, followed shortly by a clinic, staffed for now by the Sisters of St. Anne from Tucson. Fanny was especially delighted half our front parlor was no longer a hospital. Occasional dust-ups aside, Tombstone was becoming more civilized every day and our business was booming. So much so, I began to look around for other opportunities.

I went to Bisbee again and investigated business there, but instead Fanny and I decided to buy land and open a bigger hotel and restaurant in Tombstone. To do so, I sold the Arcade and we began construction. Around the same time, an investor named Joseph Pascholy partnered with me to open Russ House, both set to open for business in the fall.

God and all the saints were looking out for us, because three weeks after I sold the Arcade, it burned to the ground one night, much to our horror. I felt badly for the gentleman who'd bought it from me but there was little I could do. We doubled our efforts on the new projects, and the Russ House opened first, and the Delmonico a month after that. My commitment for both wasn't just "The Best Meals in Tombstone" but also the most sanitary. Teaching my kitchen staff the necessities to make that happen was always a challenge, but one I insisted upon. No one was ever going to get sick from the food from my establishments, not something that could be said in other restaurants, fancy or not.

The older children started school and that made life easier for Fanny and I, with just William and Frances, who was still in the cradle. We didn't just supervise, we worked alongside our people every day. There was no rest for the weary in the Cashman sisters' businesses, particularly our own. The first time I heard Fanny cough my heart stopped for a second.

"Are you all right?"

"Of course, Nellie, don't be silly," Fanny said and continued beating the cake batter. "Must've swallowed a gnat. Can't have those in the kitchen, can we? Good thing I was here."

I looked away. I didn't think it was a gnat. It was something else entirely. That night I went to Sacred Heart, lit six votive candles and prayed like I'd never prayed before. God couldn't be cruel enough to take my sister and I would do anything in my power to make sure he didn't.

I sold my interest in Russ House to Mr. Pascholy a few days later, and concentrated all my efforts on Delmonico's. We would make plenty of money with just one enterprise that was doing a great business, and we could both take some time off, with just one place to run.

"You know, we don't need two bosses here after the morning preparations, Fanny. I think it intimidates the staff and they're not sure which one of us to answer to when a problem comes up. It's best if it's just me for the afternoon and dinner rush. Besides, that way you're home for the children."

She smiled gratefully. "Nellie. You aren't fooling me in the least but I love you. I could use more time with them. I do get tired in the afternoon."

I made sure Fanny was home by two and waiting for the children when they came home from school, and the nursemaid was there to mind them all.

For now, that was all I could do. God would have to take care of the rest. For the first time in my life, when I entered Sacred Heart in the quiet of the desert night, and knelt by the candles I'd lit, I told him just what I thought about some of his decisions, ones I didn't agree with.

"I know you always do what's right. But, don't be takin' my sister. It's not time for her or those children. You don't need to have her, kind and beautiful as she is. You just back off and concentrate on somebody else, somebody that isn't good, somebody that deserves to go. You need to mind your business better. You owe me that much. Wasn't for me, you wouldn't have anybody coming to this church I helped build."

After the words came out of my mouth, I waited for a minute to be sure I wasn't going to be struck down right like some heathen idol there on the flagstones. I opened my eyes and the only sound I heard was a nightbird calling and a gunshot from down on Allen Street. Seems like God wasn't all that displeased with me. Maybe he was biding his time. Well, I could do that too.

CHAPTER 14

Business was booming. With the cooler weather, people were out and about and all of Tombstone was bustling. Delmonico's was popular, and I had to hire on two more waitresses, since Conchita and I couldn't keep up with the orders. Fanny seemed better, a bloom on her cheeks I hadn't seen in a while, and TJ and Michael were under firmer rein with her there in the afternoons. Those rascals got up to shenanigans unless firmly told no.

Unfortunately, there was additional turmoil and the Cowboys had grown bolder, knowing John Behan wouldn't prosecute them for any infraction at all. Virgil Earp, on the other hand, had established a firm "No guns in town limits" policy, and for the most part that edict was being followed, and a fine thing it was. Still, there was a lot of posturing and threatening. I had banned most of the Cowboys from Delmonico's after repeated incidents, but I heard they were up to their old tricks in any establishment that hadn't, and that included all the saloons and gambling palaces, always eager to take their money and had no scruples where it came from.

Mayor Clum stopped in for lunch, as he often did, and

warned me to keep the children under close eye and not be out in the street often myself.

"Trouble's brewing, Nellie," he said, spooning up his tortilla soup. "Those damn Cowboys don't listen to anybody. They're about to run afoul of Virgil Earp and that's not going to be a good thing for anybody, especially children that get in the way."

"Don't worry, John," I said. "Those rascals are under our thumbs, I assure you. For me, I am going to do whatever I need to do without being afraid of some men who think laws don't apply to them. Never have before, and that isn't going to change today."

He shook his head. "I worry about you sometimes, Nellie, I swear."

I laughed. "I've heard that one before, John."

He kissed me on the cheek before he left. "I mean it this time, Nellie."

He wasn't wrong. The next morning Wyatt Earp took a gun from Ike Clanton and locked him up in the jail after an altercation the night before when Ike swore he was going to kill the Earps and Doc Holliday too. The whole town was on edge to see what would happen next. We didn't have to wait long.

The Cowboys rode into town in force, and I watched them pass by, along with the McLowrys and the Clanton brothers, including Ike, from the window of Delmonico's, all armed and headed down Allen Street. This couldn't be good. I tore off my apron and made for our living quarters behind the restaurant. The children were due home from school soon but I knew the whole town was on edge, and Michael especially was one of those children who always had to be the first on the scene to any trouble, enamored as he was with the Earps and their exploits. He wasn't there and I didn't waste a second before I tore down the street to the schoolhouse.

Virgil Earp had deputized his brothers Wyatt and

Morgan, along with Doc Holliday, who didn't usually join in with law enforcement, but there they were, the four of them, walking down Allen Street towards the OK Corral, nearly keeping pace with me. They looked serious and determined.

It was then I caught a glimpse of Michael standing beside the horse trough down the block in front of the Corral. That little devil. I broke into a dead run, leaving the Earps and Holliday behind. I grabbed him by the collar.

"What do you think you're doing?" I yelled, my temper getting the best of me, hauling him up and holding him close while he struggled.

"It's Wyatt," he yelled. "I need to be there for him. Them damn Cowboys are gunning for him."

"The hell you do," I said, surprising myself and holding tight, now to his arm as well. This child was going nowhere if I could help it. We struggled and eventually sank down onto the boardwalk, him on my lap. It was then we heard Wyatt yell "this is not what I wanted!" and the first shots rang out. We both looked up in reaction and then ducked, me pushing Michael flat.

It seemed like forever but in reality was only a minute or so before the gunshots stopped. Gunsmoke filled the air, the afternoon breeze having a hard time dispersing it. Michael was crying. I hugged him.

"It's going to be fine," I said, not sure if I was lying or not.

"Is Wyatt OK? What about Virgil and Doc, and Morgan?"

I saw John Behan walk towards the Corral and talk to a man who stood there, dressed in black, and when the man turned his head, I saw it was Wyatt Earp. Doc Holliday was on his knees, as was Morgan Earp and Virgil lay on his side. All were moving and not dead. I couldn't see much further into the Corral, but there were bodies or so I thought, on the ground. I didn't wait around to find out, and hustled Michael away.

"Wyatt is fine, Michael," I said, as we hurried along Allen Street. "I think the rest will be too. We'll find out more tonight. Right now, we're going home."

The aftermath of that day resonated through the town and county but I tried to concern myself with my family and business and stay out of the line of fire, aside from my condolences and deliveries of food to the Earp households as they recovered from the wounds they'd received that day. I did make it clear no Cowboy would ever be welcome in Delmonico's again, and that included John Behan, sheriff or no, while anyone named Earp or Holliday could count on a free meal from me.

Before Christmas, everyone seemed to mellow and tensions eased. We made a merry celebration this year, and Fanny seemed improved and happy. Our menu for Christmas Eve at the restaurant was the talk of the town. Roast beef prime rib, crown roast of lamb, fresh seafood from the coast packed in ice were our main courses, accompanied by vichyssoise, salads and stunning desserts, including a four-layer fondant and cream-filled cake that towered on the side table, dwarfing the other pies and puddings. As usual, the back door area of the kitchen hosted its own celebration, even though most of the cake didn't make it that far.

Life seemed to be returning to normal until three days later Virgil Earp was ambushed and shot on the street. John Clum brought me the news the next morning.

"They shot Virgil," he said, "this whole feud is going to get worse before it ever gets better, Nellie."

"How is he?"

"He's alive, but I don't think he'll ever use that arm again, that is if he manages to keep it." He poured more coffee.

"Starting to feel like Pioche around here," I said. "I came to hate that place but now especially with the children, I'm not very happy with Tombstone either."

"I know," he said, "neither am I. Something has to be done."

But nothing was. Although everyone knew it was the Cowboys who had shot Virgil, no one was arrested and they boldly walked around town like they owned the place while a great many of the townspeople kept out of their way. But John Clum was right, as he often was. Morgan Earp was shot and killed in March, playing pool with Wyatt. Virgil and Allie, with Louisa, packed up and left town, carrying Morgan's body in a casket to Los Angeles, while Wyatt and some of his friends accompanied them to the train station. It was fortunate they did, because an ambush was attempted. Frank Stilwell, a Cowboy suspected by many to have been the man who shot Morgan, was found dead after the train had departed.

Wyatt's posse returned to Tombstone, but not for long. They left the next day on what we'd all come to know as the Vendetta Ride. Before they left, I packed three bags of food and had Michael and TJ, thrilled to their souls, deliver them to Wyatt and Doc, along with our prayers. I never saw either of them again in my time in Arizona.

They weren't the only ones to depart. John Clum, also threatened by the Cowboys, soon sold the Tombstone Epitaph and left as well. He came in the morning before he left to say goodbye.

"Nellie, I'm going to miss you," he said, gathering me into his arms for a hug. "Your food has kept me alive and well these two years, along with that smiling face."

"I'll miss you as well," I said, blinking back tears. I felt as though the linchpins of my foundation in Tombstone were being taken away, one by one. We'd all come to this place around the same time and now I was to be the only one left.

"We've done our best here, haven't we?" John said. "Sometimes fate takes a hand and we deal with that as we can. I believe Tombstone won't be thriving much longer, even with the Cowboys on the run. The mines will play out, you know that well as I do. You don't want to be the last one to turn off the water in this place."

"Ah, you're not telling me news, John," I said. "There's still plenty of ore in this state, but 'tis true most of it isn't sitting underneath us anymore unless it's in underground rivers. Don't worry about me. I'll keep running this place while there's customers to feed and after that, well, I'll travel on."

He hugged me again. "Take care of yourself and your family, Nellie. I hope I see you again in this life. You never know where the roads might take you."

"You take care too, John, and remember, keep the wind at your back."

He laughed and doffed his hat. "That I'll do, Nellie, that I'll do.

CHAPTER 15

JOHN CLUM

I don't believe I ever met a woman like Nellie Cashman. That Irish brogue, infectious smile, bright eyes wrapped up in an indomitable spirit like I'd never seen before. This woman wasn't intimidated by anything or anyone.

She walked into my newspaper office in Tucson one morning to submit an advertisement for her new restaurant opening on the Plaza the next week. No white woman had ever opened a restaurant here before and I was a bit taken aback by her sheer audacity at her chances of success. Then she smiled at me and it was like the sun came out in that dim little office, and I didn't doubt for one minute she'd be a success. Of course, she was. I wasn't surprised because I'd faintly remembered her name from somewhere and did a little research. This was the woman who had saved a pack of miners in the Cassiar mining district a couple of years before. They called her the "Angel of the Cassiar" but when I mentioned it to her a few weeks later, she just laughed and said she'd done nothing anyone else wouldn't have done, shooing me away. She was also one of the most humble people I'd ever met. Anyone else in this world would've capitalized on that sort of fame, but not Nellie.

When word of a silver strike in Tombstone began to filter into Tucson, many of us made plans to head east to that tiny godforsaken place, which by all accounts was growing so fast it was as though buildings were springing up out of the ground, and they practically were doing just that. I sold the newspaper and opened a new one in Tombstone called the Tombstone Epitaph. I was caught up in the turbulence of this town, its poor origins being swept away by the newcomers and money people who had come to profit from the mining enterprises. It was an insane mix of hardscrabble miners looking for a fortune and sophisticates from the East hoping to profit from their hard-won fortunes.

Gambling halls, saloons, brothels and a variety of stores offering everything from caviar to French corsets dominated the main streets. One of them, Tombstone Cash Store, had wonderful produce and other goods. One morning not long after I'd arrived, I happened into the Cash Store for a cinnamon bun and a pear and found Nellie Cashman, white aproned and sporting the same mischievous smile I'd seen in Tucson, asking me if that was all I needed.

"Mr. Clum, how nice 'tis to be seeing you again," she said in that surprisingly strong voice. "I see we are of a like mind. Would you be having a cup of coffee to go with your fare?"

Thus, we renewed our acquaintance and deepened it from there. Nellie became a frequent guest at my home for dinner, and a welcome companion to my wife Mary, pregnant and in need of a friend. Nellie was that for us, and when Mary passed away after the birth of our daughter Elizabeth, who followed her into that shadowy vale shortly thereafter, it was Nellie who helped me find my way out of the dark halls of death and depression. While I didn't embrace it, her Catholic faith was a guiding light and comfort to me and many others.

Nellie was a tireless crusader for a Catholic church and a

hospital, arranging plays, musical entertainments and dances where all the fees went to the fund for both. I supported the building of both those institutions to the fullest, writing about them in the paper. They were needed in Tombstone, no question about that. Many a night my pockets were emptied, along with the Earps and Doc Holliday's. Nellie had a sixth sense intuiting when someone had a good night at the gaming tables and when the hat came around, we threw in, some of us worried about the fires of hell if we did not, although she never mentioned a word of that fate, only the soft plea of those who needed our help, which, who knew, could include us at some point. One should never discount the future need of faith and succor, to say nothing of medical attention.

After the trouble, I came to realize I too was on the Cowboys' list of people that needed to be eliminated, especially after the aborted stagecoach holdup where I was the only passenger on the road to Benson. After Morgan was killed, I sold the paper and made plans to leave. One of the people I would miss more than anyone was Nellie Cashman. Having breakfast with her a few mornings a week, and often dinner as well, was one of the great pleasures of my life in Tombstone. I'd often thought of courting her some months after Mary passed, but if there ever an independent woman who had no interest in marrying anyone, it was Nellie Cashman. She was her own woman, come what may. I respected that although it only made me wish she was more pliable. That, however, was not a word in Nellie's vocabulary.

The morning I wished her farewell, I found it very difficult to not tell her how I felt, but I managed. Besides, she had her hands full. Her sister and five nephews and nieces had descended on her the year before and I knew Fanny was in poor health and perhaps soon Nellie herself would be additionally tested with the sole care of those children. She would never have left her family under any circumstances whatsoever.

That would never be who she was. Nellie Cashman was an indomitable spirit, a force of nature, if you will. Life takes many turns, and it may well be our paths might cross again, unlikely as that seemed that cloudy morning when I left Tombstone forever. A woman like Nellie only comes along once in hundred years, maybe more. I left hoping she lived a good life, and knowing that she wished me well on my own road. That was a blessing I carried away from my years in Tombstone and one I gratefully acknowledged.

CHAPTER 16

The silver was shrinking, or perhaps just getting depleted by all the people digging it out from its home in the earth where it lodged. Water was filling the tunnels under Tombstone as fast as the miners could pump it out, making the silver even more inaccessible than before. Life went on in Tombstone regardless, even if the easy days of the years before now were behind us, it wasn't a subject anyone wanted to dwell on. Business was still thriving and more people kept coming.

My sister had good days and poor ones and we all became fairly used to that. As long as the good ones outpaced the bad, we all smiled, prayed and went on. The children were happy here, especially the boys, always up for an adventure. I had to keep an eagle eye on them, which wasn't always possible, so sometimes I had to trust to luck and the Almighty to fill in. We all missed the Earps and John Clum and no new heroes for TJ and Michael had arrived in town to replace them, nor likely ever would. Michael became fascinated with baseball, a game introduced to children in Tombstone with the arrival of the Flynn family, Irish miner transplants from New York City. Michael and his pal Colin Flynn organized a group of kids who played on the vacant lot behind the restaurant, no doubt because they could always stop in for cookies after their efforts.

A frequent customer was Mr. E. B. Gage, superintendent of the Grand Central Mining Company, who seemed to enjoy my daily offerings. One afternoon he came in with Mr. William Brophy, who worked for Phelps Dodge in Bisbee. Mr. Brophy was a charming fellow, another Irishman, and Mr. Gage was quick to sing my praises to him. We hit it off immediately. Brophy was a forthright man, who saw the future of Arizona. He became a frequent customer as well, even getting to know Fanny and the children.

After dinner one evening, he lingered over his coffee and asked me to sit with him. The restaurant was empty, and the kitchen staff was busily cleaning, the clatter of pots heard from the back rooms.

"You're a very enterprising young woman," Mr. Brophy smiled. "Have you ever thought of venturing into business in Bisbee?"

"Truly I have, a few times," I said, "but the time never seemed right."

"Well, you never know when things will change," he said, and sipped his coffee. "If you decide to head in that direction, stop in and see me. You see, I've heard about you from my friend John Clum. You're the woman who nearly singlehandedly amassed the funds for Sacred Heart Church, which is no surprise, since you're also known as the 'Angel of the Cassiar'."

"Oh, that," I scoffed. "Anyone else would've done the same. I don't like people talking about that. It makes me look like something I'm not."

He gave a full-throated laugh. "Miss Cashman, that is never something I'd think about you. You're one of a kind, from my estimation. Regardless, the offer stands."

I thanked him and stowed that conversation away for

future reference. You never knew where life might take you and Bisbee wasn't far away.

As we readied for the dinner trade one fall afternoon, Fanny came into the restaurant in a flurry.

"Nellie, I can't find Michael and TJ anywhere," she said, her breath short. "Sam Lee over at the laundry said he saw them riding off on their burros around two o'clock, but he didn't think anything of it. But they aren't back, and neither are the burros."

This wasn't good, but first things first, I thought. I took Fanny back to the kitchen and sat her down with a cup of tea. The air smelled enticingly of chili verde and cornbread, as well as the beef roast and spiced chicken in the oven.

"I'll find them," I said, taking off my apron. "You take some tea and calm down. You know I always do what I say I'll do, Fanny. I'll have those rascals back here before you know it." I patted her hand.

"Francesca," I called to my head cook. "Fanny will be in charge of the dining room tonight, and make sure the girls give her everything she needs."

"*Si,* Senora Nell," Francesca said, and issued rapid orders in Spanish. Fanny was in good hands. I headed back to the dining room. William Brophy, dressed elegantly in a three-piece suit as usual, had seated himself at the front table as usual and looked up as I rushed past him.

"Nellie," he said, "I couldn't help but overhear. Why don't you take my buckboard to look for the boys? It would be an honor to help you. Would you like me to go along?"

Was he serious? I stared at him for second or two. I figured he was. "No, I'm fine on my own, but if you're serious about the buckboard, I'll gladly take that."

"Out in front, the bay horse," he said. "I'm at the hotel, just in case you're not back before I finish dinner. *Vaya con dios,* my dear."

I threw on a shawl against the night chill and went out to

the street. True enough, Brophy's buckboard and horse were hitched outside. I climbed onto the seat, lit the kerosene lamp that hung from its hook beside the seat and headed north out of town towards the Dragoon Mountains.

It was full dark within five miles and I began to rethink my hasty departure but it no use going back over ground that couldn't be retraced now. I'd overheard Michael talking the other day about prospecting and some old miners he'd heard about that had a claim this way, bragging that even kids like him could find silver if they looked, things were so plentiful.

I was worried not because they were likely to lose track of time before dark but because there were roving bands of renegade Apaches all over the area, and two children would be quickly taken and absorbed into the tribe, if lucky. If not lucky, much worse could happen if they put up resistance, which TJ and Michael surely would. I tamped down my fear and anger at their foolishness like most people would do, and imagined the creative punishments in store for the miscreants. But, that didn't work, not for me. Instead, I redoubled my pleas to the heavens that I would find them.

I knew, from my own ventures into this barren area, that there was an old abandoned ranch house not far from the base of the Dragoons, and I headed that way the best I could in the dark. I could see campfires in the distance, and I knew those were likely Apaches, and not those of the children I sought, who likely were foolish enough to not even have taken matches with them.

Another hour passed before I came upon the ranch house. There were no lights, nor had I expected any. The place looked as dilapidated and empty as it ever had, but I pulled closer. Two burros were tied to a mesquite tree. I gave a sigh of relief and tied Brophy's horse to it as well before heading closer to the house. They would likely have heard someone and were hiding.

"Michael," I called. "TJ?" I didn't want to pitch my voice

too high, as the Apache campfires weren't that far away. The little imps needed to show themselves before we all ended up in the Dragoons in much worse circumstances.

Two small pale faces peered out from the broken walls of the house.

"Aunt Nell?"

"And who else would it be now, the faeries come to drag you to a revel?"

They both rushed out and enveloped me in hugs, clinging to me like the very hounds of the Wild Hunt were after their disgraced selves.

Dirty, hungry, frightened, and thoroughly chastened, two little boys sat on the wagon seat while I tied the two burros to the buckboard.

"What were you thinking?" I said, as we made our way back to Tombstone in the very dark night.

"We wanted to help. They said there was silver easy for the taking," TJ said. "You and Mama work so hard we wanted to make it better for you."

"Ah," I said. I thought for a moment. "Don't you know you make it better every single morning when you wake up happy and give us a kiss? That's the best help we could ever have, and the only help you need to give."

They were silent for a moment too. Then Michael piped up.

"Then that's what we'll do, Aunt Nell. Like we always do. Could we add in a big hug with that?"

I smiled in the dark and pulled him closer to me. "I'm thinking that would be grand, Michael. Very grand indeed."

They were asleep long before the lights of Tombstone came into view.

CHAPTER 17

1882

Christmas came, even with a few snow flurries, which delighted the children. We decorated the house and the restaurant, although things were a little different than what we'd done in Boston and San Francisco, and much more inventive.

We made wreaths from eucalyptus trees and juniper bushes, their sharp and pleasant scent filling the rooms in both the house and restaurant. The boys found good-sized dead mesquite branches which we stuck in empty lard tins filled with sand and the barren black branches were quickly filled with red and green paper chains that the children had spent many hours making, and trinkets of every sort, from Madonna lockets to metal rings the children painted with gold and silver gilt. They sparkled in the light from candles and lamps and everyone exclaimed at the stark beauty when they entered the restaurant.

My holiday menus were expansive and challenging. Cherry-stuffed goose, chestnut-stuffed turkeys, baked hams, and prime beef ribs with Yorkshire pudding (I wanted to rename it Dublin pudding but refrained at Fanny's emphatic "Jaysus, Mary and Joseph, Nellie", which she hardly ever said, and shake of the head) were the main course, with every imaginable dish to go with them. We had a Mexican menu as well, red and green tamales, chicken pozole verde, buenuelos, sopapillas with mesquite honey and brown sugar lacy cookies Francesca called little gifts from God. After one bite, I had to agree, they melted on the tongue like honey from heaven.

On Christmas Eve, we went to Mass at Sacred Heart, following the pathway we'd lit with luminarias. It had been a busy two weeks for children, and their brown paper bags filled with sand and a small flickering candle lit our pathway into the church, much as we would have wished that Mary and Joseph had a pathway into the stable haven they had found. Following an ancient tradition, I could see the pinpricks of small fires of pinon and mesquite all around the hills surrounding Tombstone. The chill air fragrant with the smoke carried in on the winter breezes. It was the season to chase away the dark and bring on the season of light.

I gave great thanks that night for my family and asked for only one thing. "Please lift the burden of consumption from my sister. She needs more time."

He seemed to hear me because as the new year dawned, Fanny was the first one up, making pancakes for everyone, and singing an old Irish tune. I kissed her on the cheek as I entered the kitchen.

"Good morning to you, darlin'," I said.

She put a cup of coffee in my hand. "It's not just a good morning, dear Nellie, it's going to be a good year."

For a long time, it was, too.

* * *

Milt Joyce and Mark Smith were frequent customers and one morning in the early spring of 1883 after the breakfast rush, they asked me to sit down with them. They had a proposal. I'd been prospecting and staking miners in claims around the area for three years now and everyone knew I had a particular interest in ferreting out new claims and strikes. They looked at each other and finally Mark launched into his speech. I suspected it'd been prepared in advance but I thought to hear it anyway. I wasn't particularly fond of either one of them but they were somewhat astute businessmen and worth a listen.

"So, Nellie, there's been a big gold strike in Mexico, in this town Muleje, across the Gulf from Guaymas. I admit it's a long journey but this strike, well," he turned to Milt. "What would you call it, Milt?"

Milt snorted. "Hell, I'd call it the biggest strike since old Ed came to the Dragoons, Nellie. No question about it. And, this ain't silver we're talking about. This is gold."

"Tell me more," I said. A little voice inside me was saying be very careful here, but I wasn't listening as carefully as I should have after I heard the word "gold".

Mark took up the narrative and turned back to me. "We know about your time in the Cassiar, Nellie, even though you never talk about it. You know gold. We're putting together a consortium of sorts to go down there and bring some back. We were thinking you might be interested. We could use your expertise, to be honest. Me and Milt here, we're saloonkeepers and ranchers, but we sure know a good thing when we hear about it, and we're good organizers but we need to know what to organize." He laughed. "You sure were good at that, from the stories I've heard, and you know gold. What do you say?"

Three weeks later, twenty-two of us left Tombstone on the Modoc stage for the long journey to Guaymas, half of them on horseback leading pack mules. This was a large expedition and I was the only woman. I'd left the restaurant in the capable hands of Francesca and Fanny, who swore she was feeling up to it, and although I had some misgivings about that, the lure of untold riches in Muleje was a siren call I couldn't resist.

Every one of us was tired and discouraged after the grueling journey to Guaymas. Sore, tired and covered with dirt, we checked into a hotel, bathed and ate a real dinner. By morning, we were restored and made plans to cross the Gulf. My backside tried to tell me I could use a couple more days in a soft bed, but my anticipation overrode it.

Next morning, we crammed onto a boat, mules, supplies and all, and landed at Muleje. From there, we planned to head west and find the gold fields. Milt pulled out a map I hadn't seen before and pored over it at our campfire that night.

"Let me see that," I said, and he reluctantly handed it over. It was a mess. Chicken tracks and dotted lines meandered all over the paper. "Are you serious? I thought you knew exactly where we were going. I can't make head nor tails out of this."

"Wait, wait," Milt said. "This is just a guide. My source told me to head west and then south at the second creek with the big hills."

Mark stood up. "Nellie, don't worry, we've got a guide here. Mateo?"

A Mexican man I hadn't seen before materialized out of the dark.

"Si, senor?"

Mark handed him the map and he looked at it for a few seconds and nodded. "Si, this is the place. The gold is there. My friends have told me."

"Satisfied?" Mark said to me.

"Not really," I said. "But we're here and there's nothing for it now but to go."

I tossed and turned that night, and it wasn't the last. I was beginning to have serious doubts about this entire venture. Still, if there was a big gold field out there, that would set up all of us for a long time, maybe for life. It was the dream I'd been chasing for years. I prayed heartily before my head hit the pillow but I had a bad feeling God wasn't listening at the moment because as St. Paul said, he likely didn't suffer fools gladly. Sometimes people had to think for themselves.

We checked our supplies and set off in the morning. It was scorchingly hot by noon, and we all cursed the sun and our unfortunate timing. Summer in Mexico wasn't a good season to travel. Following the crude map, we found the first marker, but after a day or two of sinking picks we came up with nothing but dust and aching muscles and on we went.

There was no water, no creeks or rivers in this hard-baked desert. Sometimes not even a mesquite bush. After two weeks of searching, we all sat down and pondered our options.

"Should we head north? Further west? I'm not sure anymore," Mark said, shoveling a forkful of beans in his mouth. "It's so damn hot I can't even think straight. Is there no water in this country?"

Milt took a drink of whiskey, the last of it in the bottle. "I don't know either. What do you guys think?"

Everyone offered opinions, some for going back to Muleje, others for one direction or another. I wasn't sure what to do either, but I'd learned the hard way of perhaps more pressing concerns.

"How much food and water have we got?" I said, bringing the conversation to a somber halt.

"Let me check," said Roger Conwin, one of the Tombstone men. After a few minutes he came back, frowning.

"There's only four gallons of water left," he said. "Some food, but not a lot."

There hadn't been a watering hole or a creek since we started out and the likelihood of one further on wasn't much better than what we'd found so far. There hadn't been a single animal to hunt unless you counted lizards and snakes and I wasn't particularly eager to try either one. Pandemonium ensued after Roger's announcement and when it quieted down, I spoke up.

"We need to go back, and hope to God we get there," I said. "We continue on like this we're all going to die."

"That's ridiculous," said another miner, throwing down his hat. Others murmured assent. "There's going to be water any day now. I'm not giving up when we've come this far and been through this much."

Some disagreed but the general opinion was to continue on. I tried to appeal to Milt but he shrugged.

"They've been through a lot, Nellie. They won't quit now."

Two days later, we'd found no water, much less gold. I was done.

"I'm taking two mules and I'm going to find water," I said. "We're all going to die out here if someone doesn't go."

Nobody argued, since we were down to two gallons. They all looked bad, and I'm sure I didn't look much better, but I wasn't willing to die out here looking for water or gold, neither of which seemed likely to be discovered. I took two mules and a bag of water with me and headed southeast. There had been a cross on the map I'd noticed and perhaps that meant a mission, if I was lucky. I prayed as I'd never prayed before that was true.

I came upon the whitewashed adobe walls of San Miguel de Rosa at sunset the next afternoon, having traveled without stopping. I practically fell off the back of my mule and staggered into the courtyard, greeted by two young Mexican boys and a white-robed priest who ran out of the sanctuary, holding his arms out to me in dismay at my condition.

"Senora, come with me," the priest said, and led me into the church. The last thing I remember is the glass of water he gave me before I fell asleep. Nothing had ever tasted that good.

The next morning, after some sleep, food and a lot more water, I started back. The brothers sent two of the Mexican boys with me, and another water-laden mule. It took another day to come upon our camp. I didn't figure they'd move far and in fact they hadn't moved an inch, laid out under any shade they could find or contrive.

Milt Joyce staggered to his feet as we came in. "Thank Christ, Nellie. We're about done in here."

"I can see that," I said. We quickly unloaded the water bags and everyone drank their fill, clapping me on the back in thanks and relief.

"Listen, boys," I said, "I'm heading back to Muleje and getting on a boat for Guaymas, with you or without you. I know a dry search when I see one. If there's any gold in this place, it's hiding good enough I can't find it, and I'm not going to die trying, and I don't think you should either. What do you say?"

Some of them weren't too pleased about the idea, but the thought of ending up bleached bones in the barren desert on a fruitless quest held little appeal. The next morning all of us packed up and trudged back to Muleje. The water lasted until we got there, but just barely. The big expanse of the Gulf of California looked like the Pacific Ocean to me and I'd never been so happy to see that much water in my life. We boarded the boat to Guaymas eager as hungry puppies to get away from the barren flats of Muleje as well as our dashed hopes and dreams. When the captain we'd found announced we'd sail that night, we happily agreed, wanting to waste no time in leaving Muleje.

It soon became clear we should've spent more time vetting our captain and the boat we'd boarded. After two hours, we were constantly veering off course, heading too far north or west, and in one case, close to going south.

"What's wrong with this guy?" Mark Smith said to me as we stood on the deck, unsteady on our feet. We'd just taken another dizzying turn of the tiller and we were all worried.

"Let's find out," I said, and into the wheelhouse we went. The smell of whiskey permeated the small enclosed cabin, enveloping us. Captain Vargas turned, not pleased we'd invaded his private space. He frowned, his eyes bloodshot, and he looked barely able to stand, holding the wheel with one hand and the bottle he was drinking from in the other. No wonder we were meandering all over the sea.

"*Sal, sal*," he grunted and turned to shoo us out with his bottle hand. We stood rooted in place, more from shock than any desire for confrontation, and when we didn't turn tail, he came after us, tripped and fell on his face. Two breaths later, he was unconscious.

I looked at Mark. "Don't think we got a lot of choice here. Isn't Joe Clancy a sailor?"

"That he is," Mark grinned. "A damn sight better one than this lush."

We locked the captain up in the hold, still unconscious, and took over the ship, and Varga's crew didn't make any complaint. We arrived safe and happy in Guaymas the next afternoon. Unfortunately, the Mexican authorities didn't see it our way, especially with the vociferous rantings from the aggrieved captain. They charged all of us with mutiny and by nightfall, our next accommodation was the dank Guaymas jail.

Our cell was filthy, and no thought was given to me as the lone female among my fellow miscreants, possibly because of my britches and attitude. Rats skittered here and there, looking for crumbs but their hopes were dashed for the most part, and buckets were all we had for our needs. We were given tortillas in the morning, and tortillas and beans in the evening, with two cups of water daily.

It took several days before the American consul, Mr. Willard, heard of our plight. Once he did, things moved swiftly, as least swiftly enough to get us out of our cell and onto a stagecoach headed for Tucson. We were aware that some proceedings might be in the offing, but we didn't wait around to find out, but headed for the border. If they wanted us badly enough, us dirty and smelly mutinous scoundrels, they would have to send the Army after us. That didn't happen, although I can't say we all didn't peer over our shoulders for the first day or two, hoping the poor horses could run faster. My days in Mexico were over for good, I decided, and that elusive gold would remain hidden, wherever it was, without any interference from one Nellie Cashman.

CHAPTER 18

MILT JOYCE

When we first heard about the gold strike in Mexico, somewhere west of Muleje, I was skeptical and not interested. Running the Oriental and being on the Cochise County Board of Supervisors was enough to keep me busy. But as the weeks passed, I heard more, and finally, at the urging of Mark Smith, we decided to put together a little expedition to see if the rumors were true. It was tantalizing, and a payoff like that would make life easy for a long time to come. Trouble was, neither of us knew a damn thing about mining. Mark said there was one person in Tombstone who knew a lot, and that is how I came to know Nellie Cashman.

I was acquainted with her, as was everyone in Tombstone. She was a one-woman fundraising organization, the biggest reason we now had the Sacred Heart Church and the hospital. She could talk a man out of a week's wages, with that Irish charm and those twinkling eyes, and leave him happy. She also cooked the best food in town. What I didn't know, which Mark told me, was she had a reputation. The Angel of the Cassiar, where she'd saved a bunch of men from dying, and had mined gold. Mark cautioned me she didn't like to be called that, so I was forewarned. The rest was a revelation.

The morning we met, she looked at me with those bright blue eyes and I couldn't have told a lie to save my life. This was a woman of consequence and from that moment on until very likely the day I die, I've never met anyone like her, or anyone I admire more.

She agreed to join our expedition. If Nellie had one fault, it was that she was as gold-obsessed as we were. That said, she was also smarter, and had it not been for her, we would be lying in our graves in Mexico, the coyotes' pawprints our only markers, or drowned in the depths of the Sea of Cortez because of an incompetent drunken ship's captain.

Nellie is one of a kind, and I can't sing her praises high enough. Anything she needs, all she ever has to do is ask. She's got those five children to look after now and I drop by frequently to make sure all is well, and bring whatever she might need, sometimes things I know she'd never ask for. No doubt the wine goes to Father O'Hara for communion, but I know Nellie well enough to know the Irish whiskey goes into the cupboard.

CHAPTER 19

I was delighted to be back in Tombstone after my ill-fated foray into Mexico. We slid somewhat reluctantly into the long hot summer months. For us Cashmans, it was a holding pattern for more than the weather. Fanny's cough had become much worse, and I was at a loss for what to do for her, as was the doctor. We'd tried so many remedies, none of which had a lasting effect. I felt guilty, having left her with so much to do when I went to Mexico, that disastrous decision. Even so, she'd seemed to take to the responsibility, more animated than I'd seen her, but lately she'd been very tired. I caught her one morning in the pantry, trying to hide the bloody handkerchief in her hand.

"Fanny, don't lie to me," I said, taking her into my arms. "I want you to go back to the house and lie down. We have everything in hand here, trust me. You need to rest, not worry about the restaurant or anything else. Get Mamie to read to you."

"I'm fine, Nellie," she protested, but I put my fingers lightly on her mouth.

"No, you're not," I said, "and I won't hear another word about it."

I told Francesca not to let Fanny back into the kitchen and after I made sure she was resting, I went to the doctor's office.

"She's coughing up blood, but it's not the first time," I said, "but worse than that, she's very pale and can hardly take ten paces. This is the worst I've seen her in a year. What can we do?"

He shook his head. "I wish I had an answer, Nellie, but I don't. New research is being done every day, but for now, there is no cure and little care for consumption. Fanny likely caught it from her husband, as I hear, who died of it a few years back. They say a dry climate, like this one, is beneficial, but I've not seen much evidence of that, truthfully." He looked at me sympathetically.

"She's a lovely lady, your sister. I saw her yesterday and she's failing quickly, as you know. I think all you can do now is make sure she's as comfortable as can be."

So that is what I did, because it was all I could do, except pray, and I did a mighty amount of that as well. I talked to the children as gently as I could, but I didn't sugarcoat the reality that they needed to spend as much time talking and reading to their mother as they could, because her time with us on this earth was limited.

When I went to check on her early on the morning of July 2, she opened her eyes and smiled at me one last time.

"Take care of our children, Nellie," she whispered, her breath failing. "Tell them how much I love them and you, dear sister, for always taking care of me."

We buried her in Boot Hill Cemetery on July 3, not far from the grave of Mary Clum, John's beloved wife who had passed two years before. The children threw roses on the freshly turned earth, and I think half the citizens of Tombstone turned out to trudge silently back to town with us that terrible day, in honor of the sweet and kind woman they'd come to love. There was a vacant space in many of our lives for a long time to come.

* * *

I CLOSED the restaurant for a week, spending time with the children, telling stories and and amusing them as best I could. My heart was heavy and I knew theirs was too. We comforted each other but after a time, I knew we had to establish some semblance of normality and return to the life we now had, bleaker without the luminous presence of Fanny, but the one we in which we must craft our future. For me, it was life-changing, in that I'd never wanted to marry and have children, but I found myself solely responsible for five of them, and it was quite a bit different than being "Aunt Nell" because Aunt Nell had now become the unanointed mother of five.

At least there was no pesky husband to deal with, but the responsibility for rearing and educating my nephews and nieces rested solely on my shoulders. My days as an occasional miner needed to escalate into a prosperous miner that found a strike on a claim not yet discovered, and I'd have to figure that out. The children were both an endearing gift that needed to be reared and educated and at the same time, a loving encumbrance to my roving ways.

I reopened the restaurant and business poured in. Profits were good as always, even without Fanny's gentle presence. Life went on, as normal and sad as that would be. Loss was a frequent visitor to most of the people in Tombstone, and a state we all had learned to live with. Some of my oldest friends, like John Clum and the Earps, were gone, but I made new friends every day, thanks to Billy Brophy and his business and mining contacts all over the county. He would sing my praises and tout the food at the restaurant, and new customers showed up every week, much to my delight. Mama had always said the quickest to any man's heart (or mind, for that matter), was through their stomachs, and I found she was right, as usual. Mr. Brophy introduced me to E. B. Gage, superintendent of the Grand Central Mining Company, Mr. Ben Williams, Fred

Dodge and many other prominent individuals. I was happy to meet them, fed them well, and made it a point not to engage in any discussion of politics or business with these gentlemen. My opinions may not have agreed with theirs, but we got along just fine over roast beef and Yorkshire pudding.

One afternoon just before the dinner hour, a miner turned up at the kitchen door, asking for me. Francesca tried to shoo him away, thinking he was our usual guest looking for a free meal, which most knew only happened after the restaurant was closed. He was persistent and I finally left the dining room and came to the back door. He was young, thin and by the looks he kept throwing over his shoulder, scared.

"Miz Cashman, I come to warn ye," he said. "There's a plot afoot this night."

"What sort of plot would that be now?"

There were always some nefarious deeds happening in Tombstone, but it wasn't often anyone referred to them as a "plot". He got my attention with that.

He rubbed his hand across his forehead, the dirt of the day mingling with the sweat of it and hunched over as though afraid of the gathering dark.

"Me name's Joe Parnell, sorry for not sayin' that first," he said, "but they'll kill me if they know I've told a soul. All I could figure was to come to you, since you've always been a friend to us."

He had my full attention now. "Go on, Joe."

"See, here's the thing. They plan to kidnap E. B. Gage at midnight tonight, right from his bed, the strikers will, and if he don't give in after that, they'll kill 'em, right enough."

"Get in here," I said, opening the door and gesturing to a seat at the big kitchen table. He didn't waste a second. He gave me a few more details but he didn't have that much, but enough I knew he was telling the truth.

The miners were in an ugly mood, striking for various

grievances which I personally agreed with, but kept my opinions to myself. E. B. Gage was a good man, and had always been a friend to me. If his life was in danger, and I could do anything to help, I would. Joe Parnell didn't have much in the way of more detail, except for the appointed hour of midnight. I wrote Mr. Gage a note, telling him what I knew and giving him detailed instructions, and sent it off with Michael. I knew he would believe me, or so I fervently hoped. Michael was back within twenty minutes, and handed me an envelope.

"Message received. Will follow instructions and meet you at ten o'clock. E. B. Gage."

Dinner service went on as usual, except I arranged for a horse and buggy to be ready from the livery stable. I tucked in the children and left them in the care of Sally Bronwen, the young woman I'd hired as a housekeeper and nanny, and at the appointed hour, drove slowly to the street behind Gage's large house. The backyard was full of yellowing weeds, no care taken here as many did not, no matter how impressive the front aspect of their dwelling was. It was a dark night, no moon to light my way, except for the lantern on the buggy. It would be enough.

Mr. Gage loomed up at my side, a carpetbag in his hand, his normally solemn face pale and frightened in the glow from the lantern.

"Miss Cashman," he huffed. "I cannot thank you enough."

"Get in," I said. "It's a long way to Benson."

We drove slowly back through Tombstone, just an ordinary couple out for an evening's ride, the gentleman's hat pulled down over his face, not an unusual occurrence for wayward husbands. No one stopped us or showed any interest in us and our leisurely pace.

We didn't speak much on our journey. I dropped him off

at the train station in Benson and he grabbed both my hands in his.

"I don't know how to thank you for this. You've most likely saved my life tonight, Nellie Cashman. You are an extraordinary woman indeed. If you ever need anything, anything at all, I'm at your service."

"I appreciate that," I said. "However, what I did for you tonight is nothing more than any person of faith and conscience would have done, Mr. Gage. If it hadn't been for one of your miners that alerted me to this scheme, we wouldn't be here right now. Think about that when dealing with those who toil for you."

He blinked and stared at me for a second or two. "Indeed I will, Miss Cashman, indeed I will."

I was back in Tombstone by dawn, with no disturbances on the way except for the occasional coyote or havelina that crossed my path. The night belonged to the desert creatures with whom we shared this territory. They were here first and would likely be here long after we were gone, us humans who came to dig out the treasures of the earth the creatures simply walked upon. I knew that human endeavors were finite, especially when it came to mining or many other things. God has a pattern, but sometimes we can't always discern it, much as we try.

CHAPTER 20

Truthfully, Tombstone was beginning to wear on me a little. The troubles with the Cowboys had ebbed, but there was always some commotion to be had. Towns like this were like that. When people congregated for greed and profit above all else, chaos tended to ensue, one way or another and people's baser natures were exposed.

That winter, five men were convicted of murder and sentenced to hang. They were not good men and were clearly guilty of the offenses they'd been tried for. A couple of them were Catholics and Father O'Hara at Sacred Heart asked if I would visit them in the jail where they awaited their fate.

I was skeptical at first. "Why me, Father?"

"Because you have a good heart, Nellie, and perhaps can offer them more than I can. One of their victims was a parishioner of mine and I find it difficult to give them the succor they need."

I went to the jail a few days later, reluctantly, I have to admit. I didn't have much compassion for murderers myself. But, once I saw these broken men, I knew it wasn't just the Catholics among them that needed help. When men are confronted with their own death, many of them become remorseful of the evil deeds they'd perpetrated and have no way forward to help them towards their fate.

I began my work with the two Catholics, Daniel Kelly and William Delaney, but after the first day I visited, the other three, Omer Sample, James Howard and Daniel Dowd, wanted to talk with me as well, seeking some sort of absolution for what they'd done, and peace for what was to come. I couldn't deny any of them that comfort, and I visited as often as I could. My initial revulsion had faded and it was replaced with pity.

Sheriff Ward announced they would hang on March 28, 1884. No one seemed to care much about their fate, except to celebrate it. The sound of the busy hammers erecting the scaffolding rang throughout the days. Then, something altogether different occurred. A small consortium sprang up, gleefully determined to not let this business opportunity pass them by. They were determined to turn the execution into a public spectacle, since five men executed at once was an anomaly, and apparently, to some profiteers, an opportunity to make easy money.

The group leased an adjacent vacant lot and erected a grandstand overlooking the grim proceedings, selling tickets at a hefty price to watch the men die. The higher the seating, the better view of the gallows, and the top three rows were commanding hefty prices.

I found this entire scheme disgusting and thought it should be declared illegal, but even as I complained to the Sheriff and the Mayor, there seemed to be no legal way to stop it, nor any willingness to do so. I vowed somehow to stop it, one way or another. Execution was one thing, profiting and glorifying in anyone's death was quite another. The condemned prisoners had of course heard about this and were quite agitated.

"Please, Nellie," Daniel Kelly, his bearded face haggard,"I know I have no rights after the terrible things I did, but my crimes shouldn't be profited from by such as them, who are no better in their regard for life than I sadly was."

I agreed. "Don't worry. There won't be a single person on that grandstand on the morning you leave this earth. I promise you that."

I'd made a lot of friends in my time in Tombstone, and I called in some favors. Miners, carpenters and those I'd provided for, all came to my aid. We hatched a plan to tear down the grandstand the night before the executions. I convinced Sheriff Ward that because of the excitement generated about the great occasion, we needed a curfew the night before, to have people home and in bed before midnight, to be ready for the grand event the next morning. Surprisingly, he agreed and even by eleven that night, Tombstone was mostly darker than I'd ever seen it, the populace tucked in bed, awaiting the great day. The moon was only half full, but that was enough.

My long night was about to begin. I met Conn Constable and the crew we'd assembled behind the restaurant. Every man had a hammer, a sledge or a crowbar in his hand.

"Are you boys ready?"

"We surely are," Conn said, and even in the pale moonlight, I saw a lot of grins. We set out for the grandstand. We waited until around two o'clock for the loud work to begin, having already demolished what we could without a lot of noise. Then the tools and the men went to work, and by four o'clock, we'd finished our task. No longer was there a grandstand, but only pieces of wood that would make a monstrous bonfire. I handed out whiskey and thanks, and my weary co-conspirators departed, home to bed, as did I, although I was too excited to sleep. Instead, I made a big pot of coffee before Francesca arrived, usually at five, and sat up watching the sun rise over our handiwork.

The five men were hanged that day, but there was little spectacle involved. They died as they had lived, grimly enough, but there were few observers, and no grandstand to seat those who had thought to revel in it, much less profit from it. I wondered if the eager ticket buyers would ask for refunds.

Later that afternoon, Michael sidled up to me after school. "Aunt Nell?"

"Yes, Michael?"

"Did you have anything to do with that grandstand getting broken up last night?"

"What do you think?"

He thought for a second and then grinned up at me. "I think it's likely, but I'd never tell."

I rolled my eyes. "Why ever would you think a thing like that?"

Now it was his turn to roll his eyes, imitating me. "Because I know you, maybe better'n anybody else, even my mama. It was a good thing, and you do good things."

"I try," I said. "You never know where the Lord wants to take you, but sometimes you just have to go down a clear path when he shows one to you."

He nodded, and then put his arms around me. "I love you, Aunt Nell."

"Ah, no more than I love you, Michael."

CHAPTER 21

1886

The silver was dwindling, there was no doubt about it. Instead of people coming in every day, the stagecoaches and wagons were filled with people leaving, from saloonkeepers to store owners, miners to assayers. Everyone talked about it, and everyone knew it.

Of course, Tombstone was far from becoming a ghost town. There was still plenty of ore under there, and as for me, still plenty of hungry people to feed and house. Still, every day I missed the bustle and excitement of the Tombstone that I'd seen when I first arrived. It just wasn't the same.

All the claims I'd invested in, which were quite a few, had played out, or in the case of the Big Blue and my other more prosperous mines, my partners either bought me out at my request or had left for greener pastures, or perhaps just more glittery ones. I sold them cheap to eager newcomers and sent the agreed-upon proceeds to the addresses I had. Sometimes they came back with "unknown" stamped on the envelopes but that was the mining life, making vagabonds of many.

Word of new strikes in other areas filtered into Tombstone every week, and the Epitaph was kind or perhaps cruel enough to let us know. Strikes all over Arizona, New Mexico and Colorado, even as far as Idaho and Montana, abounded and every time I read about one, my dander got up. I knew full well half of them, maybe nearly all, were short-lived or nonsense, but I still got the itch to go and find out.

That was exactly what I couldn't do. I was a responsible and prosperous businesswoman with five children under my care, not some crazy-eyed raggedy prospector on his last legs dragging a burro laden with pickaxes and dynamite towards a glory hole. Still, I yearned for it, just as so many others did. For now, I buried those yearnings as deep as the mythical gold I could only dream about. I knew hunting for gold was an obsession for me, but it wasn't about the amassing of wealth. A person only needed so much of that to live a comfortable life. To make sure others could as well, especially so many that needed education, medical care or spiritual guidance, that was the impetus that drove me. Or at least that's how I justified it, that obsession, and I was comfortable in mind as well as body to think of it that way. In fact, except for the Cassiar, I'd made a much better living from restaurants and hotels than I ever had from digging out anything, gold or silver. Most of that I'd given to St. Anne's where it did more good than it would've for me.

Water flooding into the mines had always been a problem in Tombstone, but over the years it had gotten much worse. Now the pumps ran day and night. Then one summer afternoon, disaster struck. Grand Central Mining's pump, the largest of them all, caught fire and destroyed not only the pump, but the pumphouse and the buildings around it. After the dust settled, even worse news came. Grand Central chose not to rebuild it. The price of silver had dropped to ninety cents an ounce, and for them, the largest mining company in Tombstone, the costs to rebuild outweighed the profits that could be taken from those drowning mines tenfold. From a business standpoint, I couldn't disagree with their decision.

From the perspective of a citizen of this boomtown, I was disheartened.

Still, Tombstone itself survived. Other smaller companies and groups kept on, pumping and digging. For me, as it was for many others, it was time to think of other options, but I wasn't sure exactly what those were. Francesca, the stalwart woman who ran the kitchen at Delmonico's, my right hand, had a brother in Nogales, Mexico, who ran food and grocery businesses, and she urged me to think about Nogales. Her brother Angelo said that a good restaurant and hotel could do very well down there.

My last foray into Mexico had been a nightmare, but I didn't let that deter me, and leaving the children in Sally Bronwen's capable care, and the restaurant in Francesca's, I took the train from Bisbee south to Nogales.

The terrain south of the border looked pretty much the same as it did further north, but the society was considerably different. I wasn't quite sure what to expect, but when Angelo Martinez met me in Nogales, he was warm and charming, and my trepidations eased. He was a big man, with a large moustache and merry brown eyes.

"Ah, Senorita Cashman," he said, greeting me with open arms. "My sister, she has told me so much about you. Welcome to Nogales."

"Thank you, Angelo," I said. "Francesca has told me much about you as well."

He laughed. "Don't believe everything she says, only the good things. Come, let me escort you to the hotel. I'm sure you are in need of rest for now. We would be honored if you would come to our evening meal."

The hotel was small and clean if not overly luxurious. Then again, the same could be said about mine. I settled in, washed up and then followed Angelo's directions to his house. Nogales was not a large town, smaller than Tombstone, but it looked as though there had been a growth spurt in the last few years. Many of the buildings I passed looked like new construction. Copper mining was going on all around the area, as I'd heard from Fred Dodge, and with the addition of the railroad, Mexico had close ties to Arizona and the formerly sleepy little border town was expanding.

It was a short walk to a whitewashed adobe house, fronted by a courtyard full of flowering plants and a fountain, with a statue of St. Francis in the midst of the trickling water, and the evening air redolent with chili and spices, the gardens flourishing. The Martinez family had clearly been here for a very long time.

Angelo greeted me at the door, escorting me in, and introducing me to his wife Carmela, who didn't speak English, and five well-behaved children, ranging in age from four to perhaps fourteen. My Spanish was improving day by day, but I was very glad Angelo's English was so good in comparison.

I enjoyed myself immensely that evening. Maybe it was the pressure of not being in Tombstone, wondering how to keep a business going in a town I knew would not remain prosperous for me forever, or just being away from any responsibility for others, but I felt free for the first time in a while.

In the next few days, I became familiar with the town, walking it thoroughly, meeting a lot of friendly people. We picked out a location, a building that had been a boardinghouse and café before, near one of Angelo's produce and carniceria stores. On his advice, I hired some workers, mapped out what I needed, and caught the train back to Tombstone.

It was a whirlwind trip, I knew that, but exhilarating as well. I'd not been out of Tombstone, except for that awful Muleje trek, in years. It was the longest I'd lived anywhere, except for Boston. I found I had gypsy feet and they were itching to go again.

I had a long talk with Francesca, and we came to a business decision. She would be my partner in the Tombstone business, and receive half the profits, as well as an administrative fee for when I was absent. I trusted her and I knew she returned that trust, and we were both happy. She was delighted that I was going to be working with her brother.

The more difficult talk came with the children. I was reluctant to uproot them and take them to Nogales with me. New businesses often take some time to succeed, and new places can have unexpected problems. I would never forget Pioche. I would be too immersed in my activities to devote the time necessary to the children, and they'd had enough upheaval in their short lives. Sally Bronwen agreed to continue her role as governess/nana/friend as she'd been doing, with additional help from Francesca's daughters as she needed it, and it seemed a decent arrangement.

"But, Aunt Nell, can't at least TJ and I come with you?" Michael said. "Not the babies, of course, but we're nearly grown up. We could be a big help. We're a big help here."

At the note of pleading in his voice, I nearly gave in. My common sense won out over my emotions. I would miss all of them terribly, but especially Michael.

"Not for a while, Michael," I said, ruffling his hair, which he usually hated, but this time he leaned into my hand instead. "Give me some time to get the lay of the land, you know? Like an Indian scout, reconnoitering the territory? Then, when I have things figured out and know how everything will go, we'll talk again."

He looked down and I saw a single tear plop darkly onto the light chambray of his trousers.

"None of that, little man," I said. "At least not for this. I'll only be a few hours away, and come back often to visit, or whenever you need me."

"Whenever?" he said, brightening.

You always needed to watch your words with children. "Well, not exactly "whenever", but if there's a problem, of course I'll come. Is that all right?"

He nodded glumly, knowing his cause was lost.

"And, Michael?" I said. "You said it before I could: you are a big help, and Sally and Francesca will need you."

He raised his head. "Yes, they do."

I hugged him. What a precious child he was.

"Remember, Aunt Nell, if there's a next time, I'm going with you."

"Solemn promise," I said. Those words would come back to haunt me.

CHAPTER 22

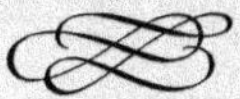

Nogales started out well. I'd ordered linens and supplies for the small hotel, and Angelo had made sure the restaurant was filled with staples and had the produce and meats on order. I hired two waitresses, a cook, along with a hotel clerk and a housekeeper, but I oversaw all of it. It was demanding, but I was used to that. In fact, it was a new challenge I looked forward to and one I found quite satisfying.

I did miss Tombstone, oddly enough, something I hadn't expected, especially the daily chatter of the children and seeing all the people I knew so well, but in Nogales, every day I was meeting new people, some of whom quickly became friends, and that helped cement me into this new and foreign place.

I only had eight rooms in the hotel, and once word got around, the rooms were rarely empty. The same with the restaurant, which featured both American and Mexican food, because here on the border, the clientele was mixed, with a lot of Arizona and California people coming and going, and the mining business, especially with the train, was exploding.

It wasn't very long before I'd made back my initial investment, but I really had no interest in expanding. Sometimes, as

I'd learned, staying with a profitable enterprise instead of extending yourself perhaps beyond the ability to recoup, was the wiser strategy. I'd made impetuous mistakes in the past and I wasn't going to do it here. I was operating on a slim but livable profit margin and it was going well.

Angelo came in one morning, wanting to talk, and he was clearly unhappy. We sat down at an empty table in the restaurant with coffee.

"Problems?" I said.

"*Si, muy malo*," Angelo said, "there is this man. Well, not just a man. He thinks he is a lord, him and his band of renegades. He calls himself El Lobo. He thinks he controls everything in this place. Now he has gained control over the man who distributes the produce and meat, and he is raising the prices of everything we buy three times the usual price."

"What?" This wasn't acceptable.

"As I said, Nellie. He has already killed two men I know who are shopkeepers and independent farmers, and he won't stop there."

"Can no one arrest him, or stop this?" I was fuming and stood up from the table. "He can't be allowed to do this, it's robbery."

Angelo shrugged. "Not if he pays them off. Which, of course, he has."

"No. Someone needs to arrest him. People just can't go around threatening and killing people and doing whatever they like." I flashed back to Wyatt Earp and his brothers and sat back down, taking a deep breath.

"Nellie, this is Mexico, not Arizona. These things happen."

"Yes," I said. "They do. So what do we do, Angelo?"

"I cannot fight them, Nellie, nor can you. Our only option is to raise our own prices. Such is the way of things."

My heart sank. If I raised prices at this point in my fledgling venture, my customers would drop off, finding cheaper places to stay and to eat. If I didn't, the profit margins on the restaurant especially, which carried the majority of the income, would drop. I was caught between the proverbial devil and the deep blue sea, as was he.

Angelo lowered his eyes, and I could see he was dismayed and maybe embarrassed at his own compliance towards those who would steal from us. Still, he had a family to think of, and I knew how quickly violence could erupt in situations like this. It was highly unlikely a champion would ride in and vanquish the gang. Law enforcement in Mexico was unreliable. I put my hand on his where it rested on the table.

"It's all right, Angelo," I said. "It won't last forever. These people come and go, and often die as they have lived. We will just have to wait it out."

He looked up at me. "You are a compassionate and understanding woman, Nellie Cashman. Yes, we will have to wait it out."

It wasn't more than a week later that a tall man and his three companions strode into my restaurant like they owned the place, seating themselves at the largest table. I'd never seen any of them before. I was at the hotel desk, talking with Miguel, my hotel manager when they came in. The restaurant was adjacent to the hotel lobby, just an open archway separating the two rooms. I had an intuition that perhaps these were some of the same men that Angelo had spoken of, so I hurried into the restaurant.

"Welcome, gentlemen," I said, standing beside their table. They were an interesting group. The tall man, clearly the leader, grinned at me, his teeth very white against his dark-complexioned but very handsome face. His moustache was luxurious and well-maintained, as was every other aspect of his clothing, including the silver spurs on his boots. His companions were equally well-attired but more ordinary looking.

"*Buenos dias*, senora," he said, looking me up and down.

"We have come to sample your food. What can you offer us today?"

One of the men snickered, mumbling something to another of his tablemates. I ignored both of them, keeping my eyes on the leader.

"I have a varied menu," I said. "I will have the waitress bring it to you. Then you can make your choices."

"Ah," he said. "So, then you must be Nellie Cashman. I have heard of you, the Irishwoman who came to town with such big plans."

"Indeed I am. And you are?"

"They call me El Lobo," he said, "but you may call me Rodrigo."

"Pleased to make your acquaintance," I said, and signaled to Evangelina, one of the waitresses, hovering by the kitchen door. "Menus, *por favor.*"

She hurried out and handed all four of them the printed sheets. They took them and I could immediately tell that at least two of them couldn't read, either Spanish or English. El Lobo looked displeased and Evangelina hovered nervously, shooting me an apprehensive glance.

"Perhaps I may be of assistance," I said. "We have a special today, albondigas soup and chicken enchiladas. Would that suit?"

El Lobo snatched the menus from the other men and handed them to Evangelina, embarrassment avoided. "*Perfecto.*"

I retreated to the hotel lobby as Evangelina delivered their food. They devoured it quickly, and then even quicker the tray of sopapillas and honey I'd asked her to deliver when they finished their meal. My stomach was churning while theirs seemed satisfied by the time they came through the archway, looking much more content than when they'd arrived. El Lobo waved the other men through the front door and turned to me.

"Muchas gracias, Nellie Cashman. Your food is as excellent as I've heard."

"*De nada*," I said. "But I have also heard that it may become more expensive, that food you enjoyed. What can we do about that, Rodrigo?"

He gave an elaborate sigh, throwing open his arms. "We live in a world where costs may rise so that others may make a living. It is the way of the marketplace, Nellie Cashman." He smiled, but his eyes were cold. "I am but a tiny piece of that, as are you. We all play our part and adapt to changes as they come. If we do not, things could go awry. I have heard stories."

I wanted nothing more at that moment than to punch his smug smiling face but while sometimes impulsive, I've never been suicidal.

Instead, I forced a smile. "I've heard such stories as well, Rodrigo. Many times they don't end well, those tales. Or so I've heard."

"As have I, but this one will, I am quite certain." He turned on his heel and within a minute, they rode out, laughter trailing behind them.

My hands were clenched into fists at my sides and I slowly opened them, stretching the tension from my fingers. Angelo was right in his assessment and he was right to be afraid, as much as I hated to admit it. Still, I wasn't ready to let El Lobo win, not quite yet.

I sent an order to my old suppliers in Tucson. Angelo might lose most of my business, but unless I could keep prices down, I'd lose mine. A week passed and I was running low on fresh food, and no word from Tucson. If the order took much longer, I'd have to go to Angelo and pay his new prices.

The next evening, as I was closing up, Angelo came in. He looked unhappy, and I poured us both a cup of the last of the evening coffee, gesturing to a chair.

"Nellie, I have bad news."

"I can tell that from your face, my friend. Is everyone well at your house?"

"Yes, that's not it." He sighed, staring down at the coffee. "You ordered supplies from Tucson, didn't you?"

"I'm sorry, I had no choice," I said, guilt washing over me. "I was going to talk to you about that, but actually, they haven't come. I'm not sure what the delay is."

"El Lobo is the delay and you won't be getting your order, only it's worse than that. They killed the freight driver."

I dropped into the chair like a deflated balloon, his words a slam to my stomach. My arrogance and defiance had cost a man his life. Mother Mary, how could I have not foreseen the consequences my actions might have?

I put my hands on my head, as though to shake some sense into myself. Angelo watched me, his eyes sad.

"It is not your fault, Nellie."

I stifled a sob. "Oh, yes, Angelo, it is very much my fault. If I had heeded your words of warning about how dangerous these men could be, that man would be alive right now. Do you know his name?"

"I believe they said he was called Red Bloom…something, I am sorry to not remember it all."

My heart sank further, if that was possible. I knew Red Blumenstein, he'd driven many orders to me in Tombstone. He had a wife, Rachel, and two children that he always talked about. This just kept getting worse.

I put my hands on the table. "I knew him. He had a family. Oh, Angelo, I am such a fool." I pushed myself off my chair, ignoring his murmurs of consolation. I deserved none.

"Thank you for coming tonight," I said. "I appreciate that. I promise you, my friend, I will do nothing more to add to your troubles. For now, I need to go speak with Father Juan over at the church. I will see you in the morning."

I threw a shawl over my head and shoulders and walked

the two blocks to the adobe church, the purple and orange skies of the sunset highlighting the curved adobe bell tower.

Candles flickered, lighting the interior walls in a golden glow, and the faint scent of incense wafted before me. Father Juan looked up and smiled at me as I entered, but he knew immediately I wasn't there for a solitary prayer, not that evening. He took my cold hands in his as I approached him at the altar.

"I need to make my confession, Father."

He peered into my eyes and nodded. "Yes, I can see that."

I entered the small confessional booth and waited until I heard movement behind the screen on the other side of the wall. I took a deep breath.

"Forgive me, father, for I have sinned," I said. "It has been too long since my last confession and I am now burdened with my transgressions." It had been far too long and I'd lost sight of exactly who and what I was.

* * *

Two months later, as much as I tried, the restaurant was losing money as I couldn't keep raising prices for the meals and El Lobo was running a thriving business in Nogales and the entire area. I was down to one waitress, and I'd had to let the hotel manager go as well. People knew I was a target for Rodrigo and many nights the hotel was empty as no one wanted to tempt fate or retribution by staying there.

Soon, it became clear that it didn't make sense to stay here and lose my investment completely. I arranged a meeting with Angelo and some of his friends.

"Thank you for coming," I said, gazing around at the eight men sitting at the tables. "I have decided to sell my business here and return to Tombstone. There is no point in telling all of you why, because you are all aware, and I know this has been a difficult time for you as well." Eight pairs of eyes stared at me, and murmured translations of my words, as I was speaking in English, were supplied to some of the men.

"What I am hoping is that by banding together, you might have a consortium of sorts to buy me out. I will give you a price that is more than fair. It is my hope that by leaving Nogales, some of the tension and division that I have caused, while not meaning to do so, will be alleviated and life may be somewhat easier for all of you."

More murmurs and nodding heads followed these words.

"Perhaps," Angelo said hesitantly, "if you would not mind, we would like to discuss this between ourselves for a time, Nellie?"

"Of course," I said, grateful that they were even considering my proposal. "I will be in my office behind the hotel desk."

I sat at my desk, fidgeting and fingering my rosary beads as they talked. It was too far away to understand their words, and most of it was in Spanish anyway. I was nervous but becoming resigned. I was leaving Nogales, that I knew for certain. Whether I left much poorer than I'd been when I arrived or at least back to where my finances had been when I started was the question. I knew there definitely wasn't going to be any profit from this venture. Worse than mining, this had been.

I was into my second rosary at "Hail Mary, full of grace, the Lord is with thee--" when Angelo poked his head into the office.

"Nellie, could you please return?"

Happily, I thought, the suspense was torturing me.

I walked into the room and sat down. I waited for them to say something, but that wasn't my natural self. However, these months in Nogales had taught me some patience, at least there was that.

Angelo cleared his throat and stood up. "We have talked

this over. Together, we can come up this much to buy you out."

He pushed a piece of paper towards me. The figure written down was less than I'd hoped for, but I knew these men, at this time, were doing the best they could. I looked at the paper for a minute and I could feel the tension in the room building. I couldn't expect more. In fact, I was grateful they'd been as generous as they were able to be, considering the pressure that was being generated by the outlaws. I hoped that among themselves, they could stand up to this tyrant and emerge victorious, gaining back their autonomy and self-respect. I felt confident they would.

"Yes. I will do this."

Smiles bloomed on each face, and each one shook my hand before they departed into the night. I watched them go, leaving just me and Angelo in the empty restaurant.

We looked at each other and he hugged me.

"Nellie, we will make sure your efforts have not been in vain," he said. "You have done your best, believe that."

"Gracias, amigo," I said, my tears threatening to spill over. This man had been so kind and supportive, even now at the end.

"De nada," he said, slipping into the night.

Three days later, I boarded the train, with little more than I'd arrived with. There would be other ventures, of that I was certain. This one had taught me a great deal, and for that I would always be grateful.

CHAPTER 23

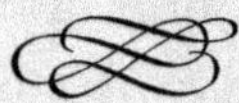

"Aunt Nell!"

I hadn't taken three steps inside the restaurant doors before small bodies hurtled into me, wrapping their arms around my skirts and jostling for position. They were all there, even little William, who seemed to have grown a foot since I'd been gone. Francesca came out of the kitchen, wiping her hands on her apron, a wide smile on her face.

"*Ninos, por favor,*" she said firmly. "Give the poor woman space to walk. She is home now."

Ensconced in a chair, the children gathered around the table while Francesca brought me a cup of her wonderful coffee, full of cream and cinnamon, her specialty, along with a heaping plate of sugar cookies. For a few minutes, their questions were stoppered by the cookies in their mouths while I took a welcome sip of the coffee. Francesca was a wise woman.

Home. The word resonated through my mind. Odd as it may have seemed to me ten years ago, this wild desert town was home, and from the minute I'd set foot on the same familiar streets, I'd known it was true. Tombstone was home, and a very welcome sight.

After an hour of questions, some insightful and others quite amusing, I kissed them all and shooed them off to the house. Brushing the crumbs from my skirt, I went to talk with Francesca.

"How has it been?"

She gave her usual shrug, which with Francesca could mean many things.

"Good, it's good overall," she said, putting down the spoon she'd been stirring the large pot of soup with on the counter. "You will find that revenues have taken a small dip, but nothing we both hadn't anticipated. People are leaving, and fewer are coming."

"Silver," I said, and she nodded.

There was nothing either of us could do about that. The reason I'd left was to be able to establish another business that I could use to pump more money into the maintenance of the Tombstone business and the care of the children, since I knew eventually the silver would dwindle to the point where we couldn't maintain a business that made enough to do that. For the moment, I put those thoughts aside.

"Angelo wrote me," Francesca said, frowning. "A bad business, what is happening down there. You are wise to have left. I worry about my brother and my family."

"I know," I said. "As do I. Angelo and his friends seem to think waiting out the bandits is their best strategy, but I worry as well. We can only hope and pray they are right."

Francesca shook her head. "My brother is a patient man, I've found, but perhaps not that patient. I want them to come north, but I don't think they ever will."

I patted her on the shoulder and kissed her cheek. "Thank you for taking such good care of the place, my friend. I know I am asking a lot of you."

She laughed. "Yes, but you are paying for it, Nellie."

I laughed too. "Oh, I know that. It's more than worth it,

for me to keep this business going in your capable hands, and have a place to come home to."

I spent the evening telling stories, some real and some in the misty land of the fairies, tucked in covers to chins, and finally settled on the porch watching the bats swoop to and fro against the moon, with a glass of whiskey, an unusual indulgence for me, but one I had found brought great solace at times. I took a sip, the warmth sliding down my throat, and snorted softly. Angel of the Cassiar, was I? Even angels have their weaknesses now and then. Let's take Lucifer, for one. I'd have to go some to be as fallen as that.

Things settled into the usual routine, cooking, supervising the restaurant, running the hotel and raising children. Every day I missed Fanny with a literal pang in my chest, and I knew the children, especially the older ones, did as well. She was such a loving and kind soul, without my impatience and impulsiveness, and every day I vowed to be more like her.

Francesca was right, revenue wasn't at the levels of a few years ago, but it was still quite good and our food was a draw around the area. The mining business was booming in southeast Arizona, especially Bisbee, and further north into Florence, Miami and Globe and further south as well. I'd already investigated Bisbee and Globe, and nothing there was enticing enough for me to undertake another venture in those areas, Bill Brophy and became good friends, me confiding my fears and worries about the children's futures, and he telling me of his dreams and plans for future business possibilities.

"Ah, we Irish," he said one night after dinner, as we sat having coffee. "Aren't we a pack of dreamers, Nellie?"

"Indeed we are," I said. "But that is how realities and even empires are born, 'tis it not? Fortune goes to the bold, my friend." I refilled his coffee cup and topped it off with a sprinkle of the cinnamon I knew he loved, the pungent spice filling my nostrils as well.

He laughed. "Well, there's bold and then there's foolhardy. But, yes, Nellie, I cannot disagree."

I raised an eyebrow. "Don't judge me on Muleje. Even I admit that was a fool's errand, but at least I persuaded my fellow fools to save their own lives."

"Angel of the Baja? Or perhaps Angel of Tombstone?"

I swatted him on the arm. "Never say any of those words again and I'll continue to feed you." I truly detested these monikers the yellow journalists and even the respectable press had used to talk about me. He continued to enjoy his dinners at Delmonico's. Bill Brophy was a very intelligent man.

* * *

THE RESTAURANT and hotel were still solvent, but I knew it was time to look further afield for income opportunities. There were many towns that had bloomed when mining came to the forefront of their income, but none as close by as Kingston, New Mexico. I pored over the newspapers and gathered information from the people that came and went and I kept going back to Kingston.

The place was booming. From everything I'd heard and read, it was like Tombstone had been in 1880. People were arriving in droves, fancy retail businesses and restaurants had taken root, including an opera house, and telltale signs of prosperity, like ice cream parlors and bowling alleys, had blossomed almost overnight. The mines were prosperous and showed no signs of water issues or waning strikes. When I heard about a hotel for sale, I went to investigate.

Not more than three months later, I was the proud owner of the newly renamed Cashman House, an upscale hotel and restaurant, purchased on a loan from one Nigel St. Clair of San Francisco, who had clearly had enough of the southwest.

Nigel was what my mother would've called a "fancy man", which had a few variables, from overdressed in the French fashion to somebody who preferred wearing satin and lace gowns and consorting with his pretty male friends. I couldn't have cared less what his proclivities or style choices were. All I was interested in were the papers in front of me.

We agreed upon what I felt, as did Nigel, was a fair price, with payments to be sent to his solicitor in San Francisco. He took my hand in his rather damp one and quickly withdrew, pulling back on his kid gloves.

"Thank you, Miss Cashman." He smiled and touched his lace handkerchief to his lips. "I hope you enjoy Kingston much more than I have." He studied my face and rather mundane garments, especially in comparison with his own pink silk. "In my humble estimation, I think it may suit quite well."

Within six months, the monsoon storms hit. The roof began to leak, but we got it patched up several times, and I was assured it would hold until the winter when we could a more thorough assessment and repair. I was skeptical, but there was little to be done. One evening, at the height of the dinner service, the entire south corner simply gave way, drenching the second floor rooms, and cascading down to the kitchen and restaurant, nearly drowning the customers trying to eat their steaks. Even better, the stove blew up, catching the restaurant on fire two weeks later.

I had no choice but to temporarily close for repairs. Those repairs turned out to be demolition and reconstruction of a third of the property, including the kitchen. I simply did not have the money to do it. I was going to have to sell it back to Nigel and take the loss, and I fervently hoped he'd let me do that.

I sent a letter through my lawyer in Tombstone to Nigel St. Clair, but it was returned with a "not at this address" stamp. From that day on, I never heard from him again. I'm not quite sure Nigel was even his real name. I berated myself once again for an unsound business decision and left

Kingston, returning to Tombstone once again wiser but quite chagrined. I needed to make more money and I wasn't quite sure how to go about that.

I fell asleep on the nights before I left Kingston, but it was a battle, staring at the water-stained ceiling above my head, my cotton nightgown tangled in my legs, frustrated sweat on my body. Nellie, I said to myself over and over, maybe in a dream, or maybe just my own mind telling me what I already knew. You need to go back to what you know. What's real, what you can touch and feel, what you know has value, what you have built already. Dreams of a future business that will be miraculously successful are just that. You have to be smarter. And so I vowed to be.

CHAPTER 24

Changes. That's what life is made of, especially if you really live it, instead of sitting in an armchair and watching it happen outside your protective window or your cocooned safety nest. At least, I've always thought so. Worried about the future, I thought I had to boldly escape my established routine, but I came to find that I didn't have to take a step outside Cochise County, Arizona to make a difference for me and my family. I can't deny that if there had been a Cassiar gold strike nearby, I wouldn't have given it a good try, but there was not. There was, however, a good deal of change to be had in Tombstone.

The children were delighted to have me home again, and I was as happy as they were. Changes, indeed. Children grow and develop so fast that it's taken the time away from them to show me just how much. TJ was almost a man, his voice deepening, and Michael wasn't far behind him and quite the know-it-all. Mamie was blossoming into a young woman and her artistic abilities amazed me. I hung her latest water color of cactus blossoms in a prominent place in the restaurant. William strutted around in a small cowboy hat and was crazy about horses, and dear little Fanny was the most endearing child I can ever remember seeing, her face a replica of my much-missed sister. All of them were quite independent, but that didn't surprise me. They'd also learned to depend on each other. They'd been through a lot in their short lives, uprooted and experiencing loss, even if the younger two didn't realize just how much, and had seen things many children would never be exposed to, as much as I'd tried to shield them. Looking back, I thought perhaps that wasn't such a bad thing. People are an amalgam of their histories and it makes them into the adults they become, given the right parameters. I think I had provided that, and I vowed to continue on that path.

On a practical note, to do so I needed to make changes of my own. I sat down with Francesca to discuss the finances of the business.

"Nellie, it's not as good as it was two years ago, there's no question. But, it's not bad, either. Maybe we need to think about ways to make more money with less customers." She laughed. "Of course, that's what every business person in Tombstone is trying to do."

She was right. That's exactly what we had to accomplish. The saving grace was that Tombstone was the county seat of Cochise County, no matter if the silver wasn't producing like it had. Everyone came here at one time or another to visit the courthouse or file legal papers, some more often than others.

I started with the restaurant and hotel. Paint was a miracle worker, and the buildings were in dire need of a fresh coat, inside and out. Then we painstakingly redid the signs, and TJ had a dab hand at intricately recreating the lettering and bringing it to life in black paint against the new glossy white background, with the "D" in Delmonico's elaborate. I was amazed at the difference in the exterior and signs alone. It was as though we were breathing new life and vigor into the place on that alone. But we didn't stop there.

I let Michael and Mamie choose the colors for the restaurant walls and the hotel rooms. They made brilliant choices, and I even gave William his favored turquoise for one of the walls in the restaurant, a great background for two more of Mamie's paintings of desert flowers and cactus.

Next, Francesca and I redid the menu. No more fancy food, at least not on the scale we'd done before. For instance, the beef Wellington was a standby and easy to prepare, but the cherry-stuffed quail with bourbon sauce was regretfully left behind, along with its Italian risotto, full of expensive ingredients that we didn't need. Apple pie and whipped cream cake became our usual desserts, and the seven-layer raspberry chocolate torte went the way of a wistful memory. Steaks, chops and Mexican food were the most popular menu items anyway, and we implemented many more vegetable dishes, because they were less expensive, poring over cookbooks I ordered from New York. After that, I wanted to try Italian pasta dishes, but Francesca vetoed it immediately.

"There are no Italians here, Nellie," she said.

"Of course there are, there's plenty of Irish, Spanish and Englishmen. Foolish to think there's no Italians in the mix."

"Name one." Francesca sat back on her chair and waited.

"Well, there's…" I thought about it for a minute and gave up. "You're right, there are no Italians here that I can think of. Still, that spaghetti sounds really wonderful."

She snorted. "Not on our menu."

Just to be stubborn, I said, "What about Chinese food? There's plenty of Chinese people around here."

This time she rolled her eyes, something I'd rarely seen Francesca do. "Ever seen one come through those doors?" She gestured towards the dining room. "I like their food too, but they only eat at their own cookshops. They think we eat like ravenous barbarians, so Song Lee tells me."

I accepted defeat on the new suggestions. Silently I vowed to make some pasta and try it for myself, if I had to do so in the dead of night. I smiled at her and she shook her head.

Francesca knew exactly what I was thinking. If I couldn't trek to new discoveries, I'd make them in my own kitchen. Just the thought made me happy and I imagined breathing in the smell of garlic and oregano, remembering passing by the DeMotti's trattoria in Boston.

We put out "Grand Re-opening" signs on the front of the restaurant, the windows covered with paper, to build up suspense and anticipation. Then, with a facelift, new menu and just the faintest scent of paint, overpowered by the candles of pine and sage, we re-opened two weeks later. We only served breakfast from six until nine in the morning, and dinner from 5-9 in the evenings. TJ and Michael were now waiters, and just me, Francesca and her niece Juliana worked the kitchen.

The response was gratifying. Every night, and soon every morning, people flocked in, from Cornish miners still around, to the townspeople and those from all over the county. They'd missed us. The new menu was a resounding success. Most people didn't miss aspic or elaborate pastry-encased meats. Meatloaf and mashed potatoes with plenty of gravy made them happier, along with Juliana's spectacular apple pie, its crust golden brown and decorated with little hand-formed apples. Profits climbed nearly back to the boomtown days and Francesca and I were delighted and relieved.

The Birdcage Theater, struggling, was doing the same thing as I'd done. They brought in traveling theater troupes, performing everything from Shakespeare to new plays from New York, the actors stunningly good, especially to our untrained eyes and ears. I took the children to see Romeo and Juliet one evening and they were enchanted, especially Mamie, who turned to me with tears in her eyes at the end.

"Oh Aunt Nell," she said. "Is love always so sad?"

"No, my dear," I said, hugging her. "It doesn't have to be. It was not that way for your mother and father, nor is it for most. Don't forget, Mr. Shakespeare creates drama that he knows will affect his audience. Real life doesn't usually work like that. Never be afraid to love, Mamie."

I didn't add that it certainly had never been that way for me. But then, I'd never allowed it an opportunity to show itself. I guarded my heart closely and never had been tempted by Eros or anyone human to let down my vigilance. I had too much else that had called to me and now, too much else to attend to.

Shakespeare was the tip of the iceberg when it came to entertainment, though. The Birdcage brought in circus-type acts, dogs who could do amazing things with hoops, balls and even riding on the back of a pony; magicians who made things appear and disappear in a cloud of colored smoke and seemed to saw ladies in half, (a particular favorite of Michael's, who devoted himself to finding out the secret of how this lovely woman could've survived the cruel blades.) I always expected to see a few white rabbits that seemed to appear and disappear scuttling around the alleys, but I never did. After all, it was magic.

The biggest money-maker, though, and it brought great crowds to the town, and to my restaurant and hotel, was the Cornish wrestling matches, which they said were reported in newspapers as far away as England. I only saw one the first evening they were presented, and I left before the match was over. For me, they weren't entertaining but brutal, but everyone in town was enthusiastic in their support and the revenue was high. I preferred my entertainments to be more musical or melodramatic, rather than leaving the venue with my clothing sprinkled with the blood or sweat from the efforts on display. I'd seen enough of that in real life and I figured wrestling was likely easier and more profitable than working in the mines, so I couldn't begrudge them that. Besides, business was great.

One of the things I'd always loved about running a restaurant and hotel was meeting my customers. Many were local, some were nearby and some I never saw again, but on any given day, you never knew who might show up. I truly loved that, and maybe it was the Irish in me, as my mother used to say, but I took every opportunity to chat with anyone that welcomed it and always had. Even back in Boston, I met interesting people working as an elevator operator, and now, those that came to my premises. I learned to read people and knew who wanted to chat and who had no interest in talking to me or anyone else.

That said, one morning I brought a breakfast special to a nice-looking gentleman who was, to my dismay, holding Fanny on his lap. I turned abruptly to call for Sally to take her away, when the man's laughter, mingling with Fanny's, echoed through the place. I put the plate down before him and leaned down.

"I'm so sorry, sir. She's a devil when it comes to getting her way, and going where she likes. Let me take her."

"No issue," he said, smiling at me. "She's just what I needed and I'm enjoying her company, isn't that right, Fanny?"

Little Miss Pert looked up at me. "Yes, Aunt Nell. Mr. Parker and I are having breakfast this morning, aren't we?"

"Indeed we are," he said. "If that is fine with your aunt. From all reports, you must be Nelly Cashman. My name is Robert Parker and I've been enjoying the hospitality of your fine town, but until this morning, I had no idea how delightful it could be. If you would allow me, Miss Fanny here has just told me she is quite fond of biscuits with strawberry jam. Could that be arranged?"

I vacillated, but only for a moment. "Yes, it could, if Miss Fanny behaves." I gave Fanny a stern look and to her credit, she lowered her eyes for a second but nothing could suppress this child for long.

"Biscuits and jam, coming up. Perhaps it might be more convenient if you both had a chair," I said, and Mr. Parker nodded and smoothly slid Fanny into the chair beside him, still smiling. Fanny was elated. So was I, because I'd avoided one of her monumental temper tantrums, while the other diners looked on with great amusement. If they'd been subjected to this child's wrath, they wouldn't be amused at all.

Mr. Parker paid his bill and Fanny was disappointed he was leaving, but he assured her he'd return. Sally arrived, breathless, and apologetic, and took her off to her lessons.

"I've taken a room in your hotel, Miss Cashman," he said. "A double, since my friend Mr. Longabaugh will be arriving tomorrow. We'll only be here a day after that, but I know he will enjoy the accommodations and your superb cooking as much as I have. We're on a bit of a holiday."

Well. I'd have to be sure Miss Fanny was properly corralled tomorrow morning instead of roaming through the restaurant looking for handsome friendly gentlemen to dine with. Children. At least she'd chosen a nice one in her first foray.

As I would come to learn not long after Mr. Parker and his friend departed, I'd fed and housed Butch Cassidy and the Sundance Kid. Sheriff Behan was quite unhappy with me for not realizing who my customers were, but I didn't care. I didn't like Behan, he was a liar and a grifter.

If those two kind and courteous gentlemen were outlaws that I should fear and betray, then I wasn't sure exactly who the good people were anymore. Sheriff Behan had always struck me as someone who took advantage of those who couldn't defend themselves, and supporting those who paid him to do so. Wyatt had always thought so, as had the rest of the Earps, and Doc Holliday too. I judged people on who they were, not what they were accused of doing, and even if they were found to do criminal acts, I always thought more thought should be given to the former, not the latter. God always has a way of sorting that out, and I trusted him more than any sheriff or anything a wanted poster said.

Butch and Sundance weren't the first, nor would they be the last outlaws that passed through my doors. Delmonico's was open to everyone, whether you were a copper baron, a banker, a shopkeeper, a miner, a cowboy coming to town, or, even yes, a bank robber. As long as you were kind and respectful to me and mine, I'd give you a place to sleep and food to fill your belly. What happened to you after that was up to God and the saints. I would never presume to be your judge.

CHAPTER 25

MAGGIE FLAHERTY

I never chose this life, being a whore. I knew most of us didn't. I grew up on a farm in Colorado, and I always thought I'd marry some man with a grin and merry eyes and we'd do pretty much the same, maybe a place a little bigger and better than my parents, but the grandchildren would make them happy and content.

The handsome cowboy with the grin and merry eyes came along too early and left the next morning. I was fourteen and when my father saw my belly four months later, he packed my clothes and threw the bundle out in the yard, pushing five dollars into my hand before he shut the door. I guess he wouldn't have been content with his grandchild unless he came with bonafides.

I had the baby too early, in a cabin in northern Arizona and he died, and I nearly did too. The couple that took me in buried him and patched me up and I ended up in Tombstone, looking for work. There was only one thing available since I didn't know how to do anything worth money but milk a cow and pull weeds, and that's how I came to be at the Silver Belle Saloon, working the upstairs rooms, spreading my legs for miners and cowboys. I had to work off my debt for the two cheap purple taffeta dresses they gave me and somehow that debt never got paid no matter how many customers I had, whether they lasted fifteen minutes or all night.

The first time I met Nellie Cashman was when a miner beat me up so bad I had two black eyes and two broken ribs. My friend Sally told me about Nellie and how she took care of whores with no questions and no recriminations. I showed up at her back door and she took me inside and put me down on a bed. She bandaged my ribs, put ice on my eyes and fed me chicken soup that I swear was the best thing I'd ever tasted. I remember waking up the next afternoon and seeing her face like it was that of an angel, those braids across her head like a halo, and those blue eyes that seemed to look into your soul.

Nellie went to the Silver Belle and told them I wouldn't be coming back and demanded my wages. Dell gave her twenty dollars which surprised me, but now that I know Nellie, it shouldn't have. I went to work a few days later as a waitress at Delmonico's, Nellie's restaurant.

Nellie Cashman, to me, wasn't just an angel. She was a saint and saved my life.

CHAPTER 26

Mornings were always chaotic. Grumpy children being woken to meet the day, whether it was school or summer; a busy kitchen cooking eggs, bacon, potatoes, biscuits and all the trimmings for a restaurant full of hungry customers; and me, a ringmaster for all of it, issuing orders to Sally for the children's day; making sure the panes were fingerprint-free on the glass front door, the outside flowerpots watered, the tablecloths clean and the plates spotless and countless other tasks. It usually started around five in the morning and there wasn't a break until ten, and then we cleaned up and planned for the dinner/supper hours, which began at five in the afternoon.

It wasn't quite the adventurous life I'd envisioned for myself but it was a satisfying one for the most part, the tedium broken by the children, with their constant inquisitiveness and the delight of watching them grow into the adults they would become. For that, I wouldn't have traded any mining claim in the world. Watching them was a bonanza on its own.

I missed my sister so much it was a constant ache in my heart, one that manifested itself even physically if I let it, only to be diminished by a few deep breaths and a look at the nearly always blue sky above me. Often I found solace at Sacred Heart, lighting candles for her and Tom, talking to God and Father O'Hara. I think that priest understood me more than I did myself. I hoped God did too.

Bill Brophy was a frequent customer at the restaurant, along with E. B. Gage and Bill Douglas, coming to the courthouse for one thing and another, even though their headquarters were in Bisbee and points south. Brophy and Gage had been paying for tutors for the older boys for some time, not listening to my protests, and I was secretly grateful they hadn't. TJ and Michael were maturing rapidly and had a grasp of knowledge that was far behind their peers at the Tombstone school. Sometimes I felt that keeping them here was slowing down their progress but I wasn't ready to relinquish any of the children to the outside world. Keeping them close was a promise to Fanny that wasn't a responsibility I was willing to leave yet either.

The Fourth of July parade was a welcome diversion, the streets hung with red, white and blue bunting and flags. The Tombstone Fire Brigade led the effort, the horses prancing as they led the wagon down Allen Street. Next came the official Tombstone marching band, a motley collection of musicians made up mostly with brass and drums that manfully executed a new Sousa march as well as a selection of Civil War tunes, always a favorite. Then a float of the few miners holding on, brandishing picks and shovels came by. The highlight of the parade was a double wagon full of dancing girls in red, white and blue costumes, replete with a piano player.

My restaurant featured barbecue, corn on the cob, and apple and cherry pies as an homage to America. For us, it was an easier than usual day, just one meal in the afternoon, although lots of it.

The climax of the day was fireworks. They were dazzling, lighting up the night and the surrounding mountains against the dark desert sky. Most of the spectators had never seen them before, and I was one of them. The children were enchanted, never wanting the day to end after that. Neither did I, truthfully, but eventually we all fell asleep, content with our dreams, spangled with the bright stars of the pyrotechnics.

The next morning dawned too early, it seemed. I'd given Francesca the day off before but she was in the kitchen long before me, pans of biscuits already in the ovens.

"There's some men outside on the front porch," she said. "I don't know who they are, but they've been there for a while and they haven't left." She didn't sound happy about it.

I sighed. Sometimes we had drifters or drunks sleeping on the porch amid the flowerpots but usually by the time the sun came up, they were long gone. After the celebrations yesterday, I wasn't terribly surprised. I peered out the windows. There were three of them, hats pulled down enough to obscure their faces, and they seemed quite content, and at least two of them seemed asleep. I'd have to move them before we opened. No customers would want to step over that, nor should they have to.

I opened the door, the familiar morning scents of mesquite and sage in the morning breeze that flowed into the restaurant, overpowering even the smell of baking biscuits.

"Gentlemen," I said. "You'll be having to move along now. My porch steps are not a hotel. Down the street you'll find accommodations to your liking to be sure, but 'tis not here."

The closest man stood up, doffing his hat and bowing. "Nellie Cashman, I'm not here for your porch steps, darlin'. I'm here for you." He raised his head and that familiar grin warmed my heart.

"Patrick Sullivan." I flung myself into his arms and he caught me in his usual bear hug.

"In the flesh, darlin', in the flesh," he said, twirling me around like I was a mere feather. "Long time, eh?"

"Lord, yes," I gasped out. "Put me down, you big oaf."

He did so, still grinning and so was I, as I reached up and

kissed his cheek. I couldn't believe how good it was to see him. Memories of the Cassiar flooded into my mind.

"What are you doing here?" I nudged his sleeping companions with a booted toe. "And who are these likely reprobates? Friends of yours, I hope?"

He laughed. "Very likely, Nellie. Although one you already know, and one you've yet to meet."

He did more than nudge, giving each of the sleepers a soft kick. Both grunted in sleepily outraged response, sitting up. The second man's hat fell off and I squealed in delight like a little girl, unable to stop myself.

"Tim Rickman, is that really you?" I held out my arms.

He stood up and readily took me into his much larger ones, planting a kiss atop my braided hair. "Course it is, dear Nellie. So happy to see you again."

The third man needed another not so soft kick from Patrick, before waking. He pushed his hat back on forehead and two bright green eyes stared up at me from behind a mop of wavy black hair.

He cleared his throat and stood up, all six feet of him, holding out his hand. I nearly took a step back but there was nowhere to go. "Michael Sullivan, Miss Cashman. My brother's told me stories about you for years. Very happy to meet you at last." The smile brought out the dimples on that devilishly handsome face.

I shook his warm and calloused hand and for the first time in my life I began to get a glimmering of why women actually fell in love with the male of the species, a notion that so far had completely eluded me. At the same time, I wished Patrick Sullivan had stayed in Canada or Colorado or wherever he'd last come from, along with his companions, much as I enjoyed seeing at least two of them. This could be trouble I surely didn't need.

Both Patrick and Tim showed the years on their faces and for a flash of a second, I wondered if that was true of me as well, something I'd never really given a thought to before. Mining was a hard life, there was no question about that. I'd missed them a great deal and couldn't wait to catch up.

I brought them inside and sat them at a table with a full pot of coffee, and went back to the kitchen to finish helping Francesca with breakfast. There were still no other customers, as we weren't officially open yet, when I brought out three plates full of eggs, bacon, potatoes and biscuits. I left them alone to eat, only interrupting with a platter of blueberry pancakes. All of it was demolished in short order.

"Christ Jesus, Nellie, I remember your cooking like it was yesterday," Patrick said, "it was the best I ever ate, and it hasn't changed a whit."

Pleased, I laughed and kissed him on the cheek. "You devil, you know the way to my heart is complimenting me on my food. Remember when it was lime juice and onions?"

"How could I ever forget?" Patrick smiled. "The worst and best thing that ever passed my scurvy lips. You saved my life, coming out of the snow like a screaming banshee with that wolf dog of yours. You, and this reprobate here," he nudged Tim Rickman. "To the day I die I swear I don't know how you did it."

"A lot of sweat and tears," Tim said, pouring another cup of coffee. "But, mostly Nellie's sheer grit, and a wee touch of Irish luck."

Michael hadn't said a word during this exchange, just watched us all with those bright green eyes, quietly sipping his coffee.

I sat down at the empty seat. "So, where've you been these years since?"

Patrick put his cup down. "Where haven't we been, eh Tim?"

"Montana, Idaho, Colorado, last Kingston, New Mexico, where I hear we just missed you," Tim said. "It's had its ups and downs. The best money we cleared was in Leadville, but that's playing out, like they do."

"And this boyo showed up about then," Patrick said, clapping Michael on the shoulder. "Mother's little darling he is. Went to school in Boston, then teaching those Easterners all about mining minerals, not like a one of those dandies would ever deign to muddy their lily-white hands actually doing it." He snorted his disdain and Michael chuckled.

"Teaching them about it doesn't mean I gave them any practical instruction on how to do it," Michael said, speaking for the first time. "'Tis true hardly any of my former students will ever cross the Mississippi, but I wasn't running a school for hardrock miners, just teaching them what there was hiding in the earth. If they chose to try and actually find it, that was a choice they could make. Like I finally did."

"Good thing I always wrote Mama, so's you'd know where to look for practical experience," Patrick said, "and then one morning, there he was, green as grass in his new duds and boots, standing on the platform in Denver."

With no animosity, they all laughed at the memory, Michael as much as the other two but his cheeks were pink. He shook his head.

"I really was green as grass, wasn't I? I hate to even think back on it. But," he looked at Patrick and Tim, "it didn't take long for you two to school me. You have to at least give me credit for being a quick learner."

Tim and Patrick raised their coffee cups in a toast, and Michael clinked his to theirs.

It was quiet for a few seconds. Then Michael turned to me. "I've learned a lot and heard a lot of stories in the past few years, but the one that is told everywhere we've been is about you, Nellie Cashman. It's an honor for me to sit here with you this fine morning."

I found myself blushing, the heat rising in my cheeks, and for maybe the first time in my life I was at a loss for words.

"With reason," Patrick said, and Tim nodded.

I stood up. "Gentlemen, as wonderful as it is to see you, I regret I have other duties." The restaurant was filling up, and Michael, TJ and Maggie were taking orders. Francesca would be way too busy.

"Where are you staying?" I asked Patrick.

"We've not a place yet," he said. "What about here?"

"I would love that," I said, meaning it. "But we're full, it's a small hotel. I suggest the Cosmopolitan, down the street. Are you all right for that?"

Tim knew what I meant right away. "We're golden, Nellie. But we surely will see you around suppertime?"

"I very much hope so," I said, meaning that too. "Starts at five."

I hugged each of them in turn as they left and made their way to the street. I stood there for a moment and watched them as they made their way down the thoroughfare. This was a morning to remember for certain.

CHAPTER 27

In the next few days, I saw a lot more of Tim and the Sullivans, and learned a lot more about their mining adventures since we'd parted in the Cassiar. They in turn, learned quite a bit from me about the silver claims and possibilities in the Tombstone and southern Arizona area.

So many places across the Southwest were playing out and what we called simple mining just wasn't possible anymore. Gold went to silver, silver gave way to copper and so it went. It took mining companies to dredge out those riches, replete with heavy machinery, water pumps and many underpaid workers. What we'd all started with was hard to find anymore. Even many of the mining companies had pulled out, as they had in Tombstone.

Miners like us weren't the only ones who kept hoping for the next big strike, like the Cassiar, Placerville, Tombstone, and so many other places. Gold fever, so people had rudely termed it, making it sound as though anyone who was fascinated with the finding of rich minerals was a lunatic, was truly a real thing. I was certainly infected with it, as were the Sullivans and Tim Rickman and many others. I couldn't speak for all, but for us it wasn't greed but the excitement of discovering the riches the earth could offer, as no one had done before us. I can tell you there is nothing like the feeling of holding a gold nugget as big your fist that you found in an icy stream to make your heart beat faster. For my part, I gave most of the money I'd ever earned mining to the church and its hospitals, my way to make life better for others, not out of any sense of guilt, but because I wanted to. I loved the undying tie of the earth divulging its treasures to give succor to the humans that trod upon its surface. To me, a never-ending circle, all within God's tender hands. Well, and mine.

A few nights later, the four of us sat outside on the porch of the restaurant, sipping whiskey. My back ached, and it had been a busy day, for which I was grateful but there was always a cost, I'd found.

I must've groaned slightly, and Patrick began to rub my back, the way he used to do at Dease Lake, knowing just the right spots to put pressure on after a hard day of digging. It was old and familiar to us, but I saw Michael glance up and away, a frown on his face. For some reason, I shrugged Patrick's hand away with a grateful smile.

"So did you find anything interesting in your explorations today and yesterday?"

They'd been venturing around the area, from Mule Gulch to the Chiricahuas, on the hunt for anything that had the earmarks of another strike, or at least a rich vein.

Tim shook his head. "Nope, not a thing. Seems like the trolls have sucked it all away, back to the center of the Earth. Maybe there'll be an earthquake or some such and throw it up again." He looked discouraged.

Michael chuckled at that. "Not likely, Tim, but I like your thinking. The reason it's surfaced in the first place… well, it might've been trolls. Just as good as the other explanations, and sure better than any about why it's going away." He sipped his whiskey. "I heard an old prospector over in Sonoita yesterday who said it was the old Apache gods, enticing the greedy white men here to be slaughtered with the promise of easy riches, but I guess we've been too many for them, so that didn't work out very well, as least not yet."

"Praise God and pass the tatties," Patrick said. "We've not had any of that sort of trouble in any of the places we've been, although I heard a few boys talking about the Flatheads being pretty unhappy up in Idaho, but they're pretty tame these days."

It was getting pretty dark, just the lights from the saloons illuminating the dusty street. A man in a serape and a wide-brimmed hat was walking down the street towards us. I'd never seen him before and was surprised when he turned, coming to a stop at the bottom of the stairs.

"Buenos noches, amigos," he said, his voice deep and musical. Patrick jumped up like he'd been bee-stung and threw his arms around the man. "Fabian, damn it's good to see you."

"As it is with me, *cabron,*" Fabian said, punching Patrick playfully but firmly in the arm. Both Tim and Michael greeted him warmly as well.

Patrick turned to me. "Nellie, let me introduce you to our friend, Fabian Vega. He's got a nose for gold, this one. Fabian, Miss Nellie Cashman."

Senor Vega removed his hat, took my hand and bowed to me as though I was Queen Victoria. I nearly giggled but swallowed it quickly. He was quite charming.

"Miss Cashman, I am honored," he said. "You are a legend."

"Oh, stuff," I said, "I'm just a woman like anybody else. Pleased to meet you, Mr. Vega."

He was a handsome devil, Fabian Vega. Large brown eyes, a mischievous smile and lips that seemed to naturally curve in a smile. He was also, according to Patrick, a bloodhound on the trail of gold, human-style. Vega pulled out his flask of what smelled like tequila, took a sip and sat down on the steps.

"Just where did you meet up with these Irish rogues?" I said. "Colorado?"

"*Exactamente,* Miss Cashman," Fabian said. "But we are on the trail of new and bigger opportunities, right, Patrick?"

Patrick raised his glass. "Absolutely. So, you're late. We expected you days ago. Hope it's because you've got good news."

Fabian smiled, his teeth white in the gathering dark. "I do." He took another sip from his flask.

"There is gold. It is in this place of the Harquahala Mountains, west of Prescott. A new discovery, well, almost new. But there aren't too many there yet. If we hurry."

Michael and Tim had been leaning back on their elbows and now sat up straight, as though Fabian's words had stiffened their spines. Maybe they had. Mine was twitching a bit too.

"Hell, we can leave in the mornin'," Michael said and Tim nodded enthusiastically, downing his whiskey.

Patrick held up his hand. If anyone was in charge of this group, I'd already sensed it was him. "Whoa, give us a little more, Fabian," he glared at Michael and Tim. "Before these boyos go off half-cocked and ride out of town like they're seeking vengeance on Mad George himself."

Fabian laughed softly, and pulled a sheaf of papers from under his serape, handing them to Patrick. At that, we all decamped into the restaurant where there was light enough to read them.

The soft glow of the kerosene lamps illuminated the pages Fabian spread out on the tabletop.

"Assay reports, maps and testimony from Isaac Worth, who first discovered this vein on the south side," he said, and we all read them greedily, passing them from hand to hand around the table. It looked legitimate to me, and clearly to the other three men seated beside me.

A silence fell, and I poured more whiskey.

"Votes?" Patrick said.

Three hands raised, but not mine, since I didn't think I was entitled to one. I was simply the hostess of this get-together, not a participant in their decisions. But Patrick turned to me.

"What do you think, Nellie?"

"What does it matter what I think, Patrick? Your mining ventures are of no interest to me. I'm just a businesswoman in Tombstone, Arizona now."

Patrick laughed, and smiles appeared on the other three faces as well. "I'd be surprised if you weren't on the first stage out of here long before we fell out of bed tomorrow morning. You can't fool me, Nellie. You're just as much in the game as you ever were. Now, tell me what you think, please."

"Well," I said, and took a sip of whiskey. "Here's the truth. It wouldn't be the first stage. Don't insult me. I've learned to plan."

"Ha!" Patrick said, but I held up my hand.

"As far as the stages go, I think you four should be gathering your equipment and get on the first one after you do. The reports look genuine, truly the first good news I've seen in Arizona in a long while, and even anywhere in the Southwest. But, don't put all your faith in the accounts of others, many of which prove to be false. I, on the other hand, have obligations which you do not. I may be joining you, but that will take me some time."

Sobered and more serious, they all looked at me and each other.

Michael, sitting next to me, took my hand. His green eyes were bright in the glow of the lamp on the table. "You're right, on all accounts. You take as much time as you need. If you come, we'll be there to welcome you."

He stared into my eyes and my heart gave a little flutter, just as it had when he took my hand. I didn't really want to, but I slid my fingers away from his and back into my lap.

Nellie, I said to myself, *you're acting like a schoolgirl. There won't be any more of this nonsense.*

And there wasn't. They were busy, took a day buying supplies and planning, and left on the first stage the two days later.

Patrick took my hand. "I wish you were coming with us right now, Nellie. You're the best good luck charm anyone could have, and you seem to have a direct line to the big man, so that's likely why it's so." He laughed. "You're a life-saver, you are."

"Ha," I said. "Maybe if you went to confession a little more often, as in at all, his ears might open for you as well, Patrick."

The others sniggered at this, as they knew it was true, and likely for all of them. I hugged them all, none more so than the other, waving goodbye while I stood on the street and watched them go, filled with a longing for both them and the adventure that awaited them.

I didn't doubt for a minute there was gold in the Harquahalas. I knew there was, and this wasn't the first report I'd heard, just the first one they had. It had intrigued me for some time. However, after the trip to Muleje, I'd learned to be cautious, even if this one was prefaced with assay reports and other bonafides. In the hunt for gold, nobody could be trusted, I'd found, even those who seemed to be of the utmost honesty when reporting of it. This was an occupation that inspired the imagination, followed by cupidity and greed, and then the lies began.

As far as I was concerned, I knew there was a way to make money in the Harquahalas, but it wasn't solely at the end of a pick, or draining a sluicebox on my muddy knees. I'd learned better. Those methods sometimes provided value, but I knew a way to provide profit.

CHAPTER 28

1888

Dawn was breaking as I left Prescott, the four mules pulling my heavy wagon much livelier than I was despite two strong cups of coffee. It was much cooler up here than in Tombstone, thankfully, and the early morning chill had me wearing a jacket which I knew I'd soon discard when the sun was full up.

I'd ordered merchandise and supplies to be delivered and warehoused in Prescott before I left Tombstone, and arranged for the wagon and mules with Patrick before he left. He'd been true to his word as always, when I arrived at the livery. Four handsome mules and a sturdy large wagon were there waiting.

I spent the day supervising the loading of the wagon, and then walking around Prescott, admiring the Courthouse and noting the bustling businesses and saloons surrounding it. This was a town with a future, and a nice climate to go with it. I could've left that afternoon, but I knew it was nearly seventy miles to the Harquahalas and I didn't want to spend two nights on the road. One was more than enough and too many people already knew how much valuable cargo I was carrying.

There was nothing to be done about that but put my trust in God and myself. I held out a vague hope four mules rather than two would make faster time but I wasn't foolish. The road was rough and steep as it neared the mountains and in the dark of night, with a driver who'd never traveled it, a risky proposition, one I wasn't keen to wager my life on.

I'd given serious thought to bringing TJ and Michael with me, but in the end discarded the idea and I was especially glad of it now. This trek wasn't for children of any age. I'd arranged for all five of the children to live with the Brophys in Bisbee until I returned. Sally had accompanied them because I knew how rowdy the younger three could get and they needed a firm hand. Bill Brophy had generously offered, and I could think of no better place for them. They were a good Irish Catholic family, with many of the same traditions and values the Cashmans had. Michael in particular had bonded with this kind man, eager to know more of business and there was no one better to educate him on that score. I smiled just thinking of it. The boy who had idolized Wyatt Earp had a new hero, a man of commerce. I had heard tales of Wyatt, and it sounded as though he'd embraced business himself. I wished him well.

Francesca had the restaurant and hotel well in hand, as usual, and I had little worry on that front. That woman was a wonder, sort of a Mexican carbon copy of me, I sometimes thought with amusement. While she'd never venture out for mining opportunities, she kept a firm no-nonsense hand on her own demesne, and I knew there was no one in the world better than Francesca to partner with.

It was lovely up here, northern Arizona new territory for me. The cooler pine-scented air was still spiked with mesquite, and there was certainly more trees than I'd seen in a long time, along with green ground cover. Still, by noon, the sun beat down on me and those poor mules with relentless fury. I'd been keeping an eye out for any trace of water, and when I saw some sycamore trees ahead, I knew a creek could be close by, and turned them accordingly. It wasn't much of one, but it was enough. I walked the mules into the shallow bed and gave them a few minutes, but not too long. I didn't want them bloated out. They weren't too happy about leaving, being mules, but I had a stronger will and soon we were back on the road, such as it was. I munched on an apple and a big roast beef sandwich. The hotel restaurant had supplied me with a hamper of food, more than enough for two days.

We made better time than I'd expected, somewhat familiar with wagons. Still, we kept going until it was nearly full dark. As the shadows lengthened, I began to worry there wouldn't be any place suitable for spending the night. Then I saw an outcrop of large boulders, twice my height, and I pulled the wagon over beside it. The sky was clear and no clouds were in sight, but I rather liked the idea of having something solid at my back besides just darkness.

I had no idea exactly how far we'd come. I hoped it was at least halfway and we'd be in the boys' camp in the Harquahalas before the sun set tomorrow, but I truly had no way to know that. I'd been on the road since five in the morning so that was at least fourteen hours on the road today, for whatever measurement that could give. Tomorrow would hopefully bring me into the camps of the gold field.

I built a small fire, ate some cold potatoes and fried chicken, and fell asleep almost immediately on a couple of blankets. I figured the mules would alert me to predators, marauders and rattlesnakes. At least I hoped so. In my opinion, they were more reliable than horses and didn't spook as much, even though they liked having their own way.

I woke just before dawn. All was quiet, as it had been throughout the night, or perhaps I'd been so tired I wouldn't have heard a bear walk through my tiny camp anyway. I harnessed up the mules and we were back on the road before the sun broke over the hills. We found another stream not far down the road and I let the mules drink for a few minutes while I filled the canteens.

The way became steeper the further west we went and the road rougher. I hadn't seen another soul so far, which struck me as rather odd, given that a lot of people were headed to the Harquahalas for the same reason, more or less, as I was. By mid-afternoon, that destination looked no closer than it had in the morning, and I sure wasn't looking forward to another night on the trail.

I recalled the livery man talking to a couple of other men the morning I left. I hadn't paid much attention at the time, but in retrospect, I wish I would have. They'd been talking about outlaws on the road, robbing miners. No names or locations were mentioned, and I'd been in too much of a hurry to get moving to inquire further. *Sometimes, Nellie Cashman*, I said to myself, *your impatience does you no service.* Ah, well, no point in worrying about a boogeyman that likely would never appear except under the bed. I'd never carried a gun before and this trek was no exception. I figured God had need of me and he wasn't done providing protection just yet, since we both knew I had further things to do. It was a bargain we'd struck some time ago and we'd both held up our ends of it.

I came around a particularly tricky curve, the mules protesting, and as we came out onto a small flower-dotted meadow, four men on horses ran at me, two on each side. Well, shoot. I sure hoped God was on duty for me this afternoon because this didn't look too good. I knew trouble when I saw it and it looked as though the boogeyman had just crawled out from under the bed, after all.

"Hi there, sweetheart," said a red-haired man riding a buckskin stallion, pulling the horse up beside me as we trotted along. He seemed to be the leader, or at least the spokesman. "I like those braids on your head like you're some sort of princess. What you doing out here all alone except for your pretty self?"

His companion, who looked Apache, looked slightly bored and just stared at the mules, while the other two horsemen pulled up on the right side of the wagon. They both could've used a good bath and I could smell them from as far away as the wagon seat.

"Yeah," one of them snickered, "you sure got a load on there for a little lady. Maybe you could use some help."

My hands were shaking inside my leather gloves, but steady on the reins and the mules just kept on going, as did the riders pacing us.

"Cat got your tongue, missy?" Redhead said.

"No, I just see no need for your help or conversation," I said, keeping my eyes on the road. "Didn't ask for it, don't need it. Ride on."

He laughed. "Well, that's just plain rude, don't you think, boys? Here we are, fellow travelers on this mean road of life, offering assistance to the gentler sex and we are rebuffed like we aren't gentlemen of substance. Now that just plain hurts my feelings."

I said nothing, just kept my hands on the reins, the mules plodding along, until he grabbed the reins out of my hands quick as a rattlesnake and pulled them to a halt.

"Get down."

I just stared at him and shifted my back further back on the wagon seat. He shook his head.

"Let's not make this harder than it has to be," Redhead said, nodding at the two men on my right. "You're getting off that wagon, one way or another. Depends on how you feel when you're on the ground. Up to you."

I had no wish to be manhandled down from that wagon, so I stepped down and stood with my back beside the canvas-covered cargo on the wagon bed.

"See how easy that was?" Redhead said, getting off his horse. "Arms up."

Dutifully, I put my arms skyward. He patted me down, taking particular care here and there. Typical and I hadn't expected anything else. No point in feminine hysterics, even if

I knew how to do that. It's always rather mystified me. Boiling mad was another matter entirely.

He stepped back and shook his head. "Lady, you're out here with this load and you don't even carry a gun? You think there's some sort of angel on your shoulder? I swear, you must be crazy."

He leaned in close and I could smell his breath, which wasn't pleasant. "We are going to have some fun due to your foolishness."

I spit into his face and raised my knee to his privates. He howled and jumped back as though he'd been rattlestruck, falling into the dirt. His companions dismounted and rushed to his assistance, which only seemed to make him angrier. I just stood there as I didn't have anywhere to go. I thought about jumping back onto the wagon but it wouldn't take them long to catch up and they had guns.

Red got his feet, shoving off his friends, staggering a bit and backhanded me across the face. It was a good hit and I went down just about as rapidly as he had. I'd never been violently attacked by anyone in my life and the ferocity of it felled me just as much as the physical force of it. God help me. I struggled to my feet just as he grabbed my shoulders and shoved me back hard into the side of the wagon.

"You'll pay for this," he snarled, and threw me back into the dirt. "I was just going to leave you out here but now it's different. You need a lesson in manners. We'll have some fun tonight."

I didn't feel that any of those words required a response that wouldn't end badly for me and my face hurt like the devil, so I kept quiet.

One of the smelly followers climbed onto the wagon seat and picked up the reins of the placid mules. "You want to put her up here, Trace?"

Red nodded at me and I scrambled up onto the seat, since there was no other option except another smack to the face, staying as far away as I could from Stinky. I hunched down a bit, thinking if there was any opportunity, I'd roll off the seat and start running. It seemed a feeble hope, but there weren't any other options I could see. They tied the spare horse onto the wagon and turned the mules back the direction we'd come from. Guess they saw no point in heading where somebody might know them.

Before the mules taken more than a dozen steps east, Stinky's head exploded in a haze of red droplets and he dropped the reins as his body slumped forward. I grabbed up the reins, wiping the coppery reek of his blood from my face, and halted the mules while more shots rang out around me. All I could think to do was drop into the foot space below the seat and pray. Somebody didn't care for these men or what they were doing, but I had no way to know if they were friends of mine, or just more outlaws out to steal my wagon. Waiting it out seemed the best option unless I wanted to end up shot like Stinky, getting more fragrant by the moment beside me since his bowels had let go along with his life.

More gunshots followed, along with yells and the sound of horses coming near and I kept my head down. I don't remember being more frightened in my life, not in the Cassiar, faced with raging rivers and ice dams, or in fear of my friends' lives. This was something entirely different. Nature was cruel, but mankind could be much worse, and now I knew that first-hand. The world could be a wicked place.

"Nellie?"

Patrick Sullivan's voice sounded like a clarion call from the heavens. I raised my head and there he was, Michael beside him, his arm bloody, both brandishing Winchester rifles. A half of dozen other men rode beside them. They looked like angels to me. I flew off that wagon seat like I nearly was one myself, embracing both the Sullivans.

Michael gently put his hand on my bruised face and swore softly. "Oh Nellie, I wish we could've only been here sooner."

His touch was soft and caring, especially given that he must be in pain. I put my hand over his and pulled it gently down. "But you're here now, and that's all that matters."

God forgive me, I stepped over those dead bodies like they were rocks on the road to perdition. I took some sour comfort over the red-haired one. He'd made his own demise, and his greed was the instrument of his destruction, not me.

I'd pray for him, but not for long.

The men buried them where they lay, and no mention of their lives was left.

CHAPTER 29

"You got any a them brown boots left?" First customer of the day. His boots looked pretty bad but he'd come to the right place. 'Course it was the only place.

I smiled and held the tent flap open. "Sure do, come on in, pal, and let's get you outfitted."

He walked away, almost prancing on those new boots that were a long sight better than the rest of his kit, but at least he'd gotten the most important part. Another satisfied customer, which always made me happy. Besides, I'd made ten bucks.

Michael walked in and handed me a cup of coffee. I took the warm cup in my hand, and his warm fingers were an added benefit that made my heart beat just like a little faster.

"Mornin', Glory." His smile enveloped me like a ray of sunshine while at the same time I felt silly and unexpectedly, vulnerable, which always gets my back up. I'm Nellie Cashman. I don't need any man or anything he's got to offer. I can do it myself. But that was a smile to be reckoned with, all right. And those eyes. Well. I took a deep breath and then another sip of coffee.

"How's your shoulder, Michael? Better?"

He shrugged him arm. "Yes, Nellie. It was just a graze, you know that, a lot of bleeding and no lasting damage. Stings a bit but that'll pass soon. How's your face, since we're askin'?"

"Sore," I said. "It sure looks like it, doesn't it?" Purple bruises on both sides of my cheeks and my jaw were still vivid in the little mirror I'd hung up on the tent pole even after a week. At least I'd not lost a tooth and for some reason, no black eyes. Guess it took a higher hit for that one. Still, it was no pretty picture.

"Sure does," he agreed. I was taken with the fact that he knew me well enough to know I didn't relish pity when it came to my condition. I was also glad he had a cup in his hand and he didn't reach out to touch me as he had when they'd rescued me. I wasn't sure how I'd react to that.

As Patrick had told me that day on the way to their camp in the Harquahalas, driving the mules and ordering me to sit and rest, they knew I was coming and decided to ride out and meet up with me, even if they had to go as far as Prescott. Trace Batner and his gang had been waylaying miners and suppliers along the road to the Harquahalas for weeks and everyone was scared. No one had been traveling alone, but only in well-armed groups, both coming and going.

It was good timing they'd come along when they did. I thought it might also have been God's handiwork, but I didn't mention that. Patrick was a Catholic, but I don't think he took any comfort in prayer or wanted to hear about it from anybody that did. That was fine with me, as I never saw a need to proselytize. I was only grateful for the help that had saved me, as this time I'd sure needed it.

"Hey Nellie," said Hobbs, a miner who'd been a frequent customer. "You got any more of them peaches?"

"Surely do," I said, pointing to the cans laid out on the

shelves. "Help yourself, and look around a little, too." More people were wandering in.

Michael smiled, and lifted his cup in farewell. "I can see it's time for business. I'll see you at dinner."

I nodded absently, my attention on the customers. "All right. Tell Patrick I'll be out tomorrow."

The store was always busy in the early morning hours and then in late afternoon, both times when the miners weren't out working their claims. A town had sprung up out here, if you could call tents, quickly dug privies, an assay office and now my store, a town. So far there wasn't a brothel, but I heard a wagonful of whores infrequently come and spend a day or two. Some of the miners slept rough out by their claims, but quite a few came together in the evenings to talk about their days, eat and have a drink, sometimes much more than one or two, depending on the finds of the day. Sometimes it was elation, but more often than not, it was a little something and some days, nothing at all to keep them going except for hope tinged with desperation. In the short time I'd been here, I'd seen all of it, and it wasn't any different than what I'd seen before.

The night before they left Tombstone, I'd confided my plans to Patrick.

"Mining is all well and good," I'd said. "But I know the sure money is to be had in supplying goods to those doing it. I'll strike a deal with you, Patrick Sullivan. I'll buy the supplies and haul them to the Harquahalas. You will set me up with the means to do it in Prescott, and file a claim for me up there. I trust you to pick a likely location."

We'd been sitting in the restaurant, alone late at night. The candlelight played on the harsh angles of his face, one I'd come to trust, based upon our experiences in the Cassiar.

He'd raised his whiskey glass. "And what do I get in return, dear Nellie?"

"Five percent of the profits on the store."

"Ten." He'd smiled and taken a sip of his whiskey.

Highway robbery, but I'd raised my own glass and clinked it against his. "Done."

One of the better deals I'd ever made. Of course he was worried about me driving up from Prescott because his profits were on the line as well as mine, although I knew Patrick cared about me and my welfare likely more than the money. Still, being the businesswoman I am, I was tempted to grind my teeth a little when I thought of Hobbs's boots this morning, watching ten dollars become nine dollars just like that. Then again, if Patrick and company hadn't shown up when they did, I wouldn't have had the opportunity to make a nickel out of those boots. Good old Trace would've had his fun and left me for the vultures, I was pretty sure. Making a deal with Patrick Sullivan had turned out well. When I saw my claim tomorrow, I'd know for sure.

* * *

Michael had agreed to mind the store and Patrick and I took off at first light. It was only about half a mile to the claims he'd staked, his and mine. A creek trickled through the rocks on the hillside, and it was about ten inches deep where we stood.

He pointed to the left. "That's you over there and me on this side."

One didn't look much different than the other to me, just water, rocks and trees. "So what've you been getting?"

"Some flakes, a couple of small nuggets, but nothing to make your mama smile so far," he said. "Course, as you know, that can change in a minute if the rock's of a mind."

"True." I gathered up my pack. "How far does my claim go?"

"Up to those trees on the crest, about 200 yards below the stream, and about a quarter mile down the creek. There's a real big pine tree that's a boundary. You can't miss it. Meet you back here for lunch?"

"How much digging have you done, or just working the creek?"

"Some," he said. "I haven't ventured too far up yet, but I'm thinking today's the day. You're my lucky charm."

Lord save us both. He'd likely set off a rockslide because he looked like a mythical dwarf mining for diamonds, swinging that pickaxe on his shoulder. I waved and walked away. I wanted to look at the terrain before I put a pick to anything. I didn't know if he'd reconnoitered much of my side but I suspected he had and chosen the one he'd thought more likely. I trusted Patrick but he was a miner with gold fever, just like me, and I'd suspected nothing less. That was fine. Rock was very good at hiding its secrets but I was very good at discovering them.

After twenty minutes or so, watching the stream and the rocks for something likely, I stopped. I couldn't hear the sound of Patrick's pickaxe anymore, and I liked the look of the hillside above me. It was pocked with boulders, but one had a seam that had been covered with water not long ago and I saw a lighter quartz vein running through it. I hefted my pickaxe and went to work.

I'd forgotten just how hard it was to do this. The little pick mining I'd done around Tombstone was nothing like the Cassiar, and it'd been a long time. My muscles were used to carrying heavy trays of food and slinging bags of produce, but this was much more intense. For an hour I smashed that rock with a hammer and pick, watching the chunks of rock head down to the creek, where the water flowed over them where they lay.

Finally, I stopped, leaning on the handle of the pick. I hunkered down on my heels and wiped the grit and sweat from my face. I took a drink from my canteen and looked at the crumbles that lay at my feet. The sun glinted off one and I pounced on it like a cat on a mouse. I knew before I even touched it. My hand twitched where it lay there on my palm like it was a live thing. Gold.

I stuck it my pocket and grabbed up the pickaxe. For another hour or two I hacked away at that rock face like it was a devil from hell and I was an avenging angel, aches and pains forgotten. I picked up a few more nuggets and climbed back down to the creek where the bigger pieces had landed. Many more glints caught my eye and I knew there was a lot more work to be done here. Add to that, working the creek bed itself, given that was where the water had flowed down from my rock above, was likely to prove very profitable with a sluice and even a pan, and was going to yield much more.

For right now, all I had was this day. To be truthful, I hadn't expected to find what I did. While some miners here had struck good veins, most were still looking. I'd assumed the Harquahalas, like most of the new finds in Arizona, was a surface win and then proven to be nothing in the long run. I didn't know how long this run would be, but I was here now and I was going to work it dry, or at least to bedrock. I was going to need some more help with the store, that was one thing for sure, because this claim was going to need more of mine.

I met up with Patrick for lunch, trudging back upstream. He was elated. He'd found a promising vein himself, and bringing up a couple of good-sized chunks of gold veined quartz from his pocket, showed me.

"What did I say, Nellie?" He clapped me on the shoulder and I winced but didn't say anything. "You really are my good luck charm. This is the best day I've had."

I felt somewhat ashamed, but I didn't follow suit or show him what I'd found. I knew I couldn't keep it to myself forever, but right now, I wasn't willing to share.

We devoured the ham sandwiches and boiled eggs I'd packed this morning and set off again to our respective tasks.

When we met up and got back to camp that evening, we both had pockets full of gold, but only one of us told our friends about it, swearing them to secrecy. To share this kind of news was to invite claim jumpers and desperate miners to invade your find. While I trusted our group, word had a way of spreading or being overheard and none of us could afford that. As they say, two can keep a secret if one of them's dead.

We certainly didn't want to sleep out there next to our claims, like so many did. Even so, it wasn't long before Patrick, Michael, Tim and Fabian thought that was the best plan. As the saying goes, the pickings were good. And too many people knew it. I wasn't willing yet to leave the confines of my store and tent, but in the end I did just that. My pickings were good, too, much greater than the trouble of restocking my store. As profits went, there was no question anymore.

CHAPTER 30

Horse liniment worked very well for humans too, we found. I'd stocked some for the store and while nobody bought it for horses, we miners made good use of it. The stuff didn't even smell that bad once you got used to it, which was good because bathing facilities were limited to the creek and a bar of soap. There was many an evening where not a one of us had the energy even for that, our bedrolls more enticing than a cold bath.

It would seem an odd place for love to bloom as well, but bloom it did, much to my surprise and I think Michael's as well. The touch of his hand, a look from under those heavily lashed eyes, or just a smile sent my heart to fluttering. At first I felt like a fool and did my best to ignore the entire situation, but as the weeks passed, I had to admit to myself that I was experiencing, for the first time, an attraction to a man, one I finally thought worthy or perhaps handsome enough to justify it. Or maybe it was just what people called animal attraction or something like that. I'd never thought much about it before, because before, it had never applied to me.

Sure, I'd met my share of charismatic gentlemen, but never one that seemed to take a real interest in me and my thoughts, aside from my appearance or the gold in my pockets. This was something entirely different. Michael wasn't simply charismatic and handsome, at least to me, but he was genuinely interested in my thoughts and my welfare as well, a combination that previously had never crossed my path. At least not long enough for it to take hold. If there was anything that bothered me, it was that Michael was eight years younger than me, and while I'd never been a vain woman, I knew there was no place in a mining camp to make one attractive. Limited opportunity to bathe, clothes covered in dirt, and when I ran my hand over my hair, I flinched. There was as much Arizona dirt on my scalp as there were hair roots and it was hard to tell one from another. Not that I'd ever been a peacock over my appearance, but at least I'd been clean and shiny as soap, water and a hairbrush could make me.

One evening, sharing our meal over the fire, we began to talk about ourselves and the others, one by one, feel asleep on their blankets or drifted away to find a game of dice or somebody with a jar of whiskey, leaving us alone, a rarity in the open quarters we all shared.

We found we had a lot in common, both Irish immigrants that landed in Boston, and found our way to this place we were in now. Michael had that same restlessness that had afflicted me, and that had led him to search out his brother and try the mining game.

"How are feeling about your decision now, Michael?"

He looked at me, his eyes shining in the firelight. "At the moment, very satisfied indeed, Nellie."

"Because of the gold? You're doing very well, or so I hear."

He smiled, the firelight playing on the planes of his face, and a nice face it was. "Yes, but it's not just that. I think I may have found something more valuable than that."

I answered before even thinking. "And what could that possibly be now?"

"You."

He leaned across the space between us and cupped my face in his hands, gently kissing me on the lips. I didn't know what to do. Here I was, a 43-year-old woman who'd never been kissed before in her life. The gentle pressure of his lips on mine was insistent, and I liked it. I flung my arm across his shoulders and drew him closer. That kiss lasted a long time while I learned how to respond, opening my mouth a little and returning the pressure. I didn't want it to end, and it seemed he didn't either, only moving from my mouth to my throat and then back, while one of his hands slid around my neck and the other down my body. As to that part of me, I felt like I was on fire, a tingling in my stomach and further down, a feeling that I'd never experienced before but one I surely was enjoying and wanted to keep having.

Somehow we became entangled in my blankets, Michael's body pressing against mine, kissing and touching each other as though we were the first people to have ever done so. I certainly was, and I had a feeling it wasn't a common pastime for him either. When we heard the crunch of bootsteps approaching, we pulled apart like scalded cats, sitting up and staring into the fire.

"There's no luck no be had with the dice this evening, my darlin's," Patrick announced, flopping down on his bedroll. He hardly gave us a glance and Michael and I smiled at each other. He shrugged and held his hands out, palms up and we both lay back down on our respective blankets. I don't know how that felt for him, but for me, all I wanted to do was curl up beside him. After a few minutes, we heard Patrick's snores. Michael's hand reached out and I took it in mine.

As I drifted off to sleep, my body as tired as it was, all I could think of was the coming day and the next opportunity to be close to him again. *Nellie Cashman*, I said to myself, *you are a strange woman. Perhaps it's time to change that.*

Every morning we set off to our respective claims,

managing a touch or at least a look with no one the wiser. All day while looking for the elusive metal that had set me down in this place, I thought about him and sometimes my cheeks grew warm. Luckily there was no one around to see me. It was a torment, but one I embraced. Every evening, we usually shared dinner and talked about our day with our companions, Patrick, Tim and Fabian.

We were all doing well, but I'd noticed lately the yield, at least for me, was less and less. The Harquahalas, at least the surface mining everyone was doing, didn't have deep veins of ore we could have access to. In fact, I was no geologist, but I wasn't sure those deep veins were even there, something that others had seen in California and Colorado long before. I'd seen this before myself in the Cassiar and certainly in Tombstone. I knew the time was coming when I'd be off back to Tombstone and the children. I couldn't abandon them at the Brophys forever. Winter would be settling in, and this harsher country up on the Rim wasn't going to have the mildness of the lower desert. I'd made quite a tidy fortune and I suspected it was close to time for me to return.

While I knew all that perfectly well, the attraction to Michael, our stolen kisses and caresses and confidences, wasn't something I wanted to abandon along with my claim. Now that my desires had been awakened, I wasn't sure I could exist without that feeling that surged through me whenever we were together. Michael and I had taken to having walks together at night. Everybody came and went as they pleased, and we were pretty sure our absences weren't noted any more than anyone else's were.

Usually, we didn't take more than a hundred steps away from the glow of the firelight before we ended up in each other's arms. This night, we went a little further.

"Christ, Nellie," Michael breathed into my hair. "I can't take this anymore. I love you, woman, and this is not a place where I can show you how much."

My mind reeled. He loved me? No man had ever said that to me before, at least not one over twelve, or my brother-in-law. What does one say in response to that? I took a deep breath.

"I love you, too, Michael," I said, and his lips came down on mine as he pulled me tightly against his body. Well. I guess that was the correct response, because it was true.

Before I knew it, we had sunk to the ground, only the moonlight illuminating our forms. He pulled my shirt out of my work trousers and softly cupped my breasts in his hands, and lifting my shirt higher, bent down to kiss them as well.

"So beautiful," he murmured. "Ah, my God, Nellie."

My heart was racing. This was beautiful and wonderful and I didn't want it to stop. Then Michael began to undo my trousers and pull them down, kissing my belly.

The word popped out of my mouth before I even knew it was in there.

"No."

His warm breath was replaced by the chill night air as he pulled away from me. "Are you certain, my love?"

I sat up, tucking my shirt back into my pants. I felt somehow bereft, like I was alone now on an island where no one would ever venture again.

"Yes."

"As you wish," he said. "I love you and I would never want you to be afraid."

Somehow those last words made me angry. "Afraid? I'm not afraid, Michael Sullivan. What I am, is quite certain that I don't want to commit a mortal sin, and God above knows there's no confessional booth around here."

It was very quiet for a minute or two, only the sound of an owl hooting over his next kill, and the sound of the night breeze in the pine trees around us, the gentle susurration that put me to sleep every night.

Then Michael began to laugh softly. I didn't see anything

particularly amusing in this situation. I stood up, adjusting my clothes and brushing the dirt from my hair, and turned to walk back to our campsite. He grabbed my arm and turned me around, clasping me in the circle of his arms. He gently tilted my face up with the tip of a finger.

"There's nothing for it, Nellie Cashman," he said. "Will you marry me?"

* * *

WE HAD A GRAND ROYAL SEND-OFF, or as grand and royal as they come at a mining camp in the middle of nowhere. When we told them we were leaving and going to get married in Prescott, Patrick, Fabian and Tim looked at each other and burst into laughter. Michael and I looked at each other, somewhat surprised. That wasn't quite the reaction we'd expected.

Patrick had doubled up, his hands on his knees. He raised his head, slapped his hands on his knees and looked at us. Then he started laughing again, as did those other two loons.

"We're happy for ya both, my darlin's," he gasped out. "But you must know we've been watching this entire dance since Tombstone and now here you are, the waltz finally over, or perhaps just beginnin', and we've been an eager audience waitin' for the last act."

"Well. So all this time we've been so careful and we had no need to be? Is that what you're saying, you devil?" I looked at Michael, whose cheeks were turning bright pink. Then he looked at me and started laughing, too. Was there no hope for the male half of the human race? Perhaps I needed to rethink this entire situation, for pity's sake. Ridiculous monkeys, men were.

Patrick recovered himself first, grabbing me and Michael, and hugged us to him like a grizzly bear, kissing us both on the cheek.

"Ah, never think we didn't love you both for it. It was like watching a Shakespeare play. We've been anticipating this moment for a long time now, and it's the best thing we've discovered out here, as precious as the gold." He cocked his head and cast his eyes skyward. "Hmmm. Maybe more, but then I haven't been to assay office yet."

I kicked him gently in the shins but I couldn't hide my smile. "Thanks, brother. That means so much."

A few minutes later, Patrick pulled me aside "Nellie, are you sure about this, my darlin'? Michael's my brother and I love him dearly but truthfully, I don't know the man all that well since I left home while he was a callow boy. He's a charmer, and he's smart, he's my brother and he seems a good lad. That's all I know for certain."

I was touched by his concern. "Patrick, you are so dear to me. I appreciate your caring, but I'm happy with this decision. I love him."

"Then that's all I needed to know." He squeezed my hand. We both felt better.

They insisted on cooking us a pre-wedding dinner, not allowing me or even Michael to do a thing, for which I was grateful since I'd been doing most all of the cooking for a while now. I have no idea where they found the ingredients, but we had a most wonderful meal. Steak diablo, potatoes roasted in the fire, and fresh avocados and tomatoes from my successor, Adrian Bingham, an Englishman who'd shown up with a wagon full of wonders a week ago. My irritation at the three of them vanished with that culinary thank you. We toasted with Irish whiskey from Adrian's stock. It was very tasty and I knew he'd do well in his current career. I had a worthy successor.

Now that we'd put our feelings on display, even though everyone seemed to have a pretty good idea about them anyway, I felt exposed somehow, as though reality had intruded on our private little obsession. I'd been in a fever dream of new sensations, exhilaration and anticipation for so long that I'd put all my thoughts into what was happening between me and Michael, without giving a lot of consideration to where that might lead, until now. Here I was, on the precipice of a new phase of my life, one I'd never planned on, and had, in fact, scorned. I tossed and turned all night, my thoughts swirling. I wondered if Michael was doing the same, but I knew I'd never ask him.

The next morning, not very early, we left in the empty buckboard along with the four mules, gold, and hopes and dreams that neither one of us ever thought we'd have. We knew it would take us two days to get to Prescott, and tonight, for the first time, we'd be truly alone, if you didn't count coyotes and mules. I tried not to think about that, and I was very apprehensive, perhaps not wisely so. It was just that all these feelings were new to me, and while I welcomed them, I had lived a life without them until now and I wasn't quite sure how everything was supposed to work. I clasped Michael's hand in mine as we drove away, and he smiled at me and leaned over and kissed me.

"I know you're worried, Nellie, I can tell," he said. "Don't. I love you, and everything will be fine. We are meant for each other."

CHAPTER 31

It was a crisp autumn morning with a nice breeze and I leaned back on the wagon seat while Michael held the reins. It was rather nice to have someone else doing what I'd always done myself. Since the incident with Trace and his gang, there'd been no more assaults on the road between the mining camps and Prescott, or at least none we'd heard about. News traveled fast even here, and people came and went with frequency, so we felt safe.

Without a heavy load in the wagon, the mules went along much faster than they had on the journey before, so there would likely be only two more days for me to be a single woman, instead of a wife. The word conjured up a whole host of images in my mind, from Fanny beaming at Tom Cunningham, to vague childhood images of my mother and father, to the lovely Mexican brides clad in white lace, clinging to the arms of their handsome young husbands as I'd seen in Nogales and Tombstone. Somewhat darker ones surfaced as well, but I tamped those down and went on to romantic dinners at a dining table and cozy evenings by the fireside, nestled beside Michael. We would have a good life together because we loved each other and we'd make it so.

We stopped for a quick lunch of tortillas, cheese and beans, watered the mules and were quickly back on our journey. Michael began singing an old Irish song, one that I had a vague memory of my Father singing when I was a very small child. The words I couldn't make out. It had a plaintive melody and his sure and lovely tenor was a delight to listen to.

"What is that song?"

"Galway Bay," Michael said. "I learned it in the Gaelic before I knew the English words. My mother was a stickler for a proper education and learning your native country's language is something she insisted upon. I can sing it in English if you like. It's a very sad song, really, so you might prefer the Irish version."

"You could," I said, "but I rather like the way the words sound in Gaelic. Why is it sad?"

"It's about a man and his true love who sail away from Ireland to a new life together in a new world, but as they reach the mouth of Galway Bay, their ship is struck by a storm and goes down with all aboard."

"Oh." A tear crept down my cheek and I brushed it away. What was wrong with me? "That is sad, but I like it. Do you know others, my love?"

He grinned and put his arm around me, the reins steady in his left hand. "Of course I do. Think you're marrying an unlettered brute?"

"Well, I did wonder," I laughed, nudging him with my elbow. "We've not had much of an opportunity for cultured discussion, but you likely have more to offer than I do. For instance, I don't really know many Irish songs, so I'm afraid the music department will be you."

"Happy to oblige." He launched into the Queen of All Argyll, this time in English, a song I knew, and we made our merry way down the road.

The gathering dark had us near a creek and if I wasn't mistaken, the same large standing stones that I'd camped at on my way to the Harquahalas. It seemed a lifetime ago, but was really only months. We pulled off the road, unharnessed the mules, built a fire, and made dinner. I'd brought half a dozen pickled eggs, fried chicken packed next to some chunks of ice, a precious resource I'd gleaned from Adrian, a loaf of bread and honey. I had no intention of eating tortillas and beans, much as I liked them, the entire trip.

Michael was delighted. "Nellie, this is a delicious surprise. You are amazing."

"Thank you," I said. "Not all that amazing, just a little planning."

He polished off another chicken leg and popped an egg into his mouth. "You see? There are many reasons I fell in love with you, but your skill at organization is certainly one of them."

I swallowed my bite of chicken. Organizational skill was certainly one of my skills all right, but I'd never thought it was a particularly lovable one. I wiped my hands on the napkins I'd brought. So very organized, I was.

"You've got a unique slant for business, Nellie, not only organized but forward-thinking, always realizing the next big opportunity. Now that we've got the money from the gold we mined, I can start the shipping business I've always wanted. Boston's still the best port in America, and my friend has already leased the warehouse on the docks we looked at a year ago before I left."

The firelight lit the planes on his handsome face, and his eyes sparkled as he glanced at me while enjoying his dinner and went on detailing his plans for us. He finally reached out and grabbed my hand, not bothering to wipe it on the very organized napkin I'd provided. It was a bit greasy in mine.

"This is going to be wonderful. Mother is going to adore you, and you'll love the house. It overlooks the harbor. If there's anything Mother loves, it's having someone to help share the burden of keeping up that house, even with the staff.

Having a daughter-in-law like you will be a dream come true, one so mature and practical. You'll learn to take charge of the house, under her tutelage, and we'll have a most gracious life, especially with your knowledge of food and cooking."

I hadn't said a word for the last twenty minutes as I learned who my intended husband really was. I was stunned into speechlessness, a rarity for me. I pulled my hand away and took another bite of chicken. I nearly choked on it but I needed to do something to calm my mind before I threw the whole carcass at him. *Mother Mary, help me now like you've never helped me before,* I thought. This situation was more dangerous than any icy abyss I'd faced in the Cassiar. I had come very near to making the biggest mistake of my life. I managed a smile, still chewing my chicken.

"So, Boston? What a surprise all this is, Michael," I said. "Is Patrick aware of this plan, is he coming as well?"

He laughed. "Patrick? He detests Boston. I haven't talked to him about this, Nellie. I wasn't sure he understand. Patrick has always been a rough sort, a disappointment to Mother."

That didn't surprise me at all. "What about my children? Will they be going with us?"

He sat up, popped another pickled egg into his mouth and looked at me over the fire. "Well, no, I didn't think so. Then again, they aren't really your children, are they, Nellie? They're all old enough for boarding school here or with the Brophys, like they are now. We'll arrange for them if they want to come East when they're more educated. It's a big house, I'm sure Mother will be accommodating for a time until they find their places, if that's what you want. I know you care for them, as I will do as well."

I felt like I'd swallowed a lead ball and I could hardly look at him. "Of course. That makes sense. I mean, we have our lives to live, after all."

"You see? I knew you would understand, because you're practical and so clever," he said. "We are just starting on the road to a new life. I love you, my wife-to-be in just one more day."

"Yes," I said, because that needed some sort of response and the one I wanted to deliver wasn't likely to have me surviving the night, especially with the heavy sack of gold, ten times what his was, that I'd put in that wagon, a fact I was sure he hadn't overlooked. Michael was a charming man, but apparently a very calculating and conniving one, something I'd overlooked myself, and I had a feeling Patrick didn't know the extent of his younger brother's ambitions and plans any more than I had. I felt like a complete and utter fool, and that was not a humiliation I'd not experienced often. My emotions had led me down a path to disaster and I'd ignored every warning sign, not that there'd been many. Michael was a canny man.

We cleaned up our dinner debris and spread our bedrolls for the night, separate but close together. As we lay down, he reached his hand out to me. I took it, not wanting to give my feelings away.

"Tomorrow night, after we're married, we'll have a bed in the finest hotel in Prescott and at last, I'll be able to show you how much I care about you, Nellie. I know how much the marriage vows mean to you and I respect that."

At least there was that, my good Catholic beloved. My stomach churned but I squeezed his hand. "Thank you, Michael. I look forward to tomorrow more than you can possibly know."

* * *

As I'd suspected, without the heavy load they'd been burdened with on the first journey, the mules trotted into Prescott in the mid-afternoon, the sun still slanting its light on the town. It hadn't been a long day, but certainly one that provided me with the time to assess everything I'd learned about my fiancé.

We pulled up at the livery stable I'd rented the wagon and mules from, and the friendly proprietor was happy to see me. I settled the bill, and we took our baggage from the wagon bed. I hefted my heavy bags myself. I didn't have much except for gold but there was a good amount of it. Michael's load was noticeably lighter, just one bag and a rifle. I took a deep breath and insisted on carrying my own bags, trying hard not to show just how heavy they were. He frowned but smiled anyway.

"So, where should we go first? The courthouse, or the hotel?" He glanced at me.

We'd walked a block or so, and were in front of the Palace Hotel. It looked nice. I didn't respond to him and walked into the hotel without saying a word, stopping at the desk.

"Good afternoon. I need a room, please."

The desk clerk smiled. "Of course, madam. Is the second floor all right with you? We have a lovely room that faces the street with the bath next door."

"Perfect," I said, returning his smile. "Especially the bath nearby."

Michael came in to stand behind me, looking confused.

"Nellie, perhaps we should discuss this."

I ignored him and filled out the registration book. The clerk handed me the key.

"Excellent, Miss Cashman. Let me know when you wish to have the bath ready for you."

"Thank you. May I leave these bags with you for a moment? I have some business to attend to. I won't be long, I assure you."

"Of course, madam," the young man said, coming around and picking up my bags, wincing a bit when he found out how heavy they were. "They'll be safe with me."

"I'm sure they will," I said and turned to Michael, who was nearly breathing down my neck.

"We should go outside," I said, "the lobby is quite small here, and I am quite sure you don't want us to be overheard."

He trailed me outside to the boardwalk, his footsteps resounding behind me. There was an occasional passerby but I didn't care. I didn't want the hotel desk clerk to overhear our conversation but some random person I didn't care about. At this point, Michael was irritated, but I could see it was rapidly advancing to quite agitated, and I wasn't sure where it would go from there. I could see the sheriff's office wasn't far away and the courthouse was right across the street so I wasn't particularly concerned about my own safety. The desk clerk also seemed fairly interested, and the door was open.

"What is going on here, Nellie? You've been acting oddly for the last few minutes, not to mention hours, and I don't understand. You owe me an explanation."

He stood not a foot away from me, his face not so handsome anymore, since it was red and belligerent, which only enforced my resolve.

"You are a liar and a scoundrel, in my estimation, Michael Sullivan," I said. "I wouldn't marry you if you were the last man on earth. Now I see that the only value I have for you is my gold and what you have determined are my skills at advancing your business, whatever that might be. You, your plans and your sainted mother, can reside in the hell of your own making, as far as I'm concerned. Leave me and never contact me again."

He took a step back, clearly aghast at just how wrong his plans had gone. He raised a hand but before he could bring it down, either against me or wherever else it may have gone, I seized it in my own.

"Never threaten me or come near me again," I said. "Neither God, nor I, nor your own brother will ever forgive you."

He dropped his arm, his face paling. "How could you do this to me?"

"Easily," I said. "You lied, you schemed, and you betrayed

my trust. You have no worth. Think about that as you make your way in this world. You may go to Boston or to hell as far as I'm concerned. It certainly won't be anywhere near me. By the way? I hate Boston, and I'd likely detest your sainted mother too."

I turned on my heel and walked back into the Palace Hotel. I would have time for tears, which were threateningly close, once I got into my room, number 203. I glanced back outside the front door but he'd already left. I picked up my bags from the friendly clerk and ascended the stairs as though I didn't have a care in the world except a yearning for a soft bed and a hot bath. I had many more cares but they would have to wait, at least for a few minutes more.

The memories would last much longer. They always did.

CHAPTER 32

The sunlight streaming through the trees outside the window made patterns on the ceiling in the morning breeze. I lay there on the most comfortable bed I'd slept in for some time and watched them dancing above my head. I felt more content than I'd thought I would've, given the events of the last few weeks. Sure, I'd bathed, perhaps washing away my sins along with the dirt, the first real bath I'd had in a long time, the first since Tombstone, if you didn't count creeks and a bar of soap. Then I'd prayed, and what had come back to me was a sense of peace, as though I was finally in the right place.

I stretched my arms over my head and sat up, somewhat reluctant to leave that cozy nest. After all, there was no urgency to whatever actions I might take this day. Still, I was used to rising early, even though I could see from the angle of the sunlight that it wasn't all that early. I'd clearly needed the rest, and it rejuvenated my body as well as my mind, which was still trying to push down the betrayal I'd nearly succumbed to.

The tears had come, and I'd welcomed them. Loving someone, even if wasn't the person you should love, and losing them, even if you were the one to push them away, was an arduous business. The release those tears had brought me was cathartic.

Naked, I padded over to the mirror that hung on the wall beside the door. My freshly washed hair hung down to the small of my back, still as glossy brown as I remembered, free of the dust of mining and the trail. My face was sun-browned but clear, and my eyes, even though a trifle swollen, stared back at me. My body seemed the same as it always had, slim and strong, my breasts upright and my stomach flat. I'd never paid much attention before now, but this time I did and I liked what I saw. I stood there and braided my hair, coiling it into the coronet I'd worn for years and when I finished, pinning the last strands in place, I smiled and the mirror smiled back.

Nellie Cashman, you're a woman that can do anything you set your mind to, the mirror image said. *You know this like you know your own soul. Never doubt yourself again.*

"I never will," I said. And that was the end of my mourning for Michael Sullivan and the beginning of finally acknowledging exactly who I was, and embarking on the rest of my life.

I dressed in my dirty trousers, shirt and boots, as that's all I had, and went down to the lobby and the Palace's restaurant for breakfast. After devouring the delicious ham, eggs and biscuits with gravy, I set off to the nearest women's clothing emporium. While I rather missed the comfort and ease of movement of my trousers, I couldn't deny that dressing as a woman again had its pleasures. Surprisingly enough, they were pretty easy to move around in as well, if I didn't plan on jumping on a horse or squatting down in a stream to dig gold. I purchased three skirts, shirtwaists and pantaloons, along with a fancier pair of soft kid boots that didn't look as though I'd climbed a mountain in them.

I went back to the hotel to drop off my purchases and change my clothes, leaving the old trousers and shirts for the laundry, which they handily provided for their guests. When I strolled out an hour later, the desk clerk smiled. I was wearing some of my new purchases, a white pleated shirtwaist with long lace-trimmed sleeves and a skirt of dark blue wool, brushing softly against my new boots.

"Miss Cashman, you look lovely," he said, blushing.

"Why, thank you Jonathon," I said, finally noticing his name tag. "Very nice of you to say."

"Of course."

"Tell me about Prescott, Jonathon," I said. "I'd like to get to know the capital a bit."

He handed me a map that he pulled from a drawer. It was hand-drawn, but depicted the town, at least the business area, quite well. "This might help. Course, you know we won't be the capital much longer, so they're saying. Moving it to Phoenix this time, I hear. Any day now."

"Really? That's interesting. Doesn't seem quite right to me, even though I'm from Tombstone."

"I agree, as do most of the people in town," Jonathon said. "I don't meet a lot of people from Tombstone anymore. How are things down there?"

"Pretty much the same as ever, but it's shrinking, I'd say."

"Why's that?"

"The silver's hard to get to these days," I said. "Just like so many other places. The Harquahalas will be next, in my opinion, just like many of the finds around here. My friends and I have been up there for a time but I'm leaving that behind."

He nodded, as though he knew what I was talking about, but of course, he didn't. I picked up the map. "Thank you. I'll likely be back for dinner."

"There's roast beef and all the trimmings on Wednesdays."

Was it Wednesday? I'd completely lost track of time. I knew it was October, but that's really all I knew. It was way past time for me to rejoin civilization.

I spent the day strolling around the capital. The weather was cool and quite comfortable, unlike Tombstone this time of year. But the wheel of the year was turning, and I hadn't been there to experience it.

The courthouse was formidable, along with its square, replete with grass, trees and benches. The other side of the street was filled with saloons and some restaurants, aptly named Whiskey Row. Other businesses fronted the other sides of the square, from emporiums, one of which I'd shopped at this morning, to apothecaries and everything in between. In the blocks surrounding the downtown core, boardinghouses and private residences, some quite resplendent, were replete with green lawns, something we didn't have in Tombstone. As I strolled by, I watched children playing outside, with hoops and balls, even one house with a croquet game set up, which I watched for a time, clapping when the youngest girl defeated her opponents and raised her mallet in triumph.

I thought about my own nieces and nephews and it struck me how much I missed them. It was time I returned to Tombstone and gathered them up. I had allowed the allure of gold to lead me away from that which was most important in my life right now, along with the false enchantment of a man who had been on my mind even before I left Cochise County. More fool I.

The next morning I went to the assay office, dragging my packs inside. Quite a sophisticated place after what I'd seen in other towns. They not only assayed, they melted down and seemed quite enthusiastic with my hard-won stash. They said it could take some time, and I should come back tomorrow. I couldn't help but be suspicious after my last encounter with someone who was interested in my money, but I left, quite pleased.

The next day, I walked away with a bank draft for over $24,000 dollars, which I promptly deposited in the bank in Prescott, which looked like a stable establishment. At least my efforts hadn't been in vain, as preoccupied as my emotions had been. I had a dim premonition of returning to this town, and of course, I could transfer funds at any time. Right now, all I wanted was to go home and remember who I really was again.

* * *

TOMBSTONE LOOKED EXACTLY the same as it had when I left. It shouldn't have surprised me, but in a strange way I was thinking that I had left it as one person, and returned after a fairly short time, an entirely different one, and that somehow Tombstone would've changed too, although of course it hadn't.

Francesca gave me a prolonged hug which I was delighted to receive, clasping me to her ample bosom. We were in the kitchen, and the aroma of salsa verde surrounded us.

"I am so glad to see you, Nellie," she said. "We all missed you and your happy face. There's a few people that need your help as well, coming around every night. They will be glad, too, *mija.*" She rolled her eyes. I couldn't help but chuckle. Francesca had little patience with my makeshift medical practice and was always warning me some of my patients were not the best caliber of people. She wasn't wrong, but that was exactly why I helped them because sometimes they were too embarrassed or too hopeless to go anywhere else.

I helped her with dinner and ran the dining room that night, greeting the customers and many old friends. It was good to be back. Before we closed, I told Francesca that I would be gone for another day or two, as I had to go to Bisbee and retrieve the children. I couldn't expect the Brophy household to keep them forever. He was a very busy man.

She smiled. "It will be good to see those rascals again, too. *Vaya con Dios*, my friend."

CHAPTER 33

1890

I rented a buckboard and horses at the livery and set out the next morning. It wasn't as chilly as the weather up on the Rim, but there was a crispness to the air that signaled autumn was coming, always later here than anywhere else, but that was how things worked in the desert. I reached Bisbee by early afternoon with no incident and pulled up at the Brophy residence. I'd been here a few times.

I brushed the dust from my hat and clothes before I rang the bell. I wondered for a brief second if I looked any different from the woman they'd known before I left, but that was just silly. Of course, I didn't and I'd only been gone four months, hardly enough time to age or transform to anything other than who I was.

Sally Bronwyn opened the door, and let out a delighted yelp when she saw me.

"Miss Cashman, you're here!" She opened the door wide. I stepped in, and couldn't resist giving her a quick hug. Sally was a treasure, a delightful girl and so good with the children.

"Hello, my dear. I hope you haven't been too burdened in my absence."

"No, no, not at all," she assured me, shutting the door and

drawing me into the front parlor. "In fact, now that they're in school, I've been helping with the household. Mr. Brophy is such a nice person, I'm happy to do anything for him."

Well. School, was it? I felt like a fool. Of course, it was school, it was October, after all. I felt as though I'd been on another planet, and in a way, I guess I had. Sally ran out to tell Mr. Brophy I was here, and I settled down comfortably on a velvet sofa. It was a pleasant room, sofas and chairs arranged as though a few guests could be expected at any moment, and everyone would have a welcome place. Marble-topped tables were set here and there, with a large one between the two sofas in front of the fireplace. Afternoon sunlight diffused with silk sheers filtered into the room, and a lovely Aubusson carpet covered the polished wood floor. I remembered this room because it always seemed so welcoming.

Bill Brophy strode into the room, his hands outstretched, and a broad smile on his face.

"Nellie," he said, taking my hands in his. "So good to see you, my dear."

"No more than I am to see you," I said. "And so grateful for all the care you have taken with the children. I can only hope they haven't been too much trouble."

He laughed. "Trouble? Absolutely not. They are delightful, so well-mannered, and so engaging. They've truly been the light of the household. Since I'm to be married soon, I wanted to know what having children in my life really meant, and it is I who am grateful to you for the opportunity to discover that."

I was relieved. Recently very close friends to duplicity, I could still discern the truth in his words. He meant it all.

"Married? How wonderful for you. Who's the lucky girl?"

I could've sworn he blushed, just a little. "Her name's Ellen Goodbody, and she's truly an angel. She'll be here fairly soon, along with her sisters, Teresa and Mary. It's a good thing I've got a large house, isn't it?" He laughed. "To marry Ellen,

I'd have agreed to host half of Waukegan County, Illinois, but I didn't have to. Truthfully, between you and I," he leaned in conspiratorially, "I'm building an even bigger one just outside the town. Children need a place to run and play."

We chatted for a while over the tea and scones the maid brought in, until there was a minor commotion outside in the entry hall.

Brophy put down his cup. "It seems the children are home." He smiled and went to the doorway.

"Children, there's someone here I think you want to see."

In they came, and I found myself inundated by hugs and kisses, which I happily returned.

"Aunt Nell, we missed you so much," TJ said, dragging a paper out of his bookbag. "Look, I got an A in science."

Not to be outdone, Michael laid his head on my shoulder. "I didn't, but I do like Shakespeare." He gave me a beatific smile, to which I could only smile back.

His sisters soon followed, Mamie running her hands over my braids as though they were a royal coronet. "I missed you so, Aunt Nell. God told me you'd return soon, so I knew you were coming." Her bright blue eyes bored into mine and I didn't doubt her for a second. "I want to be a sister of St. Anne's, I can feel it." Well, that may be a little soon for a decision that big, but there was time to discuss it further.

William and Fanny, now nine and seven, climbed into my lap and clung there like limpets and regaled me with tales of their schoolroom.

They were growing, that much was certain. Children change rapidly, and when they're right in front of your eyes, you don't notice it as much. Go away for a few months and it's like a sea change. They become beings you no longer recognize, and that was true. They'd been changing right before my eyes for a long time, but put them in a new environment, and it was quite astounding how much they'd absorbed.

"So, how do you like your school? Tell me about it," I said, and five voices all began to regale me at once. I held up my hand. "Stop. One at a time, Willie, you go first."

For the next half an hour, I heard more about school and what they were learning than I had in years. Things were much livelier in Bisbee, rather than Tombstone's two rooms, that was a certainty.

Brophy returned, having discreetly left us to our reunion. He poured himself a drink from the bar and sat back down, eyeing us.

"They've been going to St. Anne's parish school here in Bisbee, Nellie. I think they like it."

A chorus of voices rose in assent, and he put out a hand, which they observed, even Fanny, quickly growing silent.

"I'm very happy about that," I said. I was about to say more, but I had a feeling that was a topic best discussed between adults, not children, even as invested as this crew clearly was.

He nodded. "I think it would be wonderful if you spent the night here, Nellie, and we can discuss this further."

I could see there was much more on his mind than a quick thank you for taking care of the children, I'll be taking them back to Tombstone now and goodbye. I had an obligation to this man and I owed him that much, and more.

"Thank you," I said. "That would be very kind."

I turned to the children. "I don't think all that much has changed, since you're in school. Take yourselves off to do your homework and tidy up before dinner, and I'll see you shortly."

The stableboy took care of my horse, and the maid took care of me, showing me to a guestroom. I hadn't planned on spending the night, likely a short-sighted idea, but here I was. I sat down on the bed. I was somewhat apprehensive about Brophy's plans, because he clearly had some. The only plans I had were to get back to Tombstone, run the restaurant, and put the children back in the Tombstone school. Assuredly, not the best educational institution, but it was significantly better than many other options out there.

I washed up and lay down on the bed. It had been a long couple of weeks and I realized I hadn't taken a breath before leaping from one thing into another. This trip was no exception. I don't remember my eyes closing but the gentle knock on the door roused me, as I must've been asleep for over an hour. I opened my eyes, splashed cold water on my face and made my way downstairs to the dining room.

Dinner was truly a wonder. Bill Brophy knew what my children wanted. It wasn't fancy, just cooking similar to my American menu. Roast beef, mashed potatoes with rich gravy, roasted carrots with honey, which I watched William devour like candy, honey-buttered biscuits and apple pie for dessert. I had to say it was all as good as mine. Well, nearly.

The children abed, we settled down in the parlor, both of us with a glass of whiskey, for the talk I knew was coming and the talk I wasn't sure I was going to like.

"Nellie. You are an extraordinary woman, the like of which I've never met before. I've known you for years and watched as you single-handedly established yourself in Tombstone, the successful businesses you've owned, and the good works you've done. I know that hospital and the church were mainly established from your generosity."

I opened my mouth to protest, but he put up a hand. "Please. Let me finish."

"I also know that you've taken on the responsibility of your sister's children and have done an admirable job, sacrificing your own needs and desires to give them the best life you can."

I couldn't help but interrupt. "Of course I have. I love them, and they have no one else. I would do it again ten times over."

He sipped his whiskey. "I know. They know. However, I want to offer you my help, not just temporarily, but for some time. They deserve a better education than they can get in Tombstone. I don't fault you at all, but here in Bisbee there are better opportunities for them, and you know that just as I do. I've watched them blossom here and I think you can see it as well."

You have a restless soul, my friend, one that needs a vision. That jaunt to the Harquahalas is clearly evidence of that. It's always about what's over the next horizon, the next find, the next place that can offer an opportunity of a lifetime. I can see that in you, and I believe, Nellie Cashman, that you can see it in yourself as well. In no way am I criticizing this, because it's trait I have as well, one that has led me here. To see that in a woman is unusual, and it's even more unusual that she's already accomplished so much."

I took a large sip of my own whiskey. How could this man see me so well? I was not very happy that he, or anyone, could. I wasn't sure what to say in response, but Brophy was a garrulous sort, and he didn't let my silence hinder him.

"I'd like to have the Cunningham children stay here and attend school, at least if that's something they all wish to do. We both know Bisbee offers educational opportunities that Tombstone has never had, and the town is dwindling with what little business and culture remain. The children are thriving, and I can already see future possibilities with TJ and Michael with my own interests. I find them all quite charming, and I've spoken to my fiancé Ellen. She is enthusiastic about the idea as well. I know this is a big decision for you, Nellie, but remember you're only a short drive away and can rescind this at any time. As for me, I love a large and lively household around me. It's been a dream for me since I came to this country from Ireland, just like you. It will in no way be a burden, but a joy."

Now I truly was speechless. This was a lot to think about. What exactly did I want to do? Go gold mining, discover the next big strike, and travel wherever the mood or news struck me. In a way, that had been my whole life before the children, and even sometimes when they were with me, guilty as it made me feel for leaving them, if only for a time. He wasn't wrong, there was some appeal to that and I couldn't in all conscience, deny it. If Brophy was sincere, the children would have opportunities here I couldn't offer them. It would be selfish of me to deny them that, even if it came with the onus of my own wanderlust.

All that may have been true, but there was also this: I loved them all dearly and it would be a wrenching decision and I already felt a large empty spot in my heart just thinking about not having them be a part of my everyday life anymore. Of course, I'd see them often, and at school holidays and at least part of the summer but that wasn't the same.

I smiled somewhat wanly over the rim of my crystal glass. "You know me better than I thought I knew myself, Bill Brophy. I see the sense of what you're saying and it's truly an opportunity I can't turn down, for their sake. So, I accept your generous proposal, and of course, I will be providing for their clothes, school fees, and I hope their upkeep, and I am sure you will keep me apprised of those expenses. However, I tell you this, and you more than most, know it's true. My gaze will be upon you, as will that of the heavens. Care for them as I would or the wrath of God will be upon you."

He didn't smile back, but he lifted his glass to mine. "Be assured I will, Nellie Cashman. This I promise you, by the grace of that same God."

CHAPTER 34

I shoved the pan of chiles into the adobe oven, taking off my padded mitts. Francesca's nephew had built this wonder of an oven behind the restaurant, and a wonder it was. We roasted chiles, corn, bread and whatever else needed roasting, including whole chickens, in that delightful creation. Our customers loved the food we made from it, and so did I.

I missed the children every day, but I went to Bisbee often, and soon they'd be here for the summer, and I looked forward to that. Christmas had been wonderful, just like previous ones, as though they'd never been to Bisbee or anywhere else. Sometimes I laughed at that. These poor children had never seen a real city, like San Francisco or Boston, and that wasn't something I could give them, unfortunately, nor could Bill Brophy, wealthy as he was. I told them stories of those places, and others, to whet their interest but actually going there or anywhere else was something they'd have to discover for themselves, if they were so inclined and adventurous enough. I very much hoped they would do that, and I was quite sure Fanny and Tom would want that too. We Irish had come across the ocean, and then a continent further on. I hoped that spirit would awaken in these children.

We'd attended mass and visited Fanny's grave on Boot Hill, putting flowers on her grave. It had been a solemn respite in our merry days so I had arranged a Christmas reception when we'd returned, and soon all melancholy dissipated, the house and restaurant filled with friends and other children, happily toasting the season, the rooms filled with delicious aromas from roast turkeys to fruitcakes, and the warmth of love and friendship permeated the atmosphere just as thoroughly as the wonderful food.

We had a lovely summer. The children helped in the restaurant, as always, and seemed to enjoy it. Francesca and I agreed we should pay them now, as they were certainly contributors, an idea that surprised them but was delightedly accepted. We spent many hours riding, having picnics and exploring the countryside, a new thing for the younger ones, who were fast becoming people, not simply children.

The week before they left for Bisbee, we sat outside around the firepit. TJ would graduate this year, and Michael, always a go-getter, would be with him, despite the age difference. Mamie hadn't changed in her devotion to the church, but she was a happy girl who knew her own mind and I couldn't fault that. Willie and Fanny were much younger and easier, but they loved their schooling and for them, all was right with the world.

"Aunt Nell," Michael said, "Mr. Brophy says TJ and I could go to work for him when we graduate, in his mercantile venture. I'd like to do that, and I think TJ would, too."

He glanced over at his brother, who nodded vigorously. "Yes, Aunt Nell. I want to be a businessman, like you, and Mr. Brophy."

I laughed. "I am more of an explorer and opportunistic entrepreneur, boys. Mr. Brophy has taken that to an entirely higher level. He can teach you a lot, and you can see how the business and financial world works just by being in his orbit, along with his acquaintances, Mr. Douglas and Mr. Gage among them. I think working for him is a grand idea."

I had always been concerned about all their futures, but as I watched their faces, their sharp features and bright young eyes, and listened to them talk, I knew that these boys were going to be fine, making their way, as were their younger siblings. I had no cause for worry, or for guilt in asking for help. I smiled to myself. I was not the only one who saw this.

Their very natures had been formed in a strong foundation of family, love, tradition and ethics, the forces that shaped children into adults who were eminently capable of forging their own futures on those values.

* * *

I BECAME RESTLESS, as I'd known I would. Tombstone was not as it had been, an old story, but one that got worse every year. The businesses were doing fine, but I was splitting the income with Francesca, and happy to do so, but I also had five children to provide for and a future to think about it.

After my previous ventures, I was a little gunshy, but that wasn't something that would ever define me for long, and first I headed north to Jerome. Mining was thriving there, up in the Verde Valley north of Phoenix. True, it was copper, but I could smell a boomtown a hundred miles away. I opened a small hotel and restaurant and it did very well. It was up on one of the higher streets in this town that was built for mountain goats, across from the sheriff's office. I wasn't exactly a novice at this game, and it didn't take long for the reputation of my cooking and clean lice-free rooms to spread.

They called Jerome the "wickedest town in Arizona" and it didn't take long to find out why. On Easter Sunday, when two gunslingers shot themselves to death, landing face down in my baked hams, blood despoiling my maple sauce, I decided to close down, sheriff's office across the street or not. One bullet had singed the braids atop my head, landing in the wall behind me as I was carving. *Dear Lord, can you not dispense some calm to these poor souls?* I thought.

Well. I knew he was a busy entity, but I had things to do, and this was clearly a sign they weren't destined to be in Jerome.

I sold out and moved on to Prescott, because it wasn't that far, and I'd liked the town before. I put any bad memories into that dark box that existed somewhere in the storage room of my mind, and opened the Elite Restaurant, advertising the "best food you've ever had". Prescott wasn't quite as bustling as it'd been a few years before, since the capital had been moved to Phoenix, but it was still thriving. The restaurant was doing very well, but the big surprise was Michael, walking in the door one afternoon.

I ran to him and enveloped him in a hug before he could scarcely take a breath. I pulled back.

"Look at you, so dapper," I said. "Haven't seen you since Christmas and here you are, quite the gentleman." He was, too, outfitted in a black suit and a Homberg hat, his white shirt crisp and dazzling.

He laughed and kissed my cheek. "I've taken a job in the Yavapai District Attorney's office, Aunt Nell. Mr. Gage thought it would be a good idea to learn how the law works, so here I am. My first day is tomorrow but my first thought was seeing you."

"Darling boy, I am so happy," I said. "Sit down, let me get you something to eat."

He laughed. "That is always the first thing you say, Aunt Nell."

I snorted. "Well, it's certainly the thing I know best, now isn't it?"

He took my hand. "I would say it's one of the many things you do best, but taking care of all of us comes first, in my estimation."

I couldn't help but blush with pleasure at his words. We spent the day and evening, interspersed with my restaurant duties, catching up on everyone's lives and progress before he left, at my insistence, to get some sleep for his big day tomorrow.

Michael stayed in Prescott for six months or so, and when he left, to go to work at Phelps Dodge in Bisbee for Mr. Brophy, I left Prescott myself shortly thereafter. We'd spent a lot of time together, and we both agreed that returning further south was where we both belonged. I missed Tombstone and Bisbee, too.

Returning to Tombstone was a boon, and it felt like coming home. Mamie, William, and Fanny came and stayed for the summer. Michael was busy at his new job, and TJ was trying one idea after another, including a soda pop bottling company which sounded promising, although TJ's ideas always sounded promising on the outset.

Bill Brophy's wife, the former Ellen Goodbody, was a lovely and delightful woman, who had taken charge of the household, along with her sister, Tessie, and they loved the children as I did, having no qualms about this ready-made family during the school year.

Francesca, on the other hand, was struggling, as were the restaurant and hotel. There just weren't enough customers anymore, no matter how good the food and accommodations were. Splitting the profits was hurting her, and I finally just signed off and gave the business to her. This was difficult for me, and I wasn't sure what to do next. My funds were dwindling the day I took the stagecoach to Globe, another mining town that had not only thrived, but had transformed into a community, much like Prescott. Like others before me, I took advantage of that prosperity and opened the Buffalo Hotel and Restaurant on Main Street, touting "A Table of Excellent Quality".

Business was good. I'd certainly prayed enough if God was

of a fair mind, so I was happy. The hotel had ten rooms, and the restaurant was quite fancy, in my humble estimation. I hired another cook and two servers so I could work the hotel desk as well. They're were long days and for the first time, I came to resent standing on feet, because they hurt, as did my knees. That was the price one pays for serving the public, I knew. There were nights I actually prayed to Mary and the saints to show me a vein of gold all my own. At least swinging a pickaxe or crouching beside a stream fed a dream of income that didn't have me on my feet, smiling when I didn't want to, or catering to someone's ego over the quality of their bedsheets or the texture of their scrambled eggs.

Was I becoming bitter in my advancing age? Or jaded? I worried I was.

Then Patrick Sullivan walked back into my life late one evening as I stood behind the hotel desk.

"As I live and breathe, it's the Nellie I've been searchin' for these long days," he said, and stood there, holding out his arms. "Come give me a hug, darlin' girl."

I flew out behind the desk and did just that, breathing in the scent of him, the road dust, tobacco and the faint scent of minerals. Bless him, he looked older, just as I knew I did as well. The years did that to all of us.

"Oh, Nell. We have much to talk about, girl," he said.

And we did, long into that night. I gave him the key to Room 201, up the stairs, and we took a bottle of whiskey with us, two Irish renegades.

"My brother's a rum one," Patrick said. "I should've known he was leadin' you down the primrose path, Nellie, but you seemed so in love with the bastard, I couldn't bring myself to say a word. He's not worth your spit, or mine, even though he's blood to me. You are someone so special, I ask your forgiveness before I say another word."

For the first time since that night in Prescott, I cried and Patrick held me as I did. Those tears were for me, and for somebody that understood that I deserved to have them, as he very well did. When they dried, I felt better than I had in a long time.

We settled in, propping our feet up on the bed and sharing more whiskey.

"I've been looking for you, because there's something you need to know. There's a gold strike, Nellie. It's up there, in the Klondike. It's like nothin' you've ever seen before, even the Cassiar, or God bless their hearts, the California one. This is bigger than all of them. Two ships came into San Francisco two weeks ago carrying miners loaded with gold and the word's out. Now that I've found you, I'm leavin' in the next day or two and headin' up there, girl."

My brain reeled. A gold strike, bigger than the Cassiar? I'd made a fortune up there years back. The thought of a better one than that was astounding.

"Are you certain?"

Patrick grinned and held up his glass, which I clinked to mine. "Would I not be here if I wasn't certain? I owe you, Nellie Cashman. You need to be there. It's who you are."

Yes, it was, I thought as the whiskey slid down my throat. That's exactly who I was and I'd denied it for too long. Even the word was magical to me.

The Klondike.

CHAPTER 35

1897

I stepped off the train in San Francisco, carrying only one bag. I'd left everything else in Tombstone under Francesca's care. If I was going north, there was certainly no point in packing excess accoutrements or dresses. Anything else I needed I'd get here, or further up points north. I'd need a lot of equipment, that was certain, and it didn't involve skirts or fashionable boots.

I looked forward to seeing my mother, who was living in dear cousin Michael's house on Nob Hill. He'd always been supportive and had helped us all a lot in the early years when we'd arrived. He'd done very well for himself and when my mother had begun to decline a few years ago, had taken her into his home, still taking care of us Cashmans, as he'd always done. I was very grateful to him and always replied quickly to his letters.

I wore a blue serge traveling dress, with a cape, but the cuffs and collar were a bit grimy after the journey. My hat was a dark blue as well, with a ruff of feathers adorning the brim. It was likely not up to San Francisco's fashion standards but was perhaps only three years out of date for Tombstone's. I'd felt like a fish out of water since I'd left the train, and it wasn't just my clothes. My ears were ringing from the cacophony of trolley alerts, car horns, whistles, and the constant din of so many people's voices. I longed for the stillness of the desert, with only the wind and the occasional cry of a hunting hawk to disturb the placidness and calm. I could say I'd become a desert rat, but I knew better than anyone that the northern reaches provided that same solitude. It wasn't necessarily the climate I craved, it was the solace of empty places, be they sand or snow.

"Yes?" the housemaid wore a starched cap and apron, no smile on her face.

"I'm Nellie Cashman," I said, "and I've come to see my mother."

Now she allowed herself a brief smile. "Please come in, Miss Cashman."

In I went, ushered into an empty parlor of stiff furniture, presumably to await the master of the house.

"Nellie, so glad to see you." Michael bustled in, taking my hand in his. I wouldn't have recognized the man, so changed he was. Portly now, his side whiskers as grey as his hair, but the smile was genuine.

"She's having good days and bad," he said, still holding my hand as he gestured to a sofa, a seat I gratefully took. "This is a good one, so let's go up and say hello, what do you say?"

He chattered away as we ascended the staircase. "Your letter said you were on the way north. Of course, you know you're always welcome to stay here until you get your affairs in order, Nellie." At the top of the landing he halted. "I hope you're not planning on traveling to the Yukon and that gold strike everyone's talking about. We hear the news and people are dying left and right, falling off mountains and drowning in rivers. That's no place for a civilized woman such as yourself."

I didn't have an opportunity to answer before he resumed

talking, leading me down the long hallway, the lights in the wall sconces seeming to lead our way.

"She talks about you all the time, you know," he said, "she calls you her 'adventurous girl' and is very proud of you. As well as concerned, you should know."

I didn't respond, and he didn't seem to care. We stopped at a door and he knocked twice before opening it. My mother lay as though in state, in a large four-poster bed, the curtains tied back, a fire burning merrily in the fireplace although the temperature here had not yet fallen frosty. The room was well-appointed, elegant even, but very warm. The windows were closed. Her eyes flew open, those eyes I remembered so well.

"Who's that?" Her voice was strong, even though her visage showed the ravages of old age. "Speak to me."

I approached the bed and took her hand in mine. "It's Nellie, Mama."

Her eyes locked onto mine and after a few seconds, her hand squeezed mine quite painfully. "You've been gone a long time, Nellie. So has that sister of yours. You girls were never mindful of other people's feelings. Only person I see around here is that nephew of mine, always telling me how to attend to my own business." Her eyes went from me to Michael.

"Not that he's not been kind to me, but I need no advice from the likes of him. Now that's you're here, you can tell him that Fanny Murphy of Ballantrae doesn't answer to some Kerry fella. Your father will be off to the drink to hear of such a thing."

I glanced up at cousin Michael and he just shrugged, a rueful smile on his lips. It was clear what the lay of the land was here. I'd had no idea.

We chatted a bit, Mama and I, and occasionally she'd remember some incidents from our past, from Ireland to Boston and onward, but for the most part, she'd close her eyes and then open them, accusing me, Fanny, or poor Michael of something none of us had ever done. Sometimes she called me Fiona, thinking I was her mother, and once she talked to me thinking I was Fanny, my sister. Finally, I assured her I loved her, and as her eyes closed, presumably for the night, Michael and I backed soundlessly out of the room, closing the door.

"I didn't know," I said, as we stood in the long hallway, the gas lamps spitting. "What can I do?"

He put his arms around me. "There is nothing, Nell, that anyone can do at this point. It's what happens sometimes. What I do is keep her here, well cared for, and I think that is all there is now."

My guilt threatened to overwhelm me. I hadn't even visited her in years. I felt like a fraud and pushed him gently away.

"Michael, there are no words to convey what I want to say to you," I said. "You are the true definition of a saint to me. Please let me know how I help."

"I need no help, Nellie, nor does she. I was worried when you said you were coming on your way to the Klondike and would stop here because I feared this would go exactly as it has. Most days, my dear, she doesn't even remember she had two daughters. It's very sad, but that's how it is. I will take care of her. You must not let this stop you from what you have to do."

I looked up at him, tears running down my face and he patted my cheek.

"You're my adventurous girl, too, and a rather large amount of other people's as well, if the newspapers have any truth to them, which is always a risky business. The point I'm trying to make here is you must not let anything stand in your way, and you must carry on as you've always done. Everything here will be fine, and if you believe in yourself, as I think you always have, you will be fine too."

* * *

In the weeks that followed, I took his words to heart. I frequented my old haunts and listened carefully to everything I overheard, reading the newspapers and the mining journals. Everyone was in complete agreement. The Klondike was the place to be if you wanted to make a lot of money mining gold. It practically jumped out of those creeks and landed in your hands, so to speak.

More than that, I began to stockpile the supplies I needed to reach the northern reaches of the Yukon, because the list was daunting and strictly enforced by Canada's Northwest Mounted Police. I was cautious, because many items were available once I landed in Skagway, but some were fetching such a fancy price due to speculators, I was aghast. Those were the things I decided to take with me on the ship to Skagway. Patrick Sullivan had already reached Dawson City, and sent me reports, so I had some idea what I was getting into. His words were cheerful but insistent and I paid good attention. I wrote to Chinay, my old friend and Tlingit guide, in whose good hands I'd left Chris years ago. Reaching native people with letters was a chancy endeavor since they had no post offices and most moved about often. Still, I could think of no one I'd rather have on my side when I reached Skagway and it was worth a try. I knew I'd have to hire men to help me carry my goods across the Chilkoot Pass, and help me navigate the trek to Dawson City. I'd mentioned I wanted a sled and dogs at the top of the Pass and there was nobody that knew that business like Chinay.

The ship I boarded in San Francisco made a stop in Victoria to pick up additional passengers, and I made my way to the Sisters of St. Anne's for a quick visit before we sailed out that evening. Sister Mary Margaret greeted me warmly, and we had a lovely afternoon, even though she was highly skeptical of my plans.

"It's a rough place you're going to, Nellie," she said, pouring me another cup of tea. "The place is full of scoundrels and sinners, some who'd take your savings and your life in less than a heartbeat."

"Don't fret, Sister," I said. "I've met plenty of those in the last few years, and I'm still here."

She snorted, very unsister-like, and I couldn't help but laugh. "You might think so, but I've heard tales, missy. That criminal Soapy Smith is running things in Skagway and he's a terrible godless man. Watch out for him. There's a man who's had no proper upbringing at all, and one who is headed for the gallows." She stopped and crossed herself. "Just thinking about you running into him gives me chills."

"I'll be fine," I assured her. "I appreciate your warning, but I'll be fine."

She rang a bell that I'd noticed on the table and a young novitiate appeared quickly. She smiled tentatively at both of us.

"Jeanne, bring me paper and pen, please," Sister Mary Margaret said. Within two minutes Jeanne appeared with the requested items.

"I'm giving you a letter to Father Judge in Dawson City. The man's a saint in my opinion. He's in charge of St. Mary's Church and has established a small hospital adjacent to it. He's the first person you need to see when you arrive there. He'll help you find accommodations and teach you what's what in that place."

She bent to her task, writing quickly. I poured another cup of tea and sat back. It didn't take long. She finished her letter and sealed it in an envelope, handing it to me.

"There." She sat back. "That is all I can do for you besides pray. I hope you survive the journey, Nellie." She didn't seem terribly convinced that I would.

I took the letter from her and pressed her hand. "Thank you. He will be the first person I contact, Sister."

"See that he is," she sniffed. "The Lord watches over you,

but I've found he occasionally needs his charges to have a little guidance."

I couldn't help but smile. "I've found that to be true as well. Be assured that when I make my first gold strike, I won't forget you and the hospital here, and it looks as though they can put my efforts to good use in Dawson City too."

She nodded. A sly one, Sister Mary Margaret, but I loved that about her. She smiled back because we understood each other very well. We finished our tea, both of us very pleased with the outcome of our visit. I needed some sort of absolution and she needed money. We both understood these things very well.

CHAPTER 36

The sea journey was much as I remembered. The deep green of the waters, fed by the ice runoff, and the occasional whale sighting, which this time I witnessed, the magnificent creatures swimming so close sometimes the crew became alarmed, but there was no cause. I liked standing on the deck, carefully holding onto the railing, and watching the water and the creatures that inhabited that realm.

Fort Wrangell was as I'd first seen it, the stately totem poles welcoming our arrival, but although our stop was brief, taking on new passengers and disembarking others, I stayed on board and still could clearly see the town itself was three times the size I'd remembered. Many more buildings, many more houses and many more people. Such was the cost of prosperity and civilization, I supposed, but it was here I realized again that I desired less of it, and felt assured for the first time that I was going in the right direction, gold or not. *You're a restless, solitary soul, Nellie Cashman,* I thought. *You must make careful choices on how you achieve your wishes.*

If Fort Wrangell was bustling, Skagway was near insanity. The moment we stepped on shore, the passengers and our goods delivered by tenders and deposited on the wharf, we were assaulted by vendors, gamblers with shell games, shady-looking men offering assistance and their services as guides. I could only imagine to what dark alley they would guide me and I brushed past them all. I definitely needed guides but not the sort that hung about here, eager to take advantage of gullible miners. I left my goods on at the wharf along with some others, guarded by a sailor we hired. The captain said we had two days at most to retrieve our supplies as he would be restocking and taking on passengers for the return journey. I walked through the muddy slush of streets to the Yukon Hotel, as Patrick had advised me, and where I'd told Chinay I would be, although not quite sure of the date.

It wasn't an elegant establishment by any means, but it looked honest, and hopefully clean. I didn't plan to be there long. Every day counted when you were part of a stampede for mining claims, and there was no doubt everyone knew that as well as I did. The lobby was crowded with people – men, women, even children, and the walls resounded with a cacophony of voices. I managed to get a room, from the looks of things one of the last ones of the day, but the clerk said no messages had been left for me. I took the key and went to my room, just needing a few minutes of relative quiet in which to think what I should do next. I knew finding Chinay was a long shot, but if he didn't show, I was going to have to get busy and find some other help, which might be difficult. It looked like every man for himself out there.

I splashed some cold water on my face and straightened my clothes, as well as my backbone. I'd made it this far and I wasn't stopping now.

Back into the fray, I found a restaurant not far from the hotel and ordered some lunch. Conversations flowed around me and I listened unashamedly. This was the best way to find what I needed. Halfway through my roast beef sandwich, George Baker, one of my fellow passengers from the ship came in and waved hello, and I gestured to the empty chair across from me.

He sat down gratefully, heaving a sigh. "What a place, eh Miss Cashman? It's a confusing town, all right."

I nodded. "Certainly is. Have you found any guides or bearers for hire yet?"

"No, but I've got a few leads. We can't be leaving our stuff on the wharf for long around here or it won't be there when next we look, that's one thing I know for sure."

"I couldn't agree more," I said. "The captain said two days, so we need to move fast."

George eyed my plate and ordered the same when the waiter stopped by, and we both listened to the talk around us as we ate. The three men at the next table seemed quite well-versed in the doings of us travelers and I finally leaned over.

"Would you gentlemen be heading to Dawson City, by any chance?"

The bearded man closest to me smiled. "Indeed we would, ma'am. How about yourself?"

"Yes," I said, "and so is my friend here. Any advice on hiring packers or guides?"

They all thought this quite amusing. "You are going up the Pass? Not many women on that trail, my dear. Are you quite sure of that?"

"As sure as I've ever been," I said, and this was answered by more condescending chuckles. Men could be so annoying.

"If you go on down to Front Street, you'll find a hall where you can hire people. They've found that helping people to their fate is more lucrative than digging for mythical riches, and who can say they aren't right about that, eh boys?" His companions nodded. "That's what we did, and we're leaving in the morning."

He held out his hand. "John Lakeman, at your service. I wish you luck and hope to see you on the trail."

"Nellie Cashman," I said, and shook his hand. "Thank you for your advice and good luck to you as well."

George and I paid our bill and headed down to Front Street. The hiring hall was easy to find, people milling about it in droves. Inside we went. Tables were set up, and men for hire were on one side, and people looking to hire them were on the other. It seemed quite well organized. Many of the men looking for work were natives, Tlingits, Chumash and Han among others. They would certainly be my first choice, as they knew this country better than anyone.

George wasn't so sure. "You ever met up with these Indians, Nellie?"

I smiled. "Many times, George. I would advise you to choose them over any white man here. After all, it's their world up here."

He raised an eyebrow. "That makes good sense. I will."

George hired four Chumash guides and headed out with them to the wharf, while I still hesitated. I wanted Chinay and I was torn. After George left, I headed back to the hotel to check one more time. I knew it was likely foolish, but I had one more day and I could always return in the morning.

I walked back through the darkening streets, a light snow beginning to fall. I entered the lobby of the Yukon, not as crowded as it'd been earlier in the day. I took one step onto the staircase when I heard someone call my name.

"Nellie Cashman, I am here."

I turned and there was Chinay, holding the leash of a magnificent black and white husky who looked just like my Chris. Chinay's normally stoic face broke into a smile. He had changed little, with only a few strands of gray in his black hair. I ran over to him and enveloped him in a hug, my head barely reaching his chest, feeling as though I'd come home.

"I am so happy to see you, my friend," I said, stifling my happy tears. "And who is this beautiful creature?"

"He is Chris's last great-grandson, and he's been waiting for your return, as have I. Now we are all together again."

I knelt down and put my hands behind the dog's ears, ruffling his fur. His blue eyes stared back at me and he licked my face. Now the tears came in a torrent and I welcomed every one of them, my face buried in the beautiful dog's fur.

CHAPTER 37

Daunting. Relentless. Terrifying. Those were only some of the words used to describe the Chilkoot Pass. This was the barrier one needed to cross to reach the promised land and it would take every moral and physical fiber of your body and mind to do so. I looked up at the dizzying ascent, the bodies of my fellow miners struggling along. They resembled nothing so much as foraging ants marching on a pile of snowy sugar, moving slowly with massive loads on their backs.

Oh dear Lord, help me now, I thought. *I've needed your help before, but never for anything like this. You get me up this in one piece and I'll help build you a hospital that will serve all those in need of it.*

I carried a pack weighing 50 pounds on my back, and Chinay and his nephews, four of them, carried even more. Even at that, it would take us not just one, but likely three trips or more each up and down this perilous route to get it all to the top. Chinay even carried the dog on his back on the first ascent.

It was a sunny morning that first day, and while that may have sounded good, it wasn't. The sunlight reflecting off the snow was blinding and hindered rather than helped. When we arrived, gasping, as were our fellow climbers, we sat and arranged our base camp. There was much more to come. We left the dog and our packs with Chinay's son and slid back down the mountain to the bottom to ready for the next day.

Two more days of the same followed, the skies now gray and spitting snow into our chillblained faces, my back and legs aching like I'd never thought my muscles could ache, trudging one step after another up the steep mountain. I watched as many a man faltered and turned back, and others, much unluckier, falling into crevasses from which no one could rescue them, their diminishing cries rending my heart although I knew none of us could help those poor souls as we would die with them. Those who had hired horses or mules fared little better, the overburdened animals' hooves unsure on the icy ground, and many went over the edge never to be seen again.

On the third night, after we'd reached the summit once again, I collapsed, only to rouse enough to hold Chris II close, waiting for me at the top. The dog seemed to sense my pain and snuggled close to me as we slept that night.

I opened my eyes to Chinay holding out a steaming cup of coffee. I took it in both hands, sitting up as Chris stirred at my side.

"Do we have to go back down again?"

He smiled fleetingly. "No, Nellie, it's all here. Now the real challenge begins. It's 500 miles to Dawson City, Nellie. But I have plans for us."

I'd known that, from looking at the maps, but sitting here in the snow after the Pass, all I heard was 500 miles and that sounded like something beyond what I was capable of right now.

I sipped the coffee and stared at him owlishly. "Is it uphill?

He laughed. "Now and then, but not like that. Do not worry. We have sleds."

Relief surged through me just as sure as the caffeine from

the cup. For me, sleds were the magic word. In this country, dogsleds were the only way to travel and I'd learned that well in the Cassiar.

"Sleds?" I said, standing up, the cup still in my hand.

"Yes, but first we have to go through the inspection with the Northwest Mounted Police."

I groaned. People got turned away from the inspection and I hoped our party wasn't going to be one that did. The NWMP insisted on a minimum of 2,000 pounds of supplies per miner, and we'd packed some extra for ourselves on the journey, to be sure there was no quibbling over the Tlingit guides who would be returning to Skagway. The list was daunting:

Food, including bacon, flour, beans, coffee, dried vegetables, vinegar and I had added sauerkraut, lemons and limes, having dealt with scurvy before; a campstove, matches, oil, cooking utensils, axes, saw, nails, canvas, shovels, picks and other tools of all kinds; blankets, towels, mosquito netting, clothing, including heavy outerwear, boots, rubber coat, and more. The NWMP clearly had no wish to have to search for, rescue or bury anyone foolish enough to not have proper equipment, and I couldn't blame them. They'd learned the hard way with the Cassiar strike and this time were prepared, and making sure the gold seekers were as well.

We passed the inspection with no incident and set about harnessing the dogs.

Three sleds, each pulled by a team of seven or nine dogs, my own Chris II leading mine, were quickly loaded with all the supplies and away we went, heading north. We followed the river, still blocked with ice. Some travelers had chosen to build rafts and we saw them as we sped along the banks. There were some stretches that were thawing, the blue water flowing swiftly among the crags of ice, some as high as six feet, crashing noisily into each other. Woe betide anyone caught in the battle of these titans of the winter.

Sometimes the river travelers portaged their rafts and supplies when the river ice closed in, and we passed them, waving as we went. Tomorrow was another day and only God could know what the temperature would be. It wasn't a bad way to go, even though much more dangerous and slower than our choice in the end. I didn't care, really, because skimming over the white frozen expanses with my dogs made my heart sing. While it was a hard journey, it was one I would always cherish and I was grateful that I was here, in this place, and experiencing this wondrous adventure.

* * *

DAWSON CITY WAS NO PARADISE, nor had I expected it to be. That said, a place to sleep and a hot bath sounded like Eden to me. I smelled like a dead raccoon and my hair, even in braids, was encrusted in unknown elements. Well, most were evergreen needles and pieces of pine cones the birds had disdained, but they were hard to dislodge without a brush and there was no chance to dig that out of the packs that sat on the sleds. Surely there was some help for this. I wasn't one for fashion, but I sure was one for cleanliness if it was available.

The entire place looked to be a miniature version of Skagway, minus most of the criminals at least that I could see, but just as rowdy and raucous. It wasn't much different from other mining towns, just a good deal muddier. From the knees down, everyone was covered or splattered in mud.

Leaving Chinay's nephews on guard of my dogs and supplies, I made my way to St. Mary's Church to find Father Judge, Sister Mary Margaret's letter still safely tucked into my jacket. The church was newly built, actually not quite finished but being utilized anyway, as was the small annex next to it, housing the medical facilities. I could still smell the fresh-cut lumber. Inside the clinic, which smelt reassuring of carbolic acid and bleach, there were ten beds or so, as well as a couple of examining rooms. I spied a slender man in a black cassock, clean-shaven with gray hair, absorbed in stitching up a deep cut on a man's arm. He looked up as I approached, eyes bright behind wire-rimmed spectacles.

"Are you a nurse?"

"Indeed, I have been, Father."

"Good. Then take a look at that other boyo out there and see what you think. I'll be done here in a minute or two."

I started to protest, given my state of griminess from head to toe, but I clamped my mouth shut and entered the other room. The young man looked to be about 20 years old, slumped in a chair, his color bad. He opened his eyes when I touched his arm.

"Hello." I said. "My name is Nellie, what's yours? Tell me how you feel."

He managed a feeble smile. "Awful, Nellie, just awful. My name's John. John Chaney."

"I'm sorry, John. Let's see if we can't get you feeling better. Would you open your mouth for me?"

He grimaced. "Sure, but it's not a pretty sight. Everything hurts, too."

His gums were bleeding, and I saw he'd already lost a tooth. I knew advanced scurvy when I saw it.

"What have you been eating the last while, John?"

"Sourdough bread and beans, sometimes a rabbit or two that my friends snared. We've been out there a ways all winter."

"Wait here."

He coughed and sat back. "Sure will. Haven't got the energy to go anywhere else anyway."

I went back to the surgery where the man in a cassock had just finished up his suturing, sending his patient on his way.

"Father?"

"Yes?"

"The young man out there is suffering from scurvy. He needs care."

"I suspected as much," he said. "Thank you, Mrs. ?"

"Miss Nellie Cashman," I said. "Sister Mary Margaret sends her regards. But for now, I have fresh lemons on my sled if you need them."

After we got Mr. Chaney into a bed and eating some sauerkraut, and after he'd swallowed lemon juice, his face squinching up like the squeezed lemon that had sustained him, we left him in the care of a nurse and stepped outside.

"So, Miss Cashman. I'm Father Judge," he said. "I appreciate your assistance back there. How may I now help you?"

I handed him Sister's letter, which he opened and read quickly. He smiled absently and looked at me more closely, finally taking in my filthy clothes and more.

"So you just came in off the trail today?"

I shrugged. "Well, yes. I thought you might be the best person to see first."

"Because Sister Mary Margaret said so. That's all the recommendation I needed."

Now he chuckled. "They call me a Saint up here, which you may appreciate, since they call you an Angel. We are both going to have to live up to those titles, I suppose."

I was tired. "I'm no angel, and I'm not sure if you're a saint or not. I need time to decide. For now, if you could help me find a place to stay while I decide what's what in this place, I'd be grateful. Maybe after my first bath in two months, a bed off the snow and a bowl of soup, I could make a more enlightened decision."

This time he laughed, heartily. "I can surely do that, my dear, and gladly. I like a woman that speaks her mind, and I know what a friend you've been to those in need of help. Now, let me help you."

Before the sun went down that day, I'd met Brenda Mulrooney, the owner of the Grand Forks Hotel, and, both

Irishwomen, we hit it off immediately. That wasn't the only reason. Brenda had come to the Klondike a year before, and established herself as the most daring entrepreneur in town. She was wealthy, a very dynamic personality and with Father Judge's recommendation, she welcomed me and we agreed on a room arrangement. The rest of my supplies were soon stored in her ground floor storage areas. She even had a kennel for sled dogs on the property, and Chris and his mates were warm and well-fed down on the ground floor.

I felt as though I'd landed in heaven that night when I slid beneath clean sheets to lay on a soft mattress, the tin tub still cooling after my bath. Sleep began to overtake me before I had more than a moment to contemplate the next day. Perhaps, as Father Judge had suggested, I needed to take a few days to recover from the trek and learn how things went in Dawson City and its environs, before heading out anywhere else. He wasn't wrong. I'd been heedless many times before, but I knew I couldn't afford that recklessness here. Dawson City felt like home already, and I had to earn my place in it. Then again, that could be the warm comfort of my body and not my yearnings, numbed by the softness of the mattress beneath me.

CHAPTER 38

A pounding on my door woke me, the sunlight streaming through the thin curtains. I threw on a flannel shirt over my nightgown and opened it a crack. Patrick Sullivan bounded into the room and picked me up in a hug.

"You're here!"

I disengaged myself and stood back. "Of course I'm here, you big lout. Now get out of here so I can get dressed."

He laughed and backed out. "Meet you downstairs. You know, I've seen you in less, bathing in the river. I'm not some slavering sourdough, so your virtue is intact from me, Nellie."

Men. Just boys grown up. I met him in the lobby ten minutes later. He was fairly bobbing on his feet with his enthusiasm.

We sat down for breakfast in the hotel's dining room. We ordered coffee first, and after a few sips, my brain seemed to start working. I had gone to sleep early but it felt like I could use another day in that wonderful bed. It would take a day or two for my arms to feel like they weren't holding the reins of nine strong dogs in my hands. I'd even dreamed of it, and aside from the aches, truthfully I'd loved every single minute of that sled running through the pureness of the white snow, the ice crystals spinning past me and the joyous barking of the beloved dogs, working their hearts out to carry me forward. I blinked and stared at Patrick across the table from me.

He seemed to understand. He sipped his own coffee and peered at me closely. "So how are you, Nellie? That was a journey from hell, wasn't it?"

"Most of it," I said. "I'm glad to be here, and even happier to see you."

The waitress deposited our plates and we dug into the eggs, ham and potatoes. It was the best breakfast I'd had in some time, and it seemed for Patrick too. I felt much better as each bite went down.

He sat back in his chair. "So. I've been staying pretty close, but there's gold pretty close, so that's worked out. While I know you don't need a guide, since you've a nose for ore that confounds me, I want to tell you how things are out there. I've got two claims already, and they're paying out. Everything they said is true, Nellie. You came to the right place, I can guarantee that."

Those were the words I wanted to hear. I smiled. "Tell me more."

The next two days, we took the dogsled with just five of the dogs, Chris leading, and we ranged the area that Patrick thought looked promising. I filed three claims that I liked the look of right off. By the time snow had melted more, I'd be more precise, but I had a feeling about these. Patrick's weren't far away and he filed a couple more himself.

I thought about opening a store or restaurant, but Spring was about thawing, and summer in the Klondike was about digging, the light lasting almost the entire day. They didn't call it the land of the midnight sun for nothing. It certainly was that, difficult to tell when to stop working unless your body told you, because the sun surely would not. I remembered well from the Cassiar but we were even further north here.

Before long, I filed claims on quite a few other possibilities, leased a couple of others, further out on Rosebud and Little Skookum creeks. I decided to set up camp on the Bonanza, beside the most promising claim. I made a deal with Brenda Mulrooney to house six of the dogs until fall, and Chinay's nephews had taken the rest. Most of the supplies we'd hauled so painfully over the Chilkoot Pass I used in my summer camp, and the rest I stored with Mulrooney as well. Chris, of course, came with me. He was my loyal friend and companion, and we fell asleep every night next to each other.

I hired small crews to work some of the claims, and along with two men, worked the Bonanza until the cold really started to settle in and the creeks froze over. I didn't want to spend the winter out there myself, as many didn't, so I'd ordered stock and supplies to open a store in Dawson once the snow flew. Some of the miners I'd hired opted to stay out, and I'd arranged to send them fresh provisions on a regular schedule. I didn't want to spend the next five months in darkness, more or less, but they didn't seem to mind.

I had another idea, which had suited me well in the past – using some of the profits from the claims, I'd found setting up businesses paid better, especially in the winter, than getting frostbite on your toes for minimal return and rooting around like a blind pig in the dark.

Father Judge found me a little house close to St. Mary's, just enough room for me and the dogs. I hadn't returned empty-handed, but instead brought contributions from the miners for the church and hospital. Father Judge was eager to have me close by whenever he needed some extra help in the hospital, which turned out to be fairly often. I didn't mind at all. In fact, I enjoyed spending time with him and watching him work. He was a rare bird, this one, the "Saint" of Dawson, and many people owed their lives to his tireless work. Our patient John Chaney had recovered enough to be on his way, and before he left he shook my hand.

"Thank you, Nellie," he said. "You saved my life. I'm

going to write books about this place but I picked out a snappier name. What do you think about Jack London?"

I agreed Jack London did sound more exciting than John Chaney and he seemed pleased, waving as he walked away.

I leased a small storefront on Queen Street, next to the Hotel Donovan, and opened a store, selling clothing, supplies, and groceries. Business was slow at first, the miners trickling back into town from their summer claims, although others were continuing to arrive every day. I needed a lure, and thought to myself, what do people want to do during what leisure time they had? I knew what I'd always been drawn to, and so I set up the "Miner's Retreat" around the woodstove in a corner of the store, a dozen chairs and benches, with a coffeepot always bubbling away on the burner, cups on a table, and always free.

Patrick was one of my first guests, pouring himself a cup of coffee and plopping down on a bench.

"Damn if this isn't the best idea you've had, Nellie," he said. "This is just what people need. I don't want to sit around in some bar with a bunch of drunk cheechakos waiting for the next fight to break out. This," he waved his hand around the chairs, "is where I want to be. A warm stove, good coffee, congenial conversation."

I grinned. That was just what I wanted to hear. We could learn from each other, share information, (as much as some of the more paranoid of the miners would share and they were legion), and make plans for the upcoming season in April, as soon as the temperatures began to rise and the sun returned. Also, it brought in business and much good will, which was what I'd anticipated. We would share, comfort, and learn from each other from the coming of the gathering dark to the days when the midnight sun returned. Sometimes I thought bears might be much smarter than humans, although I doubted they chatted much in their snug dens, waiting as we did for the return of light.

The hospital remained busy, taking no notice of our axis on the sun. Thousands of people in a relatively small place and from outside came down with ailments and injuries just like they did anywhere, and I found myself stepping in as nurse and assistant to Father Judge quite often. If I was at home, his call for assistance would sometimes be no more than a yell or a pounding on the door, we were so close, but if I was at the store, he would send a boy to get me. Everyone got used to me putting up a "Closed" sign occasionally and would wait to come back until I did. I thought about hiring a clerk, but people were so accommodating and understanding, knowing where I was and what I was doing, I didn't find it necessary.

My days had taken on a new routine. I woke in the dark, got dressed, put coffee on to boil, and went out to the half-warm shed to feed the four dogs that were spending their winter out there. I felt badly for them, and usually played with them and petted them for a half hour, both morning and when I returned. They were well, but bored with no activity except for large fenced area I'd put up for them to play in, but it was far from enough. These dogs were bred to run, and that is what they loved. They were as anxious for spring as I was.

Then I went to the store, always accompanied by Chris, who at least for a few minutes felt as though he was working, forging a trail for me through the snow. We would open the store, turn on the lamps and I'd sweep off the front steps so people would know we were open for business, make a pot of coffee, stock some shelves and wait to greet our customers for the day, Chris at my side as was always. Except when he was asleep, of course. That dog could sometimes sleep through an avalanche, I was pretty sure. However, let a harsh word pass or any threatening action transpire, all 150 pounds of him would awaken like a sleeping volcano and things quieted immediately.

After business hours, which we'd all learned to gauge mostly by our stomachs or our tired feet during the winter when it was dark a great deal of the day, I closed up and went home. Except for my additional activities at the hospital, I would go home, make supper, feed the dogs again, read, think about my claims and all the things I'd heard from other miners and fall into bed. It was a quiet time, but come spring, all that would change.

Long before that, though, came Christmas. I put up swags of evergreens at the store, lit candles, and made fruitcakes from my stock of dried fruit, which were a big success, reminding everyone of home and holidays when they were young. Many a story was shared, along with some tears from craggy miners, some of whom rarely cracked a smile in emotion, and I didn't hesitate to begin prayers in the Miner's Retreat, especially on Christmas Eve, which led to a few more wet cheeks. Candlelight mass at St. Mary's followed, and many feet trudged through the snow to the little church, Father Judge presiding.

Christmas Day, I roasted a turkey and a goose, procured from the Han people, who were quite amazing at finding me fresh game, and hosted a dinner at the Miner's Retreat for anyone who cared to stop by. The response was so overwhelming I thought about opening a restaurant next, but I really had enough on my plate.

New Year's dawned and we welcomed the new year, if not yet the sun. One morning in January, I was awakened by a pounding on my door.

"Miss Nellie, come now, Father is ill." Sam, our young assistant, was crying.

Oh God save us, I thought. Father Judge had been looking peaked for some time, but every time I suggested he let me take a closer look at him, he'd resisted.

"I'm fine, Nellie," he'd said. "Don't be worrying about me. We've got our hands full right now. There's many more in need than me, my girl."

For him, that was the end of it, no matter how many times I'd protested to no avail. Now here we were.

I entered the surgery, and there he was, laying on a bed covered in a white blanket, his face gray, and his breath coming in little gasps. It was his heart, I knew that immediately, as I'd known for some time, no matter that he'd not let me check. I also knew there was nothing I could do, because there were no options except for facilities we didn't have, and even those might do little good.

I grasped his hand and stood beside him. "Father, tell me if there's anything I can do. Anything you want to say or have me bring to you."

He opened his eyes and smiled at me. "I'm in God's hands now, Nellie, we both know that. Promise me that you'll take care of those I can no longer tend."

I squeezed his hand. "Have no cares, Father. I will."

He closed his eyes, breathed once more, and never opened them again.

I think Father Judge, the Saint of Dawson, had the biggest funeral that town had ever seen, or maybe will ever see again, no matter how large this town might grow. It will certainly never be matched in its grief, gratefulness for his contributions or its sincerity. That day I committed myself to his wish, and my fund-raising efforts for this tiny hospital and church needed by so many in the midst of a frozen land intensified from that day forward. They could call me a pest if they liked, that was fine with me. I knew my cause was just, and so did most of the people I ever asked. They knew their own future needs might reside in that hospital or that little church always there for them in their time of need.

I got word not long after that my mother had died, via a stained letter from Cousin Michael, close to the same day Father had passed. I cried and said prayers for her, my knees freezing on the cold floor of St. Mary's. I'd known she didn't have long after the last time I'd seen her and we hadn't been close in the last few years, simply because of logistics. My mother had been an indomitable force in my life, taking my sister and me to a better life in America. The courage and resilience of that woman, fleeing a famine alone with two children, crossing an ocean to an unknown continent, and not only surviving but thriving, I knew had imbued itself in me, and for the rest of my life I would feel gratitude, pride and love for her. I was her daughter, and the best way I could honor her was to follow my own dreams, just as she had, bringing Fanny and I to this country.

I longed for the spring and sunlight, to chase away the hardness, death and bleakness of that Yukon winter, my first but far from my last. I was ready for the midnight sun, its warmth and light needed to chase away the darkness of the world and my soul.

CHAPTER 39

April. In more southern climes, it meant tulips and cactus blossoms but in Dawson City, it was heralded only by slush, which quickly froze over when the sun went down, and became a slippery surface where the wrong step would land you on your backside. If you didn't look quickly, you couldn't tell the difference between April and January. Still, we knew spring was coming, we learned to smell it just like the animals and with it, the hopes of all the miners who'd been snowbound these dark months.

The winter had kept me busy, at the hospital as much as I was at the store. We needed a new doctor, but until one could get here, it was just me and the nursing sisters, and we were always needed. I wanted to get out to my claims and see how things were going, but I was waiting for the new arrival, not wanting to leave them any more short-handed than they already were.

I kept up my fund-raising efforts, and everyone in town knew when they saw me coming, I was as likely to ask for a donation to the hospital as I was to ask how their lives were going. I managed to do both, most of the time and it wasn't often I was turned away. One morning I was in Don Bright's photography studio, both saying hello and asking for hospital aid, when a voice called out from his darkroom.

"Nellie Cashman, is that you? What are you doing in Dawson?"

That was a voice I knew well, but hadn't heard in some years. "Mayor Clum, let me ask you the same question."

"Don't leave, I'll be out in a minute and we'll catch up."

We headed over to the store and the Miner's Retreat, where we sat down with a cup of coffee.

"How'd you know that was me?" I asked. I eyed him closely. He looked well, prosperous and well-dressed. John Clum was never one to miss an opportunity, but he was a conscientious and honest man. I'd always liked him.

He laughed. "Seriously, I've never to this day heard anyone with a voice as distinctive as yours, with that Irish lilt and strength of vocality."

"Hmm. Well, it's what I've got," I said. "Strength of vocality, eh? I like that, Mayor. Maybe that's why I'm so good at collecting donations. So what are you doing in Dawson of all places?"

"Working for the government, actually the US postal service," Clum said. "Just passing through, under the kind auspices of the Canadian authorities on my way to Fairbanks and beyond."

I smiled. "You are a man of many and varied talents, Mayor. And doing a little photography now?"

"Yes, actually. I find it always helps to keep a record, not only words, but the magic of a camera suits me well. You know what they say, Nellie. 'Picture's worth a thousand words.' I'm not sure I'd go that far, but it does add to things. What about you? Doing a little gold mining along with this store?"

"Of course I am, Mayor. Why else would I be here? Got a few claims out there. We'll see how they are doing this summer."

"You never change, Nellie. Good luck with that gold. If there's anybody that can sniff it out, it's you."

Before he left, he insisted on taking a picture of me, standing outside the store. He sent me a copy of that photograph a month later. I didn't have a lot of images of myself but I gratefully added that one to my small collection and hoped one day John Clum would be crossing my path again. Life's a funny thing, sometimes, and you never knew whom you might see again.

The new doctor finally arrived and I felt it was time I could leave without a guilty conscience. I posted a "Closed for the summer" sign on the store and headed out to the creeks and my claims, running the happy dogs on the last of the snowpack, the sled loaded with food for the boys that had stayed out all winter, enough to last until deep fall, along with fish and elk we'd hunt for. We wouldn't be back until there was enough snow to run the dogsled back to Dawson, and that was fine with me.

The claims were paying out, much better than I'd expected, and we were all very satisfied with the results. I set up camp by my new one, which I called the 19B, on Bonanza creek, and went to work, doing what I loved best, looking for that elusive mineral once again. I think it was the end of the second week when I hit the big vein of gold I'd been looking for. I sat down and stared at it, and let out a whoop. Chris started barking, thinking I'd fallen and broken a leg. Far from it: 19B was a bonanza.

We got more sophisticated, the money allowing us to bring in more heavy equipment, steam boilers and the like, to get through the permafrost and access and process much more ore than we had previously. I filed more claims, more leases, and hired more men, and for the next four years, we all did very well, gold nuggets in our pockets and even more in all our bank accounts.

The Sisters of St. Anne's profited nicely as well, as I added my own hefty contributions to the hospital here as well as in Victoria, not a dollar of which I regretted. I had as much as I needed, but so many did not. I didn't need silk dresses or useless jewelry when I could provide a safe haven for people in need. Greed always made me a bit angry, and I tried to always pray for those afflicted with it, rather than spit my words in their faces, which did little good that I'd ever seen. I'd always wished that people could walk a mile in the shoes of others and then by some miracle, they might understand, but that wasn't likely. For me, finally, I did have the means to visit Arizona in the winter and I did just that.

* * *

I WELCOMED the sun on my face as I walked the streets of Tombstone, now a faded remnant of what it was in the earlier boomtown days. I breathed in the dry air scented with pinon and sage, which I'd come to love. Still, the town persisted, even Francesca's restaurant, which had relocated a few blocks and went by the name of La Posada, still serving the same delicious Mexican food she'd made long ago. Now her sons and daughters ran the business. None of it made me sad, but only nostalgic for the days when the town was such a bustling place, the silver pouring out of the mines, people arriving in droves, restaurants like mine thriving and the sound of pianos, the tinkling of glasses and the laughter that poured out of the saloons filled with people, some celebrating, some drowning their sorrows in the bottle of whiskey near at hand. Time moved on at a relentless pace, and no one knew that better than me.

A few days later I headed for Bisbee, eager to see my family and the Brophys. We'd corresponded, Tessie, Michael and I, during my time in Dawson City, and I was fairly caught up on events since I'd been away. Tessie Goodbody, the sister of Bill Brophy's wife Ellen, and I had hit it off from the first minute we were introduced, she being a bit of a free thinker as I was, and she kept me well informed. I knew Bill and Ellen had a son, born before I left, and now a daughter as well, and that Michael had married the youngest Goodbody sister, Mary, and they already had two children. The rest of the children had finished school and had gone off on various pursuits, Mamie married and in Tucson, TJ a businessman himself in Bisbee, and William and Fanny finding their way, soon to be out of school, William looking at ranching and sweet devout Fanny eager to be a sister of St. Anne's. I was anxious to see them all, and I couldn't help but thinking how proud and happy Fanny would have been at the way her children's lives had gone. I took some credit for that, but I'd had a lot of help, from kind friends and from God, whom I knew without a doubt, always had his eye on the Cunningham children.

I entered the Bank of Bisbee, which Bill Brophy had started in 1900, with my own dear Michael as cashier and now Vice President. My heels clicked on the floor as I walked to the reception desk near the rear, away from the tellers and their filigreed cages.

"I'm here to see Mr. Cunningham," I smiled and straightened my hat. It wasn't a remarkable hat, that was true, nor likely a terribly fashionable one. I wasn't used to wearing one purely for decoration, because they weren't much of a fashion necessity in the Yukon. There the hats were for warmth, not admiration. I'd quickly discerned that I had to get used to dressing a bit differently than I had been ever since the steamer had docked in Seattle. The cultural mores of the United States were miles apart from those of their northern neighbor.

The young woman, primly correct with her starched shirtwaist and pompadoured hair, looked up at me and I could have sworn she sniffed, her mouth turned into a flat line which didn't improve her appearance, which should have been welcoming.

"Do you have an appointment?" she asked.

"No, I do not, my dear." Her frown deepened and my patience was quickly reaching a new level along with it. "Perhaps you might tell him his aunt is here." Surely I didn't look that much of a bumpkin. This young lady could use a lesson in manners, but it wasn't up to me to give it to her. I figured life would do that for her just as well.

"Wait here." She rose from her chair and disappeared through a door.

I looked around, but there were no chairs in the small pristine lobby, only a few potted palms, so I stood there awaiting her return. Fortunately, I didn't have to wait long.

Michael burst through the door, the receptionist trailing behind him, her cheeks a well-deserved pink.

"Aunt Nell!" He scooped me up as though I weighed nothing, swinging me around, setting me down, and kissing my cheek. "Can't believe you're finally here and so glad you are."

I laughed. "As am I, dear boy. Let me look at you." I stepped away from him. What a handsome young man he was, dressed in an impeccable gray suit and vest, his blue tie precisely tied, cuffs and collar starched white. In the wilds of Arizona, his fashion style was right up to snuff.

"Well. You look amazing, Michael. How do you like being a banking executive?"

"Very well indeed, Auntie." He laughed. "I never thought this would be my future after chasing gold on the back of a burro and trailing Wyatt Earp back in Tombstone, but I've adapted."

"Nellie Cashman." Bill Brophy strode towards me, his hand outstretched. I took it in a firm clasp, which he dropped and hugged me himself, kissing my cheek as well, his moustache tickling my skin. "Back from the wilds, I see. It's been too long, my dear. I can't wait to hear of your latest exploits, even though I've heard a glimmer or two here and there. You are a force to be reckoned with, which I've always known."

Michael and I left the bank and he took me to his house, not far away, up Tenth Street, a big place perched on the hill. As we entered, a could hear the laughter of a young child, and the faint crying of a baby. A flustered young maid trailed by a toddler brandishing a toy horse met us in the hallway.

"Sir, Jack's been very…lively this afternoon," she said, and Michael laughed.

"Jack's lively every afternoon, and every hour before and after that," he said, picking up the little boy. "Give Papa a kiss, Jack. And then, meet your Aunt Nell."

He handed me the child, who was still holding the horse. I avoided losing an eye to a horse hoof and stared into those blue eyes. "Hello, Jack. I'm happy to meet you. Let's get better acquainted but lose the horse, what do you say?"

He solemnly handed the horse to the maid and we proceeded into the parlor where we sat on the sofa and had a chat. Well, I chatted and Jack actually listened. He was an adorable child, golden brown hair and big blue eyes and I saw his father in him. Once again, I thought of Fanny and how she would've loved this time.

"He seems to know you are no one to be trifled with, Aunt Nell," Michael said, sitting across from us.

"Have you been telling tales out of school, Michael?" I kissed the top of Jack's head. "Did I not do the same for you?"

He smiled. "Of course, but it was Will and Fanny that got laps and kisses. Maybe I'm envious, but I got hugs and encouragement and I'm grateful for every single moment of it, dear Auntie."

Mary joined us, handing Jack off to the maid with a kiss. I'd not met her before but no matter. She was a lovely, kind young woman. Within minutes, we'd struck up a conversation about him and his life with me, and then about how they'd met, one afternoon at the Brophy house, and how they'd fallen in love in a heartbeat. I could certainly see why. Michael had chosen well.

We had dinner that night at the Brophy's house, at their insistence. I was delighted to see Ellen and Tessie again, and their young son, Frank, had grown into quite the little charmer, even having dinner with us rather than in the nursery with his sister. He was an astute lad, and I had no doubt he would follow in his father's footsteps. A meal of roast beef with all the trimmings, vegetables was set out and a towering chocolate cake waited on the sideboard, to which young Frank directed longing glances. We all thoroughly enjoyed the delicious food and the opportunity to share our thoughts in person, a long time coming.

"I've loved your letters, Nellie," Tessie said. "I feel like I'm right there with you at the mines, walking in the snow and all. I'd love to sit and have a cup of coffee in the Miner's Retreat."

I laughed. "That would be a treat for Dawson City, I have to say. I'm not certain how long you'd enjoy it, though. Dawson is not a genteel place but it's a lively and interesting one, I'd agree with that. Of course, it's growing every day."

I tried to picture the elegant Goodbody sisters in pants and heavy boots, but that was an image I couldn't conjure up, at least not without collapsing with laughter and this wasn't the time. Instead, I said, "I, in turn, love your letters about the family and all the latest goings on in Bisbee. Gives me a welcome taste of home."

Bill Brophy concentrated on enjoying the excellent prime rib and listened to our chatter with a twinkle in his eye. I swear, sometimes I thought that man could read my mind. He'd known me a long time, that was true.

As the dinner dishes were cleared away and the coffee poured, young Frank was clearly delighted when a healthy slice of the chocolate cake he'd been watching with an eagle eye came to rest in front of him. He wasn't alone, because I took great pleasure in that cake as well, thinking I'd ask their cook for the recipe before I left. Dawson City inhabitants and visitors to the Miner's Retreat needed to have a chocolate cake like that. It would drive away the gloomy winter days and remind them of wondrous days of the past as well as those to come.

I stayed with Michael and Mary, at their insistence, and came to know Bisbee much better than I had in earlier times. The town was growing rapidly, many more houses built on the hills that towered over the downtown business area, and the huge pit mines to the south that dizzied the eye with their descents into the earth. What an odd town this was, with its vertical ups and downs, but one I thought would endure much longer than any of the other mining towns I'd ever been to or inhabited myself. The copper was there, in much greater quantities than the gold or silver had ever been, a seemingly endless supply, and the Phelps Dodge company knew how to get to it.

I spent my days wandering about, enjoying being in a place that had a myriad of retail outlets, visiting enticing and well decorated shops, acquiring books and notions that were unavailable in the North. There were so many pretty things, which I had the sense to realize wouldn't either survive the trip north, or last long in the harsh climate where I resided, so I resisted most of them. So, little things, like strong silk thread, fine needles, silk fabric, best for underthings, to bigger items such as new copper pots, unusual utensils, and fine cotton batting for quilts as well as wounds, (I always thought about the medical side of things), and even a new supply of cups and a bigger coffeepot for the Retreat, including fine wax candles and new glass shades, all came under my scrutiny and purchase. Most of this I had crated up and sent up to a Seattle warehouse and then to Dawson City to await my return.

That return would be on a ship to Alaska and an easy, in comparison, trek to Dawson City, and not one I would have to make. No more Chilkoot Pass for me, as now there was a tramway and miners would no longer have to endure what I had to get there. They were also a little late for the best claims, so that gave me great satisfaction. The prize goes to those who get there first, their suffering a just reward for their trials.

My evenings were spent visiting at the Brophy household or mostly at home with Michael, Mary and the children. TJ popped in one evening, fresh from Los Angeles, where he'd run across a spate of new ideas for money-making businesses. None of them involved mining, which didn't surprise me.

"Aunt Nell, it's a new world," he said, his eyes bright, as we sat in the parlor after dinner. He was a handsome young man, like his brothers, but with a much more excitable personality. I hoped it would serve him well. "Michael here just wants to be a banker. Don't get me wrong, he's good at it. But me? I don't want to sit behind a desk all day. This country is alive with opportunity. I'm going to start a soda pop business, and that's just the beginning."

"What is soda pop?"

He laughed. "Oh, Aunt Nell, you won't believe this. It's a drink that comes in a bottle, full of bubbles and excitement. Isn't that right, Michael?"

Michael smiled indulgently and nodded. "It surely is full of bubbles, all right. Sort of explodes in your mouth. Quite refreshing, actually."

"See?" TJ said. "Next time you come, I'll be in business and you can try it."

I didn't delve further into TJ's business prospects, which I suspected hadn't been terribly successful in the past. But he was an enthusiastic and inventive young man, just as he'd been as a child, and I knew Michael would likely keep a keen eye on his older brother's pursuits.

By mid-March I was as restless as I'd ever been, much as I loved my family. I yearned for the simpler lifestyle of the Yukon and Dawson City and the clean fresh scent of snow that never melted from the mountaintops. Places where you never had to wear a corset, layers of skirts, a dratted hat or prissy kidskin boots that would have dissolved in the snow in three days. I would return, but I was thawed out, with plenty of desert sun on my face and warmth in my limbs and the affection and company of my friends and family. I kissed everyone goodbye and meant every hug but breathed a sigh of relief when I got on the train, settling back for the long journey that would return me to my heart's desire – the North, prospecting and those empty snowy untamed expanses I'd come to love with all my heart and soul.

CHAPTER 40

1903

On my way north, I stopped in Victoria and visited the Sisters of St. Anne, as usual, spending two calm and serene days with them, observing the ongoing improvements to the hospital and spending time in the lovely chapel there. They wished me well and sent me on my way fortified with faith. I'd found that was something I needed, now and then, these women and that place were the bedrock for me when it came to finding solace, as they had been ever since my first foray into the Cassiar, so long ago now. How much we'd all accomplished since then.

Sometimes I thought I'd have been a good nun myself, given I never had a desire to marry, except for that one incident which had made me even more certain I was destined to live alone and be much the happier for it. But then I knew better than that. My acerbic tongue, my unflinchingly need for freedom and independence, and my inability to follow the rules, no matter who set them down, divine or otherwise, would've been a disaster for me in that profession. Still, it amused me to think of it and every time I did, I laughed out loud and most times no one but my dogs ever heard me.

I decided to try breeding a couple of my dogs. Dear Chris

along with my original pack had been with me since I came to Dawson City, but huskies worked hard and didn't have the longest life span. I had a female who was half-wolf and I planned to breed her and Chris. Chris was beginning to show his age and liked nothing more than to curl up by the fire these days. I had high hopes for pups that had the best of both their characteristics, wolves living longer than their dog descendants, as a rule. My female, whom I'd named Freya, was a gentle soul, sweet and manageable, not showing some of her ancestors' independence when it came to harness. Hopefully, their pups, diluted by a quarter, had that same sweet personality she and Chris had. I pampered my dogs, and everyone in town chided me for that, but those dogs had earned every comfort I could reasonably give them and they were the best friends I'd ever known, given the meanness of some people. I didn't have time for that sort of behavior, except to pray for them to get some sense. I had a feeling God was busy because it wasn't often my pleas produced results on that front.

I unpacked the crates of supplies I'd had sent, which got there before me and reopened for business, coffee on the stove and plentiful groceries and miner's supplies, my staples. My store was small in comparison to others in town but had a dedicated following, and my Miner's Retreat area brought people in, welcome if they bought anything or not, but most usually did. It was also one of the best places in town to get news, gossip, and hear local information.

Father Adam had replaced dear Father Judge, and he was a skilled surgeon and a kind man. The hospital had many new improvements, especially an expanded surgical area that rivaled Fairbanks, in my opinion. I stopped in to say hello and bring him a letter from Sister Mary Margaret. I liked him. He had big shoes to fill because the Saint of Dawson was a hard man to replace, but I'd give him all the help I could and I assured him of that, both with my hands and donations.

Dawson City had always been, even in its early inception, a relatively peaceful place, unlike some of the boomtowns I'd experienced in America. The main reason why was the Northwest Mounted Police, who kept a firm law enforcement hand on both local and provincial crime and disorder, as Canada had learned early on, especially noting reports from the states. While I was a loyal supporter of the United States, showing an American flag in my window, I also showed the British one and was happy to have the NWMP nearby. I recalled the days in Pioche, Tombstone, and even Mexico of murders, gunshots, remembering the Cowboys and their ilk and breathed a prayer of thanks to Canada for their foresightedness. This was a safe place to walk the streets, winter and summer, sourdoughs and cheechako newcomers alike, and I appreciated that.

My claims had produced well over the winter. The boys had done well, with no scurvy or problems, and my best one, the 19B, was not only producing well but much better than I'd expected. They'd used the small steam boilers that I'd paid dearly for during the winter months, but the investment proved sound. There was no slowdown on mining in the Klondike and more people poured in every day, as they had for some time and I was open and ready for business.

One morning in May I woke up to a summons from Mary McCrae, another woman miner and one who owned a hotel. She was insisting I'd stolen her claim, one near my 19B, and she was suing me for the profits and my apparent usurpation. This was ridiculous and I angrily fumed as I dressed to meet her and her lawyers in the Dawson miner's court. I'd never had anything to do with her or her claim. She was a liar and I could see no motive to her actions except she'd move on to my 19B and claim that one next if she managed to get a favorable verdict in this one. There were vultures everywhere and I knew them well.

"Court is now in session." The judge in this case was a

bearded ex-miner from Ontario who had taken up the law when his dreams fell through, looking for the next venture. That is not to say he was uninformed when it came to his legal knowledge, but rather very uninformed as to how things were done in the Yukon.

The clerk informed me as to the words of the oath I was to take. I nodded and smiled. When it came time for my testimony, I stared at the judge while the erstwhile clerk held up a Bible.

"Do you, Nellie Cashman, solemnly swear your words to be the truth, the whole truth and nothing but the truth?"

I nodded and he handed me the Bible, which I took in my left hand, raised my right hand, and said, "So help me God, I never was there" and kissed my thumb instead of the Bible. The audience, including the recording officials and the judge, burst into laughter. All of them knew me well, and all of them knew this case was trumped-up nonsense. Within minutes, the case was dismissed. At the Miner's Retreat, I handed out free whiskey along with my excellent coffee and new Arizona chocolate cake most of the afternoon, both a success, to celebrate my own. Mary McCrae left town not long afterward and no one mourned her absence.

Spring was winding to a close and full summer was coming on. I was debating on closing the store for the summer as I usually did. Business was unusually good, and my claims were producing very well without my supervision, my boys being experts at what they did. I chose wisely and paid well, which I've found to be the two reasons business of any kind succeeds or fails, along with a good product of course. Gold was a pretty good product. Food was sometimes an even better one. I had both, but I've been in situations where I didn't have either one and that was a place I never wanted to visit again.

I'd just unlocked the door one morning when Chris, always at my side, made a rumbling sound in his throat, his version of a bark but not quite a growl. I looked up and here came two sourdoughs who looked they'd had a rough winter. As they came closer, I smiled and held out my arms.

"Patrick Sullivan, where you been for three years?" I said. "Keeping scarce."

He of that name picked me up and hugged me, setting me back down with a thud onto my wooden porch. I turned and there was Ted Brandywine, whom I hadn't seen since the Cassiar. He gave me his lopsided grin, and I hugged him just as heartily. They both smelled like dead raccoons but I didn't care and Chris seemed to thoroughly enjoy the aroma, sniffing their trousers with great enthusiasm.

"Get on in here and have some coffee, you two. We've got a lot of catching up to do, I'm thinking." I held open the door and in they came.

"Lord almighty, Nell, you've done fine for yourself here," Patrick Sullivan said, looking around the small store. "How many mines you got going out there?"

I chuckled. "A couple, you know me. I learned the hard way to never put your eggs into one basket." I stared at him and he looked away, because he knew exactly what I referring to, but no more was said. I'd never blamed him for his brother and we were at peace with that. "Where have you two been working?"

No other customers had arrived yet, as it was early. We sat in the comfortable chairs around the woodstove in the Miner's Retreat, and I kept the coffee pot full.

Patrick, always the talkative Irishman, same as me, launched into his trials and treks since we'd parted company back at Fort Wrangell. The man had a yen to see every bit of country he could and he sure tried his best.

"I been to Fairbanks, Anchorage, and then up to the Arctic Circle, way up the Yukon River to the Koyukuk. I tell you, Nellie, you think Dawson is north country? You've never seen anything like what they got up there. I swear to God there's gold up there but so far nobody's found any and I couldn't take the time, my toes were getting frostbit. I'll wait for some young sprat to be the first. Besides, I got other things to keep me busy, right, Brandywine?"

Tim smiled. "Right, Patrick." He glanced at me, the same quiet mild-mannered but effective man he'd always been. "We been working claims about fifty miles northeast of here, and they're paying pretty well. I was in Montana when I met up with this reprobate here," he punched Patrick on the shoulder, "and he convinced me to come on up here like some damn Pied Piper of gold." He shrugged and sipped his coffee. "Can't say he was wrong. We done pretty good."

He gestured towards the heavy packs they'd put beside their chairs. "Time to sock it away and get back on the trail for some more, we're thinking."

"Sounds good to me," I said. I put on the apron I wore during the day at the store and took a pan of the cinnamon rolls I set out to rise every night out of the oven on the woodstove and set it on the table. The enticing scent of cinnamon and sugar wafted throughout the store. I'd been using this as a lure along with chocolate cake since I got back from Arizona. Michael and I had enjoyed quite a few discussions of marketing and I'd learned some new things. I saw there were three or four early customers milling around the shelves.

"This might be good, too. You boys sit tight and enjoy while I go attend to my store."

Eventually, since between cinnamon rolls and exhaustion, they were nearly asleep in their chairs the next time I looked, I sent them down the street to a boardinghouse I knew that would provide them clean beds and baths at a good price. These two were not candidates for any of the fancier hotels that had sprung up in Dawson, replete with Turkish carpets and ferns. Maybe once they cleaned up and wanted to spend their money on luxury, they'd feel differently but I sincerely doubted it, since I knew they had no interest in that sort of thing. My old mates rarely did.

Patrick showed up three mornings later, having partaken of the delights, such as they were, of Dawson City.

"Ted and I are headed north to Alaska, Nellie my girl," he said, as I rang up his purchases of salt pork, sauerkraut and beans. I threw in a batch of cinnamon rolls while he wasn't looking. "I think the next big strike is up there. I'll check it out and send you a letter when we find it."

I kissed him and Ted goodbye and watched them as they departed. I wished them well. I had forlorn hopes of a letter, as Patrick had never been one of those, but if one came, I'd be delighted. Those boys always went their own way, just as all of us had done.

As the days waned into autumn, I debated about going back to Arizona for the winter. But, Chris and Freya had produced eight beautiful puppies, and the mines were doing well, my supplies for the winter in the store and the claims were stocked up, and I was vacillating. Then, one morning I woke up with a pain in my stomach that was like an iron spike driven right through me. I lay back on my pillows hoping it would go away, but Chris kept whining and nudging me, and eventually I got dressed and staggered my way over to St. Mary's hospital, pretty much next door.

I knocked on the door and Father Adam opened it. He took one look at me and began shouting orders to the nurse on duty. I don't remember a great deal after that. I had a dream that likely was no dream at all. I was laying down on a bed of some kind, someone smoothing my hair away from my face while someone else was strapping my arms down which made me near insensible with outrage. Restraints of any kind and I were not friends and never would be. Then, I experienced a rather pleasant sensation of lifting away, seeing my body below while my mind floated among lovely clouds filled my mind, the Virgin Mary taking my hand and whispering to me, although I've never remembered a single word she said.

"Nellie."

I blinked, and opening my eyes was one of the hardest things I've ever done. Focusing on the blur in front of me was likely the second. Father Adam's face became clear and I blinked a few more times. I opened my mouth but the words I spoke were incomprehensible, even to me, but I kept trying.

Father Adam smiled and took my hand. "Nice to have you back, Nellie. Don't try to talk right now, it will be difficult. Let me talk instead. You had an intestinal obstruction that became infected. I did emergency surgery and resected part of your intestine. You will be fine, everything went well. All you have to do right now is rest and recover."

I opened my mouth again and Father Adam, very gently, touched my lips with his fingers. "Dear Nellie, for now just sleep. We will talk more soon."

Sleep I did, along with recover, for a few weeks. I'd never experienced debilitating illness and it wasn't something I wanted to ever repeat. I gave thanks to God that I lived next door to a hospital and a surgeon. I didn't even want to think about how this condition would have been treated if I or anyone else was out in the wilds, unable to access the services of medical people. From that day on, as soon I was out and about, I redoubled my efforts at fundraising for the hospital, and for outreach services for those unable to make it to Dawson City or a doctor. There was nothing more important to me than saving lives if I had any say in it, and I did. Once you know, you have to act, and now I knew better than anyone, or as well as anyone that had been in my circumstances or worse.

CHAPTER 41

MICHAEL CUNNINGHAM

I have had an interesting life, more so than many, and there's much more to come, I am sure. That said, my life wouldn't be anything like it has turned out to be if I hadn't had the opportunity to have been raised since I was eight by my aunt, Nellie Cashman. Not long after I arrived in Tombstone I witnessed the happenings at the OK Corral, since Wyatt Earp, his brothers and Doc Holliday were frequent customers at my aunt's store and restaurant and their kind manner toward me and my siblings, as well as my aunt, made them my heroes. I took every opportunity to trail them around town whenever I could, my brother in tow. Most of the time, she knew every step I took but unless I was in danger, she left me to pursue my boyhood adventures.

My beloved mother was ill with tuberculosis for most of the time I remember her, but she was a tireless fighter of the disease, with stamina far beyond what anyone would have expected from her slim frame. Both she and my aunt Nellie instilled in me the courage and resilience to grow into the man I've become. When she died, Nellie became both mother and aunt to us all, briskly managing a family and her businesses, even doing the mining that captured her heart even before I was born. I never went to sleep at night without a hug, song, or story, and I knew I was loved. I try to impart that into the rearing of my children now, knowing how important it is and how grateful I am she gave this comfort to me.

Nellie ventured out mining and starting businesses that I know now provided the income she needed to raise us all. For years now she has been off in the Yukon and Alaska, following the lure of unknown places, the elusive ores and her love of pioneering new trails. She's getting older and I worry about her. When she comes to visit in Bisbee I try to convince her to stay here in Arizona, where there are more comfortable accommodations than some cold cabin on the edge of nowhere, out there staking claims and running her sled dogs which she loves to do almost as much as the mining itself. Eventually, she will sigh, kiss my cheek and stand up, pulling down her jacket and straightening her skirt in that no-nonsense manner of hers.

"Michael, I still have much to do. There are people in need and for every piece or flake of gold I find, I make sure half of it goes to them. There are hospitals to build, orphanages and churches as well, and those poor souls in purgatory that need prayers to be said. Besides that, I have people that depend on me, not to mention my dogs, which some people might not think are important, but for me, they are my companions and work harder for me than any human ever has. No, I have responsibilities, dear boy, and much as I love you, I cannot shirk them."

So my words are for naught, and back to the frozen north she goes every time. Still, I persist. This extraordinary woman who has done so much for me and so many others deserves a rest from her labors but she's like an engine that can't stop turning and those labors are the fuel she needs.

So off she goes, and I hold my breath until the next time

she arrives, often without warning. I gladly welcome her each time. I'm a lucky man but apparently not a very persuasive one as she won't stay, no matter my enticements. Nellie is the epitome of independence, indomitable and inspiring, and I count myself very fortunate she's been part of my life.

CHAPTER 42

1905

I opened the store, made the coffee and sat outside in the spring sunshine while I read Patrick's letter. He wasn't one for communicating on a regular basis so my curiosity was piqued. For good reason, as it turned out.

"Dear Nell, hope you're well down there in Dawson. Things are good in Fairbanks and I'm doing all right but you never know how long things last, as we know too well. If you're looking to make a change, Fairbanks is a pretty good place with good claims available nearby. Dawson was feeling a mite crowded and maybe tired. From boys I've met here, they say Dawson's getting too citified and the mining's not what it was but I don't know. Ted went off northwards, not sure exactly where to but up the Yukon and that. I haven't heard from him but he was never much of a letter writer but good at taking care of himself. You may not care much anymore, but Michael got himself killed in some fracas in Virginia City from what I hear. He wasn't always a rum one, but he played you false and I never forgave him for that even if he was my brother. You can reach me at General Delivery in Fairbanks if you want. Your friend, Patrick Sullivan

Well. I finished my coffee and dropped the letter in my lap. I stared out at the street where people were beginning to stir and get about their business, fragments of conversations and the sound of wagon wheels filling the earlier silence. All of a sudden, it felt like too much. Dawson City was growing, and I felt a little hemmed in. The rest of the morning, even as I smiled and rang up customers and kept the coffee going, I felt like I was in another place in my mind.

I wasn't sure how I felt about Michael's death. I held no grudge against him any longer, and it was sad he'd left this world too soon and in a violent manner, but I didn't feel any satisfaction or had "he got what was coming to him" thoughts. Rarely did that apply to anyone, but was simply God's justice to mete out. I'd light some candles at St. Mary's for him tonight.

What occupied my thoughts more were Patrick's words: "Dawson's got too citified" because I'd been thinking the same thing for some time. We even had an opera house now and once that happened, that pioneer spirit that I lived for was destined to die right there on its fancy steps. I needed a frontier. Fairbanks might be citified too, but it was a gateway to the rest of Alaska, unexplored and open territory that held endless opportunities for somebody like me.

A week later, Father Adam and Sister Joan Claude came in for more vinegar and potatoes, and indulged in some chocolate cake, sitting down with me. It was a quiet time in the afternoon and we were alone, other customers having left.

"This is the best chocolate cake I've ever had," Father Adam said, scraping his plate to get the last bit of frosting.

I smiled. "Thank you, I got the recipe from some friends in Arizona. I'm happy you like it. Another piece?" I handed him another over his mild protests and he dug in, as I'd known he would.

He finally put down his fork and I knew the cake had been a delaying tactic. I braced myself.

"I've been observing your disquiet for a while, Nellie. Tell me what's troubling you, if you would."

It was hardly a confessional but I don't think any of us

cared, especially when Sister Joan Claude took my hand in hers.

"It's just that I think it's time I moved on." I looked at both their faces and they didn't seem shocked. "Dawson's grown and I need more than I can find here." I laughed, surprisingly myself. "You might say I've outgrown it. I always yearn for those places yet to be explored, it's just who I am. I've been dreaming of expanses of white untouched snow and mountains no one's ever seen. I think it may be Alaska."

"Go on," Father Adam said. "Tell me why you're troubled about that."

"Because I don't want to leave all of you, and the hospital and everything we've struggled to build here. There's still much work to be done."

He sat back and smiled. "Oh Nellie Cashman, there's always work to be done, and there always will be. It's the human condition and life is fraught with difficulty, my dear. You have done more for this town than anyone could ever expect. I believe wherever you decide to go, into that untouched snow or wherever your desires take you, you will find those who need your help. They are always there. But you must also think about yourself and not feel selfish about that, because you could never be. Have faith, Nellie. You will never change but always be God's handmaiden here on earth, doing good work but you must not neglect yourself, for that is the well from which compassion springs. Follow your heart."

I went home that night, feeling lighter than I had for some time. In the next few weeks, I sold the store to two enterprising young men from Seattle. I settled my claims and leases among the boys that had worked for me for so long. Then, I sold the 19B for $100,000, quite the bonanza indeed. I was more than solvent after that, even after sending a large donation down to Victoria for St. Joseph's Hospital.

Fairbanks, I thought, I hope you're ready for me, because I'm ready for you, along with all my dogs and ambitions.

CHAPTER 43

Fairbanks surprised me. I'd heard it was nothing like Dawson City, but I knew that miners had been pouring in there for the last couple of years, just like they'd done in Dawson, but Fairbanks had been slower to respond to the needs of an increased population in just about every area. It had only been established when the steamer Lavelle Young went aground in 1903, stranding supplies and one E.T. Barnette, who decided to set up a trading post once he heard about gold discoveries there. It didn't take long for people to begin flooding in searching for gold, and Fairbanks grew rapidly in population if not enough in services to support it. The District of Alaska, an American territory, didn't have the advantage of the Northwest Mounted Police, and no Father Judge to take care of those who needed it, but looking at the squat log buildings in front of me, I knew it wouldn't take long for things to change, especially with the money the miners brought in.

There were a couple of large commercial stores, but I chose to rent a storefront much smaller, choosing my stock carefully, as always miners' supplies and food staples, some of which I bought from the Northern Commercial Company, but also all the fresh food I could find. The Tanana valley near Fairbanks not only produced gold, but in the summer, a lot of produce on its farms, and I bought and processed as much of it as I could. I'd already ordered supplies from Seattle, which arrived two weeks after I did. The store building was divided, providing an ample living area for me and five dogs and we settled in. Before the serious winter set in, I'd supplied miners who wanted to stay out at their claims for the winter, and had established a steady stream of customers who lived right in Fairbanks or nearby. The air was always smoky from wood-fires and I didn't care for that, but the retail opportunities outplayed it, at least for a time. It didn't take long for me to discover the Episcopal church and its makeshift hospital, St. Michael's, run by Deaconess Carter. They called her "the little angel in black" and I liked her from the first moment I met her. She reminded me of Father Judge, and I devoted some time to raising funds for St. Michael's and those it provided for.

By mid-winter, Patrick showed up, looking somewhat the worse for wear and smelling like the bearskin draped over his shoulders. He was elated despite that, considering the amount of gold he'd deposited in the new bank, and was enthusiastic about heading back out to his claim in the Tanana Valley.

"Nellie, I'm telling you, Alaska is the place we should've been looking at long before now. My claim's paying out well here, but this is a big place. The Yukon's got nothing on this, girl. Come summer, I'm going to head north and look for Brandywine."

I poured him another mug of coffee, liberally laced with whiskey. "Have you heard anything from him?"

"No, but I know if anyone can handle bad situations, it's Ted Brandywine. All of us old sourdoughs that came to the Cassiar are blessed in some way, I swear. Remember those days?"

How could I ever forget? "What's north anyway?"

I hadn't heard a word about anything worth my notice further north or west of Fairbanks than fifty miles. Nothing up there but snow and impassably long stretches of more nothing, from all I'd been able to discern. Only the natives had figured out how to survive up there. But Patrick was rarely wrong about these things.

"There's a river, the Koyukuk, branches off the Yukon way up there. A man came into my camp just two weeks ago talking about gold just lying around in that river. I thought at first he was delusional, what with being half froze and snow-blind and all, but after a few days, he didn't change his mind. Kept talking about it. There's a place called Nolan Creek that loaded with gold from what he says."

I stared at him. "You telling me there's a big gold discovery up there?"

"That's exactly what I'm telling you."

Well. That could bear thinking about. Still, I wasn't going anywhere further north in the middle of January, and maybe not any other time either, at least not until I'd learned a lot more about the area up there. Patrick wasn't so inclined.

"Come spring thaw on the Yukon, I'm heading up there. I'll try to keep in touch, but there's little chance of that, unless some sledder takes a letter."

The winter passed, and the spring thaw brought to Fairbanks a flood of epic proportions, some buildings washed away, and others relocated to the other side of the Chena River. Luckily, my place wasn't in any serious danger. the summer arrived, with its usual contingent of blackflies, more miners and even tourists. Curious, I took the steamer up the Yukon all the way to Nolan Creek, sort of a reconnoiter. We passed villages of native Eskimos, Indians and whites who'd made lives up here, all anxious to see the steamboat approaching, carrying supplies and bringing goods back to Fairbanks. It was beautiful country, the midnight sun glittering off the snow, and I was thrilled to see this wasn't complete wilderness with no other people anywhere. A person could make a life up here, and this particular person was getting itchy feet.

Back in Fairbanks, business was good, and after I stocked up well that fall, in January I left the store in charge of my assistant, Samuel Brennan, an honest young man from Montana, who'd arrived during the summer and been quickly disenchanted with digging for gold, finding employment in town an easier and more lucrative task.

I'd received a letter from Patrick, water-stained and barely readable, in September. He was enthusiastic, in some place called Coldfoot, but according to him, the gold was plentiful, and the miners few. It was an opportunity he could scarcely believe and he was stocked up and spending the winter, urging me to come and see. I believed him and I was ready to go. For now, I was headed to Arizona. I yearned to see my family, but I also needed funds, more than the store would likely provide. I wanted to head north as soon as the weather permitted and I could get my supplies in order. The dogs were ready to go even before the river was passable.

January found me in Bisbee, delightfully warm in comparison to Fairbanks, and I basked in both the sun and the love and welcome of my old friends and family.

"Aunt Nell," Michael said to me one evening after dinner. "I want you to come live here with us in Bisbee. This new Alaska venture you're doing in Fairbanks is just a step too far at your age."

As I began to protest, he held up a hand. "I shouldn't have mentioned age, because I know that offends you, being the hardy intrepid pioneer you've always been, and I respect that. But I love you and I want you to be comfortable. I doubt Alaska affords that."

I had to laugh. "Alaska is many things, but comfortable, unless you're in your cabin with the fire going and dogs around your feet, all of you fed and happy, isn't one of them.

That's a comfort that's the best in the world, if only you could experience it, you would know. What Alaska does provide is an opportunity, an adventure, a calling that I can't resist, and likely never will until the day I can't get out there on a frosty morning and work. I'm not there yet, dear boy, and I have a lot of work still to be done."

He sighed and clasped my hand in his. "I know. Brophy and I will advance you all the funds you need. All I ask is you keep in touch, dear aunt, and come see us every winter when you feel the pull toward those who love you. Will you promise me that?"

"Yes," I said. "Of course. I love my time with all of you and you mean a great deal to me. Thank you, Michael."

In April, I arrived back in Fairbanks. My next trek was one I was anxious to set off upon. First, however, I had to attend to business. I sold the store to faithful Samuel Brennan, stocked up on supplies, fueled with advice and minimal maps, and harnessed the dogs. I ordered more goods to be sent on the steamboat once the river cleared but I was impatient to set off, and I bought four malamutes to double the size of my dog team. The Yukon was in ice melt and I had no desire to attempt another river trek again. Instead, the snow beckoned along the riverbed, and I knew the sled would run fast and well, my huskies, headed by Chris of course, would make certain of that.

I wouldn't miss Fairbanks in the least. It was a growing town, and I was sure the next time I saw it, perhaps heading south for the winter, it would be even more prosperous. I didn't care. Growth and progress, as they liked to call companies moving in to replace individuals, held no enchantment or interest for me, regardless of the money they promised.

I needed pristine space, the thrill of chances and risk, and to feel as though I was the first person to step foot somewhere and find the mysteries the land beneath my feet held so closely, as well as the solace and satisfaction that came to me in that endeavor.

The sun was bright in my eyes as we set off, and so were my hopes for my future in the Arctic circle, so very far north and so very vast.

CHAPTER 44

1907

The trek was long but uneventful, and I enjoyed the solitude and peacefulness of the open wilderness. Occasionally, I would run across native villages and spend the night there with the dogs. Everyone was very welcoming. There were no run-ins with wolves or bears, which didn't surprise me. I'd had very few dangerous encounters with them. The main wildlife I saw were herds of elk, sometimes so many they covered the landscape as far as the eye could see. I always reined the dogs in and waited for the magnificent creatures to pass. At Bettles, a trading outpost and mission, about 80 miles from Nolan Creek, Patrick Sullivan had left me a message.

Dear Nellie, I am leaving this note for you hoping you stop in here. I am with Ted Brandywine and some others up the Koyukuk. Head for Coldfoot or Wiseman and we will leave word there as well. Good journey to you. Patrick

I found his words strangely comforting. While I cherished the peace being alone brought me, I knew this time I would need help to accomplish my goals up here. It would mean starting from the ground up and there was much work to be done, not just in the mining, but making a home base from which to conduct it. Already I could sense this place in the Arctic Circle was calling me to make it my home and I couldn't do it alone, much as I'd have liked to think I could. People in Alaska depended upon each other for many reasons and they were sensible ones. While I sat there by the fire contemplating all I needed to do, Chris and the other dogs, noses buried in their tails curled around themselves, all watched me. So trusting, dogs were, and my favorite companions, but they weren't terribly good at building mining equipment or cabins, although they'd likely be eager to help if they could. We needed the skills and strength of men and I'd have to hire them. I chuckled and ruffled Chris's fur. Better to hire than to be married to one who'd try to tell me what to do. I preferred being on the upside of that situation.

We arrived in Nolan Creek two days later. It wasn't much, a collection of shacks and discarded mining equipment peeking through the melting snowdrifts. There was a store of sorts, and I went in, the stale air inside redolent of coffee and unwashed bodies, a rather sour combination.

"Anybody here know Patrick Sullivan or Ted Brandywine?" I said. A few sourdoughs were gathered around a woodstove and one heavily bearded man stood up.

"Do you not recognize me, then, Nellie Cashman?" Ted Brandywine strode over to me and picked me up as though I was a feather.

I laughed. "No, I surely did not. That's a fierce beard you've got there."

"Indeed it is. Haven't shaved for the Spring Ball yet because the debutantes are scarce. Have a seat, and we'll catch you up on the doings around here."

* * *

By the end of July, I'd set up camp and hired a crew to build some cabins sort of in the middle of the claims I'd filed. I'd begun with the Fay Pup, on an offshoot creek, which I leased from a friend in Fairbanks, and with Ted and Patrick's help, filed four more. The place was thick with gold. With simple methods, the crews I hired were bringing up a good payload. Come winter, we'd try other things. Bonfires were the preferred solution up here, melting the permafrost, and bringing up placer sands to be sorted in the spring when things thawed. I was exhilarated to be back doing what I loved best.

We moved into the cabins by the time the first snow hit, Yukon stoves going, supplies stocked, and mine was big enough for a inside/outside room for the dogs that my clever carpenter friend George Loomis had designed. Everyone said I pampered my dogs, but I knew better. Huskies and malamutes worked hard and didn't have the longest life span. Those dogs and I understood and supported each other, and we understood loyalty much better than some humans I'd encountered. If I could give them a little warmer place to sleep during Arctic winters, I was definitely going to do that, despite what passed for conventional wisdom on this topic. In my opinion, if someone did an academic study, they might find these northern dogs that had some respite from the intense cold developed a genetic predisposition for a longer life. I wasn't equipped with the knowledge to do anything scientific on canine genetics, but I knew my instincts were right. Their wolf ancestors had a longer span because they knew about dens and communal sleeping whereas most of the sled dogs I'd seen in Alaska and Canada lived in outside pens, no matter the weather. Occasionally some died. I wasn't about to let that happen to my dogs, even the ornery ones.

That first winter, we got relatively meager results from our bonfires and the boys and I talked it over. Come spring, I headed south to order steam boilers and copper pipes for the next winter. That was the way to bring that placer up.

The next few years went well. We installed the steam

boilers and pipes, built more improvements onto our cabins, and watched the entire area grow with more miners, Wiseman even starting a post office. Even though more people had moved in, you would never call the Nolan Creek area well populated and about the farthest thing from crowded there could be. Those of us that had pioneered here and stayed all developed a sense of community and sharing that benefited every one of us.

We helped each other, as people should. We had no hospital, nor church or school, none of the institutions that people depended upon for help and solace but we made do with our individual and sometimes communal spirituality free from the limitations of anyone's traditions from the Outside. I wasn't a trained nurse or doctor, but I'd seen and serviced plenty of injuries and illness and I helped anyone that came to me in need of medical assistance. There were plenty of wounds from picks and axes, stitches to be done, broken bones splinted and scurvy to be treated which I could do. For internal injuries or conditions I had no knowledge of or expertise for, I sent them south by dogsled or steamboat, depending on the time of year.

I hadn't been sure what to expect when I came here but I was finally certain I'd found the place in the world that I fit into like no other before. I loved it, every challenge, every blizzard, every time I took the dogsled into Wiseman or Coldfoot or Nolan to get mail or supplies, the snow flying into my face, the clean smell of the pines, the sun glittering on the ice, the happy yelps of the dogs doing what they loved to do best. *Nellie Cashman,* I thought, *this is where you were born to live.*

In the years after we installed the steam boilers I took to returning south sometimes in the winter, to Arizona and my loved ones there. If I had to pick a second place on earth that I loved as much as Alaska, Arizona would be it. The vast emptiness of the desert, untamed and unblemished by the hand of man, much as Alaska was, enchanted me. Arizona had its own special wonders – the smell of mesquite, sage and that occasional spicy wind that blew in from Mexico preceding a storm, a scent like none other I'd ever experienced. Then there was the food. The chiles, tamales, tortillas and sauces from mole to creamy cheeses always made me think about opening a restaurant in Alaska, but the customers where I lived were few and far between, as much as they might adore my food. I contented myself every time by bringing jars of peppers and well wrapped tortillas north with me when I left. At least I would selfishly enjoy them and they went a long way to spicing up elk and venison stew on a cold night.

I so enjoyed my visits with Michael's ever-expanding family and when his wonderful wife died, I was bereft and grief-stricken with him. Once again, the Brophys stepped in, those incredible people, helping him with his five children, my great grand nieces and nephews, as they had helped me with Michael and his brothers and sisters so long ago. I swear God has a special place for this family and their kindness and compassion.

Ellen Brophy's sister Tessie and I became close, and I always looked forward to her letters when they found their way to me and I kept her apprised of events in the North as she did better than anyone concerning doings in the South. I enjoyed hearing from her, and I'm sure some of my letters must've unsettled her, at least as I discovered that when she'd return my missives with her own. When I told her I'd nearly drowned in the river when my small boat had overturned or that I'd had to head-neck the dogsled through a blizzard, she was aghast at these occurrences. After that, in order to avoid Michael sending agents after me to forcefully return my aging body to Arizona and spend my declining years in the sunshine in a rocking chair on his porch, I was much more careful with my description of events in Nolan Creek. They were dear, but they couldn't even begin to imagine what life was really like in my chosen home and there was no point in distressing them.

In 1912, we got word that the United States had a proposition to make Alaska a U.S. Territory, rather than just a District, and I was determined to vote. Into Nolan I went, and on August 13, I did exactly that. That proposition passed and now we were a U.S. Territory. Later on, I heard I was the first woman in Alaska that had ever voted. I was quite proud of that. Newspaper reporters made much of that, just as they did every trip I made to Arizona which got written up in the Bisbee paper, as though I was a society woman or celebrity but I was the farthest thing from that. All that "Angel of the Cassiar" and "Champion Woman Musher" stuff made me laugh. As though women couldn't handle a dogsled. For heaven's sake, had these people ever spent a day away from their offices? Women are able to do pretty much anything a man can, and I was living proof of that. All it took was the desire and the gumption to do it. I wish more women followed that creed. The only thing good about any of this newspaper coverage was that it might just persuade more of them to do something with their lives rather than just get married, pop out babies, launder and cook. Men can be just like little boys, but they really don't need another mother.

* * *

THAT SAME SUMMER, my dearest friend Chris died. He just got up one morning, looked regretfully at me and collapsed, closing his eyes. I was devastated. That loyal dog had sustained me since I came to the Klondike and he'd lived an incredibly long life for a husky. I liked to think it was love and caring. A month later, my old friend Chinay, his hair as laced with gray as mine was, showed up at my cabin door.

"Nellie, I heard you needed some new friends," he said, holding out two fluffy husky pups. "Chris's progeny. Word travels fast when it needs to around here."

I didn't cry often, but that day the tears ran down my face

as though someone had turned on a faucet. My joy at seeing Chinay, and the wonder of those two pups, was just too much and the pressure and grief I'd bottled up when Chris died all erupted.

Chinay stayed for two weeks, visiting my claims with me and just being there because he knew I needed him to be. Together we trained the pups, two males, and their antics raised that cloud of sorrow that had been haunting me. They were sweet and beautiful, and their very presence made me smile again.

Thus did the years pass, and they were good ones, each one a challenge and every one I thanked God for giving me. I'd found my place in the world.

How I loved it all.

CHAPTER 45

1922

Nolan Creek area was becoming more civilized year by year. Not only did we have a post office, we had stores and a couple of people had started restaurants. Cabins had sprung up like weeds everywhere up and down the Creek and the Koyukuk. There was plenty for everyone and nobody begrudged what newcomers there still were.

The boys and I had been talking for a couple of years about not just expanding with more claims, but we also agreed we needed better equipment to do that, and certainly to work new seams. The steam boilers we'd originally begun with were showing their age, and we needed more of them. The summer before Patrick and I had ventured up Nolan Creek a long way from the other claims and miners and we'd found a vein that was the biggest I'd yet seen. To mine that, we'd need equipment we didn't have. I came up with a plan, after talking to the bankers in Fairbanks and Seattle. I decided to start a company to raise the money. I'd done well since I'd come to Alaska, but much to the boys' objections at times, not to mention Michael's, I'd donated most of it to the hospitals and churches that provided the services so many people needed.

For a much bigger operation, we needed money. Our notice read:

Midnight Sun Mining Company
Nellie Cashman, Trustee
No Offices, No Officers
50,000 Shares, $2 a Share

When this didn't seem to really take off, I decided to go to New York and talk to bankers there, since the Alaska ones weren't as accustomed to dealing with this sort of venture. I took the train and greatly enjoyed the journey. I'd never seen most of the country, having landed in San Francisco via boat. It was a vast and beautiful place and even if my mining capital hopes didn't work out, I was happy I'd decided to travel this land in search of them. The great plains were a marvel, as was Chicago and the expanses before and after. What a beautiful country I'd come to. I arrived in New York City, amazed at Grand Central Station and the sheer numbers of people fascinated me, especially after the very few I'd lived with so long in comparison. Carriages, trolleys and motorcars jammed with people going about their business clogged the streets but I didn't have far to travel, as Michael had made reservations for me at the Waldorf Astoria. What an elegant place it was, the lobby magnificent with its marble pillars, ferns, trickling fountains and a tuxedoed gentleman playing a grand piano. Well-dressed people strolled casually about under crystal chandeliers, chatting about this and that, laughter tinkling on the air, as though this was their everyday milieu, which it probably was.

My room was delightful, every amenity and luxury I could've wished for. The first thing I did was take a long bath after the long train ride. After that, I dressed for dinner in my woefully outdated shirtwaist and skirt and made my way to the restaurant on the ground floor. For the first time in my life, I enjoyed Coquille St. Jacques, a lobster creation, tiny brussel sprouts and potatoes in cream sauce, with a dessert called tiramisu, which the waiter assured me was delicious. He was right.

The next morning I set about my purpose and made appointments to see three bankers, two this afternoon and one tomorrow. I knew my wardrobe was frightful in comparison to New York standards, so I stopped in at Macy's early the next morning. I walked out clad in a very sophisticated black suit and a hat adorned with black and purple feathers, along with a new pair of black kidskin boots that fit me well. They'd be useless in Coldfoot, but they were very necessary here.

Thus fortified, I stormed the towers of banking power. Even as fashionably as I was attired, thus avoiding the first lines of defense, when I presented my case, it did not go well. I left both banks feeling quite discouraged. I wandered around the city for the rest of the afternoon, strolled through Central Park, stopping to watch children having sailboat races, and window shopped on Fifth Avenue, noticing there certainly was a good market for gold jewelry if Tiffany's window displays were accurate. After another incredible meal at the Waldorf, I settled in for the night, praying for a better outcome the next day. I did look quite stylish in my new clothes, I must say.

The First National Bank was housed in an impressive building and my hopes were high, as was my trepidation after yesterday. I met with a Vice President named Colin Maxwell and from the first moment I entered his cigar smoke-laden office, I had a bad feeling. He was a slim man, hair slickly pomaded, including his Van Dyke beard. I've never trusted a man with a Van Dyke beard, they always looked like connivers to me. I took a deep breath. This might not go well at all.

"Mrs. Cashman," he said, not bothering to hold out his hand. I guess in New York they assume ladies don't shake hands. In Alaska and Arizona, no matter your gender, if you don't shake hands, you simply are not a trustworthy person. I sat down in a chair facing his desk nevertheless.

"So, I've been reviewing your stock offering and your

request here," he said, not giving me a chance to respond. "It seems to me you don't have much to offer in terms of security or guarantees on this gold deposit, except a 'hunch' and a lot of luck. Anything else?"

"First of all," I said, "it's Miss Cashman. Secondly, I have tested this site and it is as close to a bonanza as I've ever seen in fifteen years of mining in Alaska, at which, if you read more closely in my proposal, I've been very successful. To develop it at its maximum potential, I need funds for heavier equipment, including ten new steam boilers, piping and drills. Perhaps more, if the shares sell. The returns will more than outweigh the initial investment."

He stroked his beard, his fingers seemingly quite fond of his own whiskers. They didn't look that impressive to me. He glanced down at the papers in front of him, flipping through a few pages, likely a sop to me because I knew what he was going to say before he opened his mouth. It may have been the Irish accent, or the fact that I was a woman in a man's game, but Mr. Maxwell was having none of it.

"I'm sorry, Miss Cashman. This isn't a venture the National Bank can consider at this time. It's much too risky, especially when we have so many other opportunities to look into."

He didn't look very sorry. I knew dismissal when I heard it and this joker was no friend of mine, nor of Alaska mining or perhaps any other kind no matter where it might be. Risky, indeed. That word had been on the mind of every miner that had ever sunk a shaft or panned for ore for the last seventy years. If their fate had been in this man's hands, the world would be much lower in precious ores of any kind.

I stood up and held out my hand, willing him to take it. He stared at me for a few seconds, and finally held his out. I grasped it firmly and shook it. "Thank you for your time, Colin Maxwell. I wish you good day."

I turned and made my way to the door of his office, but in

the end, I couldn't resist. "You're a very shortsighted man, Mr. Maxwell. It might behoove you to learn more about mining, and likely a great many other endeavors."

Back on the train the next day, I was disappointed, of course. But beyond that, I'd enjoyed my journey and my time in the biggest city in the United States very much. To be honest, I wasn't much surprised. Midnight Sun was an idea, a dream attempted since much of the country was in the throes of rampant capitalism and new ventures. It had always been a long shot, perhaps even a cheeky one. Perhaps my Arizona friends would be willing to buy some shares even if the New York bankers were not. Still, I would figure out a way to get new boilers and take my time when it came to the new claim. The boys were stalwart and together we'd make it happen, no matter how long it took. The gold wasn't going anywhere and neither were we. Besides, I missed my dogs and my cozy cabin. Winter was approaching and I'd order as many new boilers as I could afford once I reached Fairbanks. We'd make do just fine.

CHAPTER 46

1923

We did well with our older claims during the winter, bringing up good amounts of placer gravel during the coldest months, and by spring it was ready to work. The old boilers had done fine, but we hadn't invested much time in the new claim. We were all disappointed we couldn't work the new claim like we wanted to, but there was only so much equipment to go around and we had to bet on a sure thing. It was a good summer, but when the hard cold came in, I found myself yearning for the warmth of the desert, more so than I had before. The new dogs, including the young sons of the pups Chinay had brought me, who looked just like their beloved ancestor, needed some runs. We started out with fairly small ones, up and down the creeks and rivers, and visiting the settlements, but come December and a good snow buildup, I decided to run them to Nenana, south of Fairbanks. I could leave them with a friend over the winter and journey back with them in the spring.

It was fast going, that trip. With nothing on the sled but my suitcase, supplies for the journey, and me, the seven dogs had an easy pull. We made the journey in 17 days, a 350 mile trek. Upon our arrival, people were saying it was a record but I wasn't so sure about that. I'd done similar treks before but I was proud of my dogs and the hard work they'd done. My job was simple and easy in comparison to theirs. I hugged them all when I left, and I knew I'd miss waking up to their bright eyes and unconditional love.

I spent the winter roaming here and there in Arizona, up to Prescott and Phoenix once, but mostly in my old haunts of Tucson and Tombstone, and much time in Bisbee with my family. Once again, there were entreaties to stay and this time, I was actually tempted. I didn't have the strength I'd always had in the past, I knew that well every morning when I swung my legs over the side of the bed, but there were too many people depending on me, and there was a lot to take care of in Alaska that I couldn't ignore or leave to others. Perhaps next year would be the one when I came South to stay for good, but this April was not to be the time.

Back in Alaska, I developed a case of the sniffles after picking up the dogs and sled and wasn't feeling quite up to the rest of journey by sled, so I waited for the steamboat after two days on the trail. I went aboard with just my suitcase and hired two Tlingit friends of Chinay's to take the dogs and sled to Nolan and up the Koyukuk I went. As I waved goodbye, I knew I'd done the right thing, I was feeling worse by the minute and I went straight to bed. Two days later, the captain put in at Bettles with only 70 miles to go and sent word to Sister Mary Claude at the Mission in Nulato that I was extremely ill, needed care and he felt I could journey no further.

At first, I was angry that he had made such a peremptory decision about my health, but I knew he was right. I had a raging fever and was weak as a newborn kitten. When Sister Mary Claude arrived, I was relieved to see my old friend and I could tell from the look on her face that I was every bit as sick as I felt. I don't remember very much of anything for the next few days but one morning I woke up to sunshine, lying on white sheets in a bed at the Mission. I felt better, but Sister Mary Claude assured me I was in no condition to continue on to Nolan Creek and sternly forbade it.

"You are still quite sick, Nellie," she said, her face stern. "You have always pushed yourself to the limit but this time, I insist you follow medical advice. I've made arrangements for you to go to Fairbanks, to the hospital there to continue care. They have more resources and you need more than we can provide here."

I wanted to argue but didn't have the energy to do so. I lay back on the pillows and closed my eyes. I hoped the dogs had made back it back home safely and I knew Patrick and the rest of the boys would take good care of them for me until I could return.

I sailed away on the General Jacobs steamship two days later. I kept to my cabin, tended by a nice woman Sister Mary Claude had inveigled into looking after me. At first I was reluctant but I found I really needed her help. The ship's baker baked me a cake for my birthday, writing my name on top with blue frosting, which made me smile, and it was delicious. We arrived in Fairbanks and off to the hospital I went.

It was a bad time for me. I had never been truly sick except for that time in Dawson when I'd had surgery so many years before. Time seemed to float by, and I would have good days and bad days, but I never seemed to get truly well. They had diagnosed me with pneumonia, but I just couldn't seem to fight it off completely. Finally, one day in October, the doctor admitted he wasn't quite certain how to proceed anymore.

"What would you like to do, Miss Cashman? I could suggest a type of nursing home here in Fairbanks. I know a lovely woman, a nurse, who has started one. I think it may be time to consider that you should get your affairs in order as well."

Well. That came as a bit of a shock. He wasn't the kindest

man I'd ever met, certainly no Father Judge, but he wasn't being cruel, just pragmatic. I was coming to realize that perhaps I wasn't going to be able to go to my cabin, nor was I likely to get to Arizona this winter, certainly not until I'd recovered my strength.

"Doctor," I said, "I appreciate your honesty with me. I believe what I'd like to do is go to my friends in Victoria, the Sisters of St. Anne's. They will welcome me and help me get back on my feet."

He looked at me rather skeptically but then smiled. "I think that's a sound decision, Miss Cashman." I could hear the relief in his voice. "I'll send the nurse in to make arrangements for you to travel to Victoria."

I spent the next few days writing letters, telling everyone of my circumstances. To Patrick and the boys, that I wouldn't be coming further north this winter and to take care of the dogs and claims, as I knew they would; to Michael and Tessie, that I wouldn't be coming South this winter, and why, that I would be fine but was going to stay in Victoria for a time to get better; to Sister Mary Margaret that I would be coming to St. Anne's and of my desire to recover there.

The sea voyage to Victoria wasn't difficult, the weather holding from the winter storms, and although I knew I likely shouldn't, I sat out on deck, watching the sea and coastline as we passed, enjoying the cold crisp air and the cries of the seabirds. I'd been too much in a hospital room for too long. By the time we arrived in Victoria, Captain Adams's wife insisted on accompanying me to the Sisters at St. Joseph's Hospital, for which I was grateful once we started because I was getting unsteadier by the moment. When we arrived at the hospital, however, I insisted upon walking in on my own, rather than in the wheeled chair which was offered. I'd always hated the things that signified weakness, and even though I was one of those weaker things myself at the moment, I wasn't going to arrive in a conveyance that left no doubt I was an invalid, even though I no longer had much confidence that I'd be walking out of St. Joseph's a well woman at least not for some time.

The thought that kept running through my head, much as I tried to dispel it, was that it was fitting I'd come home to die, to the people and the hospital in which I'd found such solace at the very beginning of my adventures further North. A place I'd helped to build, because I could clearly see that all that hard-won gold had gone to the right place, one that I, admittedly with some hubris, was proud to have had a hand in creating.

They showed me to a lovely room, all white, with sheer pale blue curtains on the windows, and I was only too happy to fall into the soft bed in a soft cotton nightgown, and rest. I felt like an honored guest and I guess I was.

"Good morning, Miss Cashman," the silver-haired man in the white coat sitting by my bedside smiled. "Perhaps you might remember me. I was one of the doctors that came to Dawson City to intern at St. Mary's right before you left. I'm John Barrett."

"I do," I said, but in truth he was a vague memory. It was so long ago. Still, it was nice to know that someone who knew the Yukon was here. "How am I doing, Dr. Barrett?"

"I'm going to be honest. From what I remember and know of you, you respect that above all else. You've got double pneumonia, along with failing kidneys, Miss Cashman. We can treat you with medicine that will help ease your breathing and we have help for pain, but for the rest, including a general malaise that comes when we reach a certain age, we haven't yet got any cures. Rest, nourishing food and comfort are the best remedies right now. You've always had an amazing constitution from what I can see. Miracles happen every day and I am not one to discount them."

I tried to snort but I didn't really have the breath for it.

"Miracles aside, that doesn't sound too good, Doc. Still, I've lived through worse."

He chuckled. "Indeed you have. You're a legend even down here in Victoria, did you know that?"

"No, but I hear there's lots of stories about me here and there. I've heard a few myself. Maybe half of them are true. The one about the bear is a lie for sure."

Now he downright laughed. "I'm happy you cleared that up, I've always wondered. I'm very happy to be working with you, Nellie Cashman. I'm going to send in your head nurse. Let me know if you need anything. Nurse Ellison will be with you during the day, and we have a night nurse, Sister Kinney, who's from the Klondike herself, who will be here after seven."

And so it went. I rested, I ate nourishing food, some of it tasty but mostly bland stuff that the dogs would've enjoyed but I didn't. I read a lot, I prayed a great deal, both alone and with my old friends Sister Mary Margaret and Sister Mary John, and I tried to write letters. Some of those I accomplished, giving Patrick and Ted instructions on how to handle the claims, but for Michael and my Arizona family, I simply said I was ill but getting better. I didn't want them to worry or make a frantic journey here when there was nothing they could do anyway.

I think it was the week before Christmas when I fully realized I was never getting out of this bed or this hospital. That I would never again step into my cabin in Coldfoot, dig for gold, see my family again, or hug my dogs. I would never feel the deck of a steamship under my feet with the wind in my hair, or stoke my woodstove and make coffee to prepare for a day of searching for gold, or feel the thrill of snow in my face as the dogs ran like demons into the glittering midnight sun. I felt the tears on my cheeks but I gave thanks to God who had allowed me to experience such wonders in my long life.

I was no saint, no angel. I was simply a woman who lived her life on her own terms, never regretting a single day, whether it was comforting a child, making the best food in Tombstone, bringing supplies to the Cassiar, digging out that first gold nugget and holding it my hand or giving most of it away to help others.

I was a woman. A woman that truly lived.

AFTERWORD

Nellie Cashman passed away Sunday, January 4, 1925 and is buried at Ross Bay Cemetery, Victoria, British Columbia, adjacent to the section reserved for the Sisters of St. Anne's. Her obituary, written by the Sisters of St. Anne's, follows:

St. Joseph's Hospital, the Sisters of St. Anne's
Victoria, British Columbia
Nellie Cashman – Died Sunday, January 4, 1925

A few details about the illness and death of our dear departed friend, Nellie Cashman, may be of interest to you.

Miss Cashman had been very ill of pneumonia for six weeks in the hospital at Fairbanks, Alaska before coming here; and it was only her great will power which enabled her to rally and reach Victoria, as she said, "to come to her friends, the Sisters of St. Ann at St. Joseph's Hospital."

She arrived here on October 9th, accompanied by Mrs. Adams, the wife of Captain Adams. Nellie refused to be taken to her room in a wheel chair but walked in although she could scarcely do so. The news of her arrival spread quickly throughout the hospital and the Sisters whom she knew were soon at her side. Nellie said she had been sick and "all in" and added, "I am coming home to die." She was indeed a very sick woman, still we entertained hopes of her recovery. She suffered greatly during nine weeks but was always pleasant and ready to joke. Doctor Barrett, her Dawson friend, attended her and was most devoted to her night and day. She had a day and a night nurse and the Sisters were never far from her bed of pain to encourage and soothe her in every way. She was indeed most edifying by her resignation to the Holy Will of God and her great faith and loving trust in our Blessed Mother. In speaking of the Blessed Virgin, she would often say with great reverence, "She has been so good to me. I wanted to get well enough to come here and she has seen to it that I should come. She will take care of me. If she would only come now, for I do not wish to linger, but God and the Blessed other know best."

A statue of the Blessed Virgin and of St. Ann were over in her room and when she spoke of God, His Blessed Mother or St. Ann, it was with such faith that we could almost realize their presence.

During her illness she often spoke of the past and recalled different episodes of her doings in Boston, Arizona, Cassiar and Alaska. In all these narratives we could always feel an undercurrent of self-forgetfulness in the cause of charity.

Miss Cashman received the Sacrament of Extreme Unction about two weeks after her arrival at St. Joseph's and then again a few days before her death. Both times she prepared with the greatest faith and with that beautiful simplicity which was more like that of a child's than that of one who had braved the adventures of pioneer life during more than half a century. She received Holy Communion several times and always with the same ardent faith.

On December 8th, the feast of the Immaculate Conception, after receiving Holy Communion she said, "I have received a great grace. Our Blessed Lady has told me to be resigned" and she did seem so peaceful and happy. From that day on she never expressed the least desire to recover nor gave the slightest sign of weariness, no matter how much she suffered nor how tedious the hours may have seemed.

She spoke of death as a blessing and gave orders as to her funeral. She often expressed her great satisfaction at being with her Sisters, saying "I know you will see me through". Oh, how she longed to see Our Blessed Lady and a heavenly smile like a wreath seemed to come over her features when mention was made of the Blessed Virgin or Our Lord.

The last week she spent with us was marked by a greater union with God – she often asked us to pray for her and with her and would make great efforts to answer the prayers. She received Holy Communion for the last time on the evening of the First Friday, January 2, with great piety and devotion, and made her thanksgiving with the deepest recollection. One of the Sisters in attendance recited the Litany of the Blessed Virgin. Nellie answered throughout and then whispered, "The Litany of the Saints." These she followed throughout although her voice had become a whisper, then she turned to the Sisters and said, "Now you may go to rest, I shall not need you tonight", meaning I shall not die, nurse will see to me. Neither did she die that night, although she had a weak spell and the nurse, thinking the end had come and called the Sisters. But

Nellie rallied and was there for the two following mornings to say "Good morning" if not in words, by the light of her eyes with which she greeted her friends as they came in.

By a happy coincidence her night nurse, Miss Kinney, had spent several in Dawson and the Sisters who were by her bedside during the illness and at her death were Northern missionaries, having spent a number of years in Dawson and Juneau, so Nellie felt she was in a most congenial atmosphere, as the Doctor, the nurse, and the Sisters were all of the Northern family.

In acquiescence to Nellie's desire, she was laid out in our mortuary chapel at the hospital and it is from here that the funeral cortege proceeded to the Cathedral.

A wonderful soul has passed into its eternity, a most extraordinary career has come to a close in the person of Nellie Cashman, but the memory of her charity, her undaunted courage, her daring spirit, and her unimpeachable character will live to serve as a beacon to help others on to higher spheres.

May this good and holy woman who has done so much for her fellow men rest in peace, and may she pray for us!

NELLIE CASHMAN
1925
FRIEND OF THE SICK AND THE HUNGRY
AND TO ALL MEN
HEROIC APOSTOLATE OF SERVICE
AMONG THE WESTERN AND NORTHERN
FRONTIER MINERS
MINERS' ANGEL, 1872 — 1924
IN NEVADA
IN THE CASSIAR
IN ARIZONA
IN THE YUKON
IN CALIFORNIA
IN ALASKA
BORN IN IRELAND
DIED WITH THE SISTERS OF SAINT ANN, AT
ST. JOSEPH'S HOSPITAL, VICTORIA, B.C.
JANUARY 4, 1925
REQUIESCAT IN PACE

AUTHOR'S NOTE

I first heard of Nellie Cashman from a woman who enrolled in one of my writing classes at Phoenix College, Kate Brophy, the last of the third generation of one of the pioneer families of Arizona and the granddaughter of William Brophy who established the Bank of Bisbee, among other achievements. Kate and I became good friends over the years and I came to be a frequent guest at her home in Phoenix as well as the Brophy ranch, the Babacomari, in Cochise County, Arizona and came to know some of the family. After I wrote The Lily of the West, some of it during my time at the ranch, a welcome headquarters for my research forays, Kate urged me to write about Nellie, who had such a strong connection to the Brophy family. I was busy with other projects, but one day she gave me a packet of letters, photos and memorabilia about Nellie and put me in touch with James O'Fallon, whose grandmother is Florence Cunningham Moffat, Michael Cunningham's daughter, who gave me more material. Finally intrigued, I jumped in, and "Golddigger" is the result of that decision. It's one I'm glad I made.

I usually write fiction about independent women, some of it violent and occasionally profane, so I wasn't sure Nellie and

I would see eye to eye, her a devout Catholic and me a skeptic. However, as I researched more, read her own letters and came to understand her, I also came to respect and admire this incredible woman and I wanted to write a novel not just for me and the family, but for Nellie herself. There's been a few books published about her but after reading them, none that I felt did her justice. I believe that "Golddigger" accomplishes that task, and as I wrote this book, it went from a formidable undertaking to a labor of love.

Many thanks to Kate Brophy, James O'Fallon, the Alaska Historical Society, the Arizona Historical Society, Bisbee Historical Society, posthumously to William Brophy, Frank Cullen Brophy, E. B. Gage and John Clum for their writings and documents. A most heartfelt thanks to Syric Lost, my extraordinary digital tech and photography source, who worked magic with historical photographs and layouts and really brought Nellie to life.

When people say "one of a kind" anymore, it's a trite cliché. However, that is exactly what Nellie Cashman really was: an extraordinary woman, not just for her time, but for all time. I celebrate her and all women who choose to follow their own paths.

ADDITIONAL MATERIALS

James O'Fallon, the great-grandson of Nellie's nephew Michael Cunningham, has supplied me with letters, photos and documents, as has Kate Brophy, the granddaughter of William Brophy, Nellie's friend, whose family became related by marriage to the Cunninghams. The following pages contain four of Nellie's original letters, each with a transcription as they were usually written on tablet paper in pencil and difficult to decipher after so many years. In addition, there are family photographs as well as photographs from historical societies that are included as well.

Nellie, circa 1874, San Francisco

Nellie, Tombstone 1883

William Brophy, circa 1901

Arizona Historical Society

Bisbee around the turn of the century, the Bank of Bisbee visible at lower center.

The Bank of Bisbee, 1901. Michael J. Cunningham, center in gray suit

F. C. Brophy Collection

The three musketeers: W. H. Brophy, J. S. Douglas (seated) and Tom Collins, in France.

Chilkoot Pass, Gateway to the Klondike, 1897

Miss Nellie Cashman standing in front of her store at Dawson, Yukon Territory.
Photo made by John P. Clum on June 23, 1898.

Nellie and some of her boys, circa 1915

Nellie's cabin in Coldfoot, Alaska, circa 1916

The children of Michael J. Cunningham, with Mrs. William Brophy, Los Angeles, 1930

Nellie Cashman, 1922

THE CASHMAN LETTERS

Letters from Nellie Cashman to her friend Theresa Goodbody, William Brophy's and Michael Cunningham's sister-in-law, who lived in Bisbee, Arizona, sent 1909-1917.

(First are the transcriptions, second are photos of the original letters.)

January 30, 1909, Coldfoot, Alaska

My very dear Miss Goodbody and your dear Mother:

Your dear and welcome letter came to hand of October 31st and was more than pleased to receive the same. I hope and pray that you and all your beloved family are in good health. As for your humble servant I am feeling very good thank God. I arrived home on the 10th of December. I walked from Bettes which 90 miles on foot. The trail was very bad and dogs could not travel, overflow was the cause. Anyhow, dear, I was very lucky on my long journey. Going from Valdoz to Fairbanks was a bad one. Very little snow on the trail. So we never missed a stump or a boulder. The sled was running you may say on bare ground.

We fell into the river several times and bailed out safe. It is a good thing that I didn't have false teeth or I would surely have lost them. We traveled very nearly day and night as the mail had to be in Fairbanks on the 10th of November. We made it.

On my arrival I received quite a welcome from all friends. The mail sled was surrounded by many friends in about five minutes. Everyone in town knew I landed, I am sure. You would laugh hearty if you had been by my side. Anyhow the Alaska people are very fond of one another.

My dear Miss Tessie I am so pleased that I paid you and yours that visit. I shall never forget the kindness that I received from you and yours. yes, I do feel very lonely after all of you. The tears dropped very freely all the way to Benson. Yes, my own Theresa, there is a big corner in my heart for all of you and in my little cabin you and yours are not forgotten in my prayers every night. Oh how I miss your darling Mother. May God spare her health. So that I can spend a little more of my life with her. You can get everything in this world but you can't get a mother. Watch and care for her like I did mine and you can rest assured that God's blessing and his Mother's will follow you in this life and to the great beyond. That dear Mother has seen better days and may God grant that she may see them again. If not here, she will in the next world.

Well my dear Tessie, I will tell you what I am doing. Last summer was a dry one and the boys got no water to shovel in the dirt to the boxes. So on my arrival there was no money for me and nothing to eat. So the little money I had left, after paying my expenses to here, I had to buy grub with it. And I can tell you, dear, that my living is pretty tough this winter. This I don't mind for the day will come when I will have plenty. Of course, you know this is the prospector's life. Today, potatoes and tomorrow, oysters on the half shell.

So at present, I can't sink my shaft. And when we went back to the old shaft we found it full of water. We started to take it out and my goodness it filled up again so we had to quit it. The boys must have tapped a little spring for the water is warm and won't freeze. Never mind, dear God is good and has a good Mother. She never shuts one door but she opens another.

The boys took out a little gravel out of that shaft last winter and it washed up very good. And of course, we could do the same this winter, but God won't let us. So he may have something better for me. The boys are sinking another shaft I leased to them for a short time but they are not sinking in my choice of the ground. So they are using their own judgment. Still they may strike it. They are sinking with my little boiler and it is a little peach. It is a nice little rig.

They have not struck the channel adjoining me. They are still plugging away at it. It is very hard to reach the old river bed, a lot of slide on top of it. If I could handle myself I would have it this winter. I am not worried over it for I will get that half a million dollars out of this ground. Just wait, dear, you will be here with me. I am sure of this, it is going to come to pass.

Will close at present by sending you and your dear Mother fond love and to all the family and to dear Mr. Goodbody. I remain, dear Tessie, your loving friend,

Nellie Cashman

P.S. Goodby my own dear Tessie, God love you and he does. N.C.

1

[illegible]

My very dear Miss [illegible] and your dear [illegible]

Your dear and welcome letter came to hand [illegible] and was very glad [illegible] to learn [illegible] that you and all your [illegible] health [illegible] your humble servant [illegible] thank God [illegible] your letter [illegible] The trail was very bad [illegible] friends [illegible] [illegible] little [illegible] [illegible]

2

[illegible] my dear Miss [illegible] so pleased that [illegible] [illegible] little [illegible] [illegible]

3

[illegible]

4

[illegible] I heard it [illegible] but a short time. [illegible] little baby [illegible] [illegible] just [illegible] [illegible] would like to [illegible] [illegible] the best of [illegible] [illegible]

July 12, 1909, Coldfoot, Alaska

My own dear Miss Goodbody:

I received your dear letter of May the 3rd and was very sorry to hear of your dear beloved Mother not being well – with God's help she will get better and be herself again. It is a blessing that you are well and the balance of the family. At present I am at Coldfoot – I am down 22 miles on foot over a rough trail in order to get my letters off. I am very much worried about our little nun and fear that she won't be with us long. I wrote to Rev. Mother Provincal of St. Paul, her name is Mother Seraphine, and asked her to send her to Oakland to Sister Bibiana for a few months. I hope she will grant my request, I believe she will. I also wrote to Mike to go after her himself. My dear Tess, I can't leave here for a year. The man that I left here last fall didn't do things to suit me, so I let him out and down and I am sure that our dear boy Mike will do this for me.

I was very lucky it rained here in June and of course I got out a few hundred dollars and this helped me out. I will start early in the fall and sink my shaft. So my darling child, I think that everything will come out all right. I have good ground and lots of it and I will strike it will be a big one. I have to go slow but in time I will get there. I could have money to go ahead with if I took in a partner. No partner for me. I have the ground and I am going to lick it. When I'll strike it and that any of my people comes here to see me, they can do whatever they please on my ground. There won't be any partners to stick their lip in.

I do hope and pray that your dear Mother will get strong so that I will have a chance to hand her a few chunks of gold for I do think a good deal of her, and this is going to come to pass. So darling take the best care of her. She raised a nice family and has been a dear good beloved mother. Do anything she tells you for she knows more than you or I do and my dear child I know that I am welcome to your home. We will meet in the near future. My heart flows to all of you. I don't know which of you I like best. The more I see of Mrs. M.J.C. the better I like her. There is an awful lot of goodness in her frame. She had made a good wife mother. Well, dear she has a full house, 3 queens and 2 kings. Day and night here in the wilderness I pray that God and his dear beloved Mother may share their talents and their health to raise their little flock and my prayers is going to be heard. For our Lord knows that I don't want no home on this earth but there is something I do wish and that is to see all of you happy.

For God's sake Miss Tessie don't marry any useless man. You are better off without any, that is if he is not the right kind. I hope that someday you and I will travel all through Europe. I feel that it is going to come to pass. I do feel that as soon as I will get a shaft or two down that I can write and tell you that we can go. It will be very deep diggings and it will take heavy machinery to work it. I can get this later on.

Well Miss Tessie I am in good health, my pet. While at Coldfoot I make my home at the Judge's house. The post office is in the same building. His wife attends to it. They are very nice people and they are so good to me. They are from California. They have a fine garden and I am getting a fine feed of vegetables. There are quite a few people coming in and we are going to have another store. I believe it will cause goods to be a little cheaper. We are going to have fresh beef. There is ten steers here already, the first that came into the country.

So you see the camp is going ahead. In one more year this camp is going to be better. Six of the boys left here with sixty thousand dollars each out of Nolan Creek. The camp is looking up very good. We are going to have some more new strikes on Nolan this winter and I do hope that I will be one of them. I will leave for the mines in a few days. Am waiting for the next mail to come in. The riverboats will run until the 10th of Sept. After that no more mail until the river freezes up.

Well my dear Miss Tessie I do hope you and all the family will have a pleasant time in Los Angeles. Go and see Cousin Tom Cunningham, he is one of the undertakers. Am going to address this letter to Bisbee, M.J.C. will forward it to you. Well, my darling child be good to self, will close by sending yourself and your dear Mother my fond love.

I remain, my dear Miss Goodbody, your loving and fond aunt,

Nellie Cashman

January 29,1911

My dear Theresa Goodbody:

Your welcome letter came to hand today and was pleased to learn that you and dear Mother are in good health. As for me, I am feeling pretty fair, thank God. Tonight is the first time that I heard of poor Tommie's death and had a crying spell, but I am so pleased that he had the priest before he left this world of ours. I had a letter from a friend of mine from Oregon. She told me about Tommie, poor Mike. I thought of him many a time tonight. I also felt blue.

Got down and struck the gold and also some water and my plant was too small to handle it and had to quit work. Well, my dear, no one can do nothing on a shoestring. It is the first time in all my life that I had such poor luck. It never rains but it pours. I am very much pleased that Ellen and the little ones are doing nicely. They are all bright children. I prayed day and night that our dear Mrs. Cunningham will be over her troubles before this reaches you.

My dear Tessie, be cheerful everything will be all right in time. Someday I hope I will get the yellow metal out of the ground. Well, my dear Tessie I will write you soon again. It is very late so I'll make this a short letter. Excuse pencil writing. Fond love to self and your dear Mother. I remain my own dear Tessie, your loving aunt,

Nellie Cashman

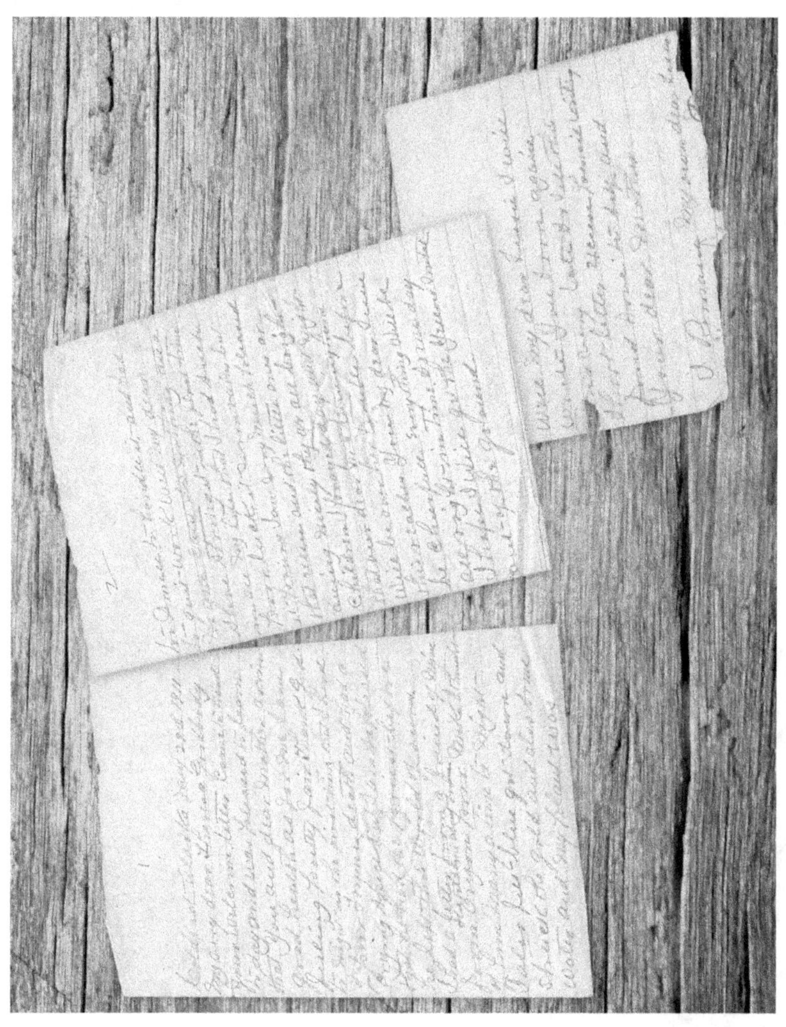

March 5, 1917 (Written on board ship to Fairbanks)

My dear Tessie:

Enclosed you will find a line or two from me to let you know that I am well and sailing along as fast as we can. It's a little rough out at sea. I landed at Seattle Friday morning and left in the evening. I wrote our dear Mike from there and told him to tell you not to send any thing that I left there in the drawers as I expect to be back in a year. And I got all the clothes I want until then. You can send those two black skirts to Kate Ward.

We will arrive at Cordova Saturday, then we will travel one day on the train, then we will take the stage for Fairbanks. It will take six days to get there and then to Gibbons on the stage fix or six days more. Then, on a dog team home about Thursday night. We are going to get a good shaking up. There is a strip between Juneau and Cordova very rough, it will last about eight hours.

I was (sic) to see our dear Ellen and she looked fine and so does Mrs. Brophy. Mrs. Brophy met me at the depot, she drove me out to Mrs. Ward. I was out at Cousin Tom's. They both asked for you. I had dinner with them. I had his car all day and saw me off on the train. Mrs. Brophy and all of them treated me very nice. I am traveling with a ladie friend of mine. She is going to Fairbanks. I am still wearing my brown suit. I am very lucky I have a room all to myself on the boat. We have a big lot of people on the boat.

Tess if you have the keys of those valises send them North to me. If I can I will write you from Gibbons. I expect Mrs. Brophy has a house by this time. The last mail will leave Koyukuk the later part of April. If I get these before the mail leaves I will try and send out a letter. You can write and I will get it in June. I heard they have a cold winter in the north.

Well, dear Tess I will say goodby by sending you and all the family fond love. Remember me to all the ladies and also dear Mrs. Jones. I remain your side partner.

Nellie Cashman

PACIFIC COAST STEAMSHIP COMPANY

ON BOARD S.S. March 8th 1917

About the Author

Kathleen Morris is an aficionado of American and Western history, a graduate of Prescott College in Arizona and lives and writes in the desert Southwest. She loves being able to immerse herself in the lives of her characters, especially bringing to life the charismatic women of the West, both real and imaginary. Meticulous research and dedication to detail are the hallmarks of her work. Her debut novel, **The Lily of the West**, the story of "Big Nose Kate" Haroney, was published in 2019 to critical acclaim and won the Peacemaker award for "Best First Western Novel" from Western Fictioneers. More books and more awards have followed. She is a member of Western Writers of America and Western Fictioneers. Visit her website at www.KathleenMorrisauthor.com.

www.ingramcontent.com/pod-product-compliance
Lightning Source LLC
Chambersburg PA
CBHW071409200726
48294CB00002B/329
* 9 7 8 1 7 3 7 9 8 6 6 8 3 *